Life at the Club

Life at the Club

Adrianne

URBAN BOOKS

www.urbanbooks.net

Urban Books, LLC
300 Farmingdale Road, N.Y.-Route 109
Farmingdale, NY 11735

ISBN 13: 978-1-64556-373-0
ISBN 10: 1-64556-373-1

First Trade Paperback Printing November 2022
Printed in the United States of America

10 9 8 7 6 5 4 3 2 1

This is a work of fiction. Any references or similarities to actual events, real people, living or dead, or to real locales are intended to give the novel a sense of reality. Any similarity in other names, characters, places, and incidents is entirely coincidental.

Distributed by Kensington Publishing Corp.
Submit Orders to:
Customer Service
400 Hahn Road
Westminster, MD 21157-4627
Phone: 1-800-733-3000
Fax: 1-800-659-2436

Life at the Club

by

Adrianne

Book Remarks

I want to thank my readers for their undying support throughout my writing career. I want to give a shout-out to my amazing publishing company, Racquel Williams Presents. Thank you for always believing in me and allowing me to be under your seasoned umbrella. I hope you all love this novel as much as the others, and I promise I have more great reads to come! Special thanks to the incredible Carl Weber for taking a chance on me. I have complete admiration for your craft, and I appreciate you very much. I want to give a special shout-out to Ms. Neka Bellamy. You stayed up late at night and brainstormed this concept with me. I hope I did us both proud. I love you, sissy!

I want to give a special dedication to two incredibly special people I lost in 2020. My aunt Yvonne Holden. Thank you for always believing in me and loving me unconditionally in every aspect of my life. You always had a kind word for all of the family, never picked sides but loved us equally. And even when you felt your worst, you were always concerned about our feelings instead of your own. I will always miss you, and I hope I continue to make you proud of me. I love you always and forever!

My homie, Travonne Lancaster. Man, I don't have a problem giving you a shout-out in one of my books, but never did I imagine you would be gone so soon. Twenty-plus years of memories, laughs, and cries that could never be replaced or erased. Thank you for always checking me and checking up on me. A real friend will always call you on your shit, right or wrong, and you did that time and time again. I am so thankful to have had the opportunity to know such a great guy, and it still hurts my heart to know that you are gone. I will never forget you, friend. Living legends don't die, they just rest in peace! Rest on, my friend, right on! Love ya, Von!

1

Nova: My Beginnings

My body melted like butter in his arms. Montezz Raymond was the man of my dreams, and more than anything, I wanted to be the only woman in his life. He kissed me slowly and with the passion of a vigorous lion hunting its prey. I tightened my arms around his neck and dug my nails into his muscular back. We both moaned with such ecstasy while we succumbed to one another time and again.

Hello, and welcome to the good part of my life, the part I worked so very hard to achieve, although I'm not proud of everything. I've made some mistakes along the way. But I had to do what I had to do for my son, Markus. His no-count daddy created a new life and not with him in it.

But enough of all that. Where are my damn manners? My name is Nova, Ja'Nova Majesty Jacobs. I was born and raised in a small town in Alabama, population "just family" and north of farmland. My mom died after having my little brother, Jacques, and Daddy worked like a dog to support us. By age 16, I had dropped out of school and got a job to help Daddy with the bills. Jacques was the nerdy type and thrived in all his classes. I wished for better days but knew that those dreams would have to be on hold because my family needed me. Daddy did his very best, but there were times that I knew how much he missed our momma. He would play old records, look at family pictures, and cradle a fifth of Jack Daniel's. Those were the times that I stayed locked up in my room or down the street at Phillip's house.

Phillip was my childhood sweetie and best friend. His mom worked the night shift, so it was easy to sneak to his house when Daddy got weird. Phillip and I experienced all of our first times with one another. But the first time we had sex was the most uncomfortable. Neither one of us knew what to put where, and Phillip busted more than one condom when he tried to practice safe sex.

"Maybe we should just give up, Nova!" Phillip nervously placed yet another condom over his shaft. I shrieked and held my stomach as I imagined his beastly member inside of my untamed guts. "We don't have to do this tonight!"

"No." I frowned and grabbed his face. "I'm ready and we might as well do it now. If not now, when?"

"Okay." Phillip was successful that time and climbed between my legs once more. "I will try to go very slow. I'm sorry if I hurt you earlier. Why did you bleed like that?"

"Chelley said that's normal for the first time you do it." I fidgeted underneath him and made sure I was comfortable. "She said it's only for the first time a guy is in the pussy. And she said it's supposed to feel better after that."

"You would ask the school slut!" Phillip snickered and placed his dickhead inside of me.

I let out a loud moan, and Phillip covered my mouth with the palm of his hand.

"How does that feel?" he whispered, and I grabbed his shoulders.

"It hurts," I mumbled. "But it does feel better than before."

***

Life is never like the fairy-tale crap we as girls watch on our color TVs. Me and Phillip had some great times together, and he was there for me when my family life got rocky. But we were young, and life got the best of us at times. After two years of fucking, we slipped up and got pregnant. I wanted an abortion, but Phillip talked me out of it. He said he didn't want to murder his seed. He was supposed to graduate from high school that year. Phillip was an all-star in football and awaited college offers from a few schools. I maintained my assistant manager position at a local grocery store. Jacques was a sophomore in high school and was set on becoming an attorney one day.

"How are you feeling today, Nova?" Phillip called me after another one of his football practices. The team prepared for a tournament bowl, and all odds were in their favor. "Did my son kick you today?"

"My feet are killing me." I was stretched out on the living room sofa. I was on maternity leave from my job, and my ankles were so swollen. "And yes, Markus kicked the hell outta me. He's been nonstop for the past hour now. I hope he's ready to come out soon!"

"Don't be rushin' my baby," Phillip laughed, and I heard a car door slam shut. "He will be here when he's ready."

"I'm ready for him right now!" I sighed and flicked through the television channels. "So, where are you headed?"

"Going home to take a shower," Phillip replied.

"And after that?" I paused.

"I thought I would come by and bug you," Phillip laughed. "Maybe rub your feet or something like that."

"Sounds great to me." I smiled and rubbed my protruding belly.

"Nova . . ." Phillip hesitated for a moment.

"Yes?" I smiled. "What is it? Oh, can you bring me some potato chips? You know the kind I like."

"Sure," Phillip answered. "And I have something I need to talk to you about."

"Something like what?" I questioned and sat up on the couch.

"I will tell you when I get there," Phillip said, trying his best to change the subject. "Anything else besides the chips?"

"A big cherry slushy," I blurted out. "And why can't you just tell me whatever it is? You know I don't like surprises. Just say what's on your mind."

"I just wanted to say it face-to-face," Phillip huffed, and I heard him cut off his car. "I'm just so confused about a lot of shit right now, Nova. And now, there's you and our son. I just don't know what to do anymore."

"What are you talkin' about, Phillip?" I frowned and felt more emotional. "Where is all of this coming from?"

"I was going to make the announcement this Monday." Phillip stalled. "But since we are best friends, I know I can tell you right now. I got a full scholarship to Stanford University. It's a football scholarship. They want me to come up there ASAP and start warming up with the team. Graduation is in a few weeks, and they will want me in California by July!"

"And when were you going to tell me all of this shit?" I felt lightheaded. "I'm due any day now and you mean to tell me that you will be leaving soon? So, I will have to deal with our son on my own?"

"See?" Phillip interjected. "I knew you would react like this. It's always gotta be about you, Nova! When will it ever be about me? You knew that football was my ticket outta this dead-end town. All I ever wanted to do was play ball and make a better life for me and my family. I always included you in that, but you want me to turn down this opportunity!"

"I didn't say turn it down." I halted my next thoughts because I didn't want him to leave.

"So, what are you saying?" Phillip continued. "Because if I don't take the scholarship to Stanford, I'm looking at junior college, and you know they don't have a team at all. I'm accepting the offer, I just wanted you to be the first to know. I love you, and I love our son. This will be the best for all of us, I promise you that!"

"Yeah, I hear you," I sobbed and blew my nose in some tissues. "It doesn't matter that I placed all of my dreams on hold for the ones I love. By all means, go after your dreams and be great!"

"Why are you doing this shit?" Phillip grew angry. "Why can't you see the positive in anything? Why does it always have to be about you, Nova? I swear, you can be the most selfish bitch I've ever seen!"

"Bitch?" I fumed. "I know you didn't go there with me, muthafucka!"

"That's how you act sometimes," Phillip said, defending his statement. "You know I didn't mean it like that."

"Oh, but I think you did!" I was so hurt and angry. "You know what? Please leave and have a great life in California! Me and Markus will be just fine without your in-the-damn-closet ass! I want Markus to be raised around a real man, not a man who don't know what end he wants to get fucked from!"

"That was way harsh, Nova." Phillip fumbled over his words. I guessed he had forgotten our heart-to-heart talks about his bisexuality. It was one of his demons that he fought with on a daily basis. "I thought we were best friends! I never expected you to pass judgment on me like this!"

"Fuck you, fuck-boy!" I hollered on. "Forget my number and forget about my son! We don't need your sweet ass in our lives!"

I hung up the phone and made sure all his numbers were blocked. I went out of my way to avoid Phillip even after the baby was born. After a while, Phillip stopped trying to stay in contact with us. I didn't shed a tear the day he left for California. I knew life without a father would be hard for my son, but my pride wouldn't let me admit that at the time. I would do the best I could for mine. What other choice did I have?

2

Montezz: Puppy Love

Nova was my second favorite girl next to my daughter, Myesha, of course! Hello, my name is Montezz Trenton Alexander. In case you forgot, I was the nigga who gave Nova's pussy a pounding in the beginning of this story. Yeah, I was always a pro at laying down the pipe, but I also knew that good dick wouldn't keep a chick. I guess the best way to prove that would be to discuss Myesha's momma. Now that is a story in and of itself.

It was the fall of my freshman year at Abbott High School. Me and my crew were excited about going to high school, mostly because of the high school girls. We all had older siblings, and they all had stories about how easy the chicks were in high school. I had just begun humpin' around and my hormones were all over the damn place.

"What are you wearing today, my peoples?" James joked with me that morning. He was my best friend and had been down with me since grade school.

"I got some of my Js and the Nike outfit to match." I had my clothes laid out on my bed. "What about you?"

"Same page, bruh," James cackled. "My colors are black and gold though."

"That's cool." I smiled and added a pair of fresh new socks. "I got blue and gray today."

"We gon' be the freshest niggas in the freshman class," James cheered.

"And you know this." I applauded. "I will meet you at the bus stop in a few."

"A'ight then," James replied. "I'ma call the rest of the squad, and we will see you at seven thirty."

I got dressed, sat at the kitchen table with my three sisters, and spoke to my parents about my new school situation. Everyone reminisced about their first day of school, and I tuned most of it out that day. I remember looking out of the kitchen window, and I saw her for the first time.

"Who is that?" I pointed through the window and turned my face sideways. "And why is she dressed so funny?"

"Where?" My mother turned to look and ultimately smiled at me. "That's Kyomo. She's going to be a new exchange student at Abbott this year."

"Kyomo?" I laughed. "What kind of name is that?"

"She's from China, idiot!" My older sister, Koran, threw a sugar packet at my head. "That's Ms. Sue's niece. I met her a few times at the corner store she owns on Twelfth Street."

"That's still a weird name." I frowned and threw the packet back at her.

"I don't think she speaks much English," Koran continued.

"Since she will be in your grade," my other sister, Tasha, added, "why don't you show her around, Montezz? Since she stays right across the street from us, it would be a big help to Ms. Sue. She's been so nice to us girls, giving us summer jobs and whatnot."

"So, because she helps you guys," I blurted out, "I'm supposed to deal with her ass?"

"Language!" Momma scolded me. "It's not such a terrible idea."

Pops walked in the kitchen fully dressed and headed to the coffeepot. "Good morning, all." He glanced at each of us. "What's the heated discussion about this morning?"

"The girls were just suggesting that Montezz show Ms. Sue's niece around the school and neighborhood. You know, she's a new exchange student from China."

"Sounds harmless enough." Pops sipped his coffee and grabbed his breakfast sandwich, which Momma had prepared for him. "That would be nice of you, Tezz! Well, I gotta get going. We got a lot of cars to work on at the shop today."

Momma walked Pops to his work truck and kissed him goodbye. Pops owned one of the best auto-body shops in the northern Birmingham area. He had billboards and a few commercial ads. His hours were long on most nights, but the old man loved every moment of it. He had always wished that I would get as excited about the family business, but at the moment, I was only interested in girls.

"I don't wanna be bothered with her," I pouted and finished my cereal. "My boys will be laughing and joking about how crazy she looks."

"Your friends are so childish and stupid." My younger sister, Carol, stuck her tongue out at me. "I swear, I'm more mature than they are, and I'm only twelve."

"Leave my crew alone," I defended them and washed my breakfast dishes. "Be quiet before I tell Rashad how much you like him!"

"Liar!" My baby sister balled up her fists. "You better not!"

I loved pissin' my sisters off. They were so emotional all the time. But I guess I got my best insight on chicks because I lived in a houseful of women.

"Can you please just do this?" Tasha sighed at me from the table. "It would mean a lot to Ms. Sue, and maybe she will finally promote one of us. I could really use the extra money for college next year."

"Really?" I folded my arms after I grabbed my backpack. "How much is it worth to you? I'm accepting all bribes."

"What was that?" Momma reentered the house, and it startled me a little bit.

"Oh, nothing, Momma." Koran gave a devilish smile and glanced over at me. "Montezz just agreed to become friends with Kyomo. He said he was looking forward to helping her out."

"What?" I scowled at her but then smiled at Momma.

"That's so nice of you, Tezz." Momma walked over and gave me a big hug. "I always knew that I raised the best son a mother could ever want."

"You know me, Momma!" I embraced her and squinted at all my joyful sisters.

They had definitely played me, but I would have the last laugh. Yeah, I could play the part of a good friend when my family watched me, but at school, I would just ditch her goofy ass. I called James and let him know about the situation. Of course he laughed at me.

"C'mon, Kyomo!" I called to her from across the street. "We gotta get to the bus stop."

I waited for her to join me, but she just stood there with a blank look on her face. For some reason, my heart reached out to her. I knew she didn't understand a word I had said. I looked both ways before I crossed the street and approached her. She had a delicate frame, jet-black hair in a neat bun, and a pale yellow knee-high dress with a white shirt underneath it. Her pale legs jittered with every step I took. I noticed her slender curves and felt an erection.

"Hey." I gave her a quick smile. "I'm Montezz from across the street."

I offered her my hand to shake, but her eyes stayed fixed on her feet. I said my name a few more times, and she finally looked up at me. She had the face of an angel, and her almond-shaped brown eyes had me spellbound. She glanced at my gray eyes and seemed fixed on them.

"Yeah," I joked, "all the girls love my gray eyes. They are like my trademark or something like that."

That was the first time I saw Kyomo smile, and it turned me on instantaneously. Her English was very limited, but we managed to get through the first few days of school with minor issues that week. At first, I was embarrassed by her, and I knew she could sense the way I felt. But in time, I grew to like her company, and she was around me just as much as my homeboys.

The night of our first high school party had soon approached us. The boys decided against having dates because we wanted to keep our options open for the night. None of them figured I was into their "hit it and quit it" because Kyomo was always by my side.

"How many numbers do you think you gon' get tonight, James?" Our homeboy Richard combed his fresh fade.

The game started our eighth-grade year. We would get girls' numbers, and whoever smashed the most girls would win $20 or whatever money we had.

"It's hard to say, playboy." James admired his new earring in the bathroom mirror. "Chelsea and Rhonda said something about a three-way after the party. Since my nude pics spread through the sophomore class, I've been quite popular these days."

"Oh, yeah." I laughed at James's dumb attempt to score pussy. "It was funny how that picture got into the wrong phone. How did you say that happened again?"

"That nigga asked to use Rhonda's phone." Our friend Malik laughed as he told the story again. "He said he accidently synced his photos to her shit. He's full of shit."

"Y'all just hatin' on me." James laughed at all of us. "Because I thought of that shit before y'all niggas."

We all joked and got ready for the night. I wasn't that focused on the hoes they were on. I hadn't fucked Kyomo yet, but I figured I would make my move tonight. I knew she was still a virgin, and I wanted to be her first. Them niggas was just worried about hittin' some used pussy, but I wanted something that I could mold and shape for myself.

3

Marvin: The Battle Cry

"Marv!" Lucinda hollered from the upstairs kitchen.

The sound of her voice used to give me goosebumps, but now I only felt the urge to punch a hole through the basement walls. We met after my first tour from Iraq and later married for love, or so I thought. Three kids later, I often wondered where the love had gone.

"Yeah?" I hollered back and turned down the studio equipment I had recently purchased for my man cave in the basement.

"Can you come up here for a second, please?" she replied from the top of the stairs.

"Yeah," I huffed. "Just give me a second."

Disgusted and defeated, I stomped up the stairs and found my wife seated at our kitchen table. She had a cigarette fired up and a glass of her favorite wine.

"What was the hurry?" I sighed and took a seat at the opposite end of the table.

"You know the twins have that field trip coming up," she said, beginning her speech. "Are you going to write that check for the hotel stays and all? Or do I need to do everything as always?"

"I can do it." I rolled my eyes. I should have known that her only concerns with me were about some damn money. "When is the money due?"

"The school needs the check by this Friday." She sipped her wine and flipped through her phone display. "Also, have you thought anymore about buying them a car? It would make life a lot easier on us. They both have their licenses, and I wouldn't have to take them as many places if they had reliable transportation."

"And what else do you have to do all day, Lucinda?" I let out a chuckle and watched her eyes squint back at me. "It's not like you work or anything. Why can't you take the twins where they need to go?"

"Is that all you have to say?" Lucinda finished her glass and poured another one.

She had always been beautiful, but her insides had made her so ugly and bitter. Where was my sexy caramel diva? The lady who kept me at my peak and the love I couldn't seem to live without?

"Sergeant Tyler," the sexy receptionist called my name and got my attention. "The therapist is ready for you in room number two."

I stood and followed the hourglass figure to my room in the back. She graciously smiled and walked away from the door. She smelled of roses, and I loved the way her flowing locs swayed from side to side as she walked away from me. I was definitely smitten with her but didn't know the first thing about approaching a woman.

Allow me to introduce myself. I'm Marvin Uriah Tyler Jr. I'd been active in the army since I turned 18, and after my first tour of Iraq, my superiors suggested counseling for my own betterment. I was the only survivor from my platoon. We were attacked by the enemy, and my fellow soldiers were viciously ambushed. I had been on watch in the tower, and that was the only saving grace that kept me on this earth.

"Hello, Sergeant." My therapist and friend, Miles Newport, graced me with a firm handshake. "How are you doing this week? Any changes, good or bad?"

"*About the same.*" *I shrugged my shoulders.* "*I don't mean to come off pessimistic, but is this really supposed to help me? I appreciate you listening to everything, but I just don't feel like this talkin' crap is helping me. And the pills I take, they just keep me up most nights.*"

"*I see.*" *Miles jotted something down on his notepad.* "*I can talk with your doctors and maybe tweak your prescriptions a bit. Other than that, is there anything new that you wanted to discuss?*"

"*Well . . .*" *I paused and felt my palms sweat.* "*As you know, I have reenlisted, but my superiors want a good bill of health from you before they give me a full okay. So, what do you think about that?*"

"*You have definitely made a lot of promising steps since we first spoke several months ago.*" *Miles readjusted his eyeglasses.* "*I don't see any reason why you couldn't reenlist. But I do want you to promise me something. If you need to talk or anything like that, you have my information. Don't hesitate to reach out to me or my office. Is that a deal?*"

"*Copy that.*" *I smiled and nodded.*

We chewed the fat for another thirty minutes or so, and I finally felt the courage to inquire about the receptionist.

"*So . . .*" *I paused and felt a little embarrassed.* "*What's the story on that receptionist out front?*"

"*What do you mean?*" *Miles raised an eyebrow with a coy smile.*

"*Is she single?*" *I blurted out.*

"*Oh, I see,*" *Miles chuckled.* "*Lucinda has been with us for about a year or so. She's a college grad and single as far as I know.*"

"*Oh, okay.*" *I breathed easier.*

"*I'm having a get-together at my home next week. I invited a few close friends, and of course, you are more*

*than welcome to come by. Lucinda should be there. She's
one hell of a cook. She always brings different dishes to
work for us."*

"Sounds like a plan." I smiled nervously. "I'll be there."

*I had agonized all that week on what to wear and
how to approach the sexy vixen at Miles's get-together.
I reached out to my older brother, Rodney. He was
something like a player and seemed to have the 411 on
women. He told me to be easy and make her laugh. That
should break the ice enough for me to land her number.
Sense of humor was not my better suit. I just hoped I
didn't embarrass myself.*

*Miles's home was decked out and he had the barbeque
pit going strong by the time I had arrived. He didn't
have a huge crowd, and I appreciated that aspect. I
didn't function well with a crowd. That always brought
about my anxiety. The music was chill, and the vibe felt
all right until I locked eyes on her.*

*"Marvin!" Miles waved in my direction, and I felt the
beads of sweat on my brow. "Come over here!"*

*I took a few deep breaths and tried to remember the
advice my big bro had given me earlier that week.*

"Allow me to introduce Lucinda James." Miles nodded.

*"Nice to meet you again." Lucinda's hazel brown
eyes followed my lengthy six-foot-two frame, and she
showed her deep dimples.*

*"Marvin," I stuttered slightly and extended my hand to
her. "Marvin Tyler."*

"Aw yes." She giggled joyously.

*"I see a few other guests by my deck over there." Miles
felt accomplished with his matchmaking skills. "I will
check back with you two a little later. Make yourselves
comfortable, all right?"*

*We both nodded and took a stroll along the enormous
yard. Lucinda talked about her life and aspirations of*

becoming a licensed counselor and other dreams. I listened and kept my cool for the most part. She was the oldest of three siblings, an army brat, and loved to cook when she wasn't working or spending time with her family.

"I feel like I have controlled this whole conversation, Marvin," she sighed, and we sat on the lawn swing. "So, tell me about you. I know you are in the army, but what else is there about you?"

"That's basically it for me." I shrugged my shoulders. "I've been in the army since I graduated from high school. I wasn't the most academic person, and I didn't want to risk getting into trouble on the streets, so the military seemed like the best route for me."

"I appreciate your service." Lucinda saluted me, and I smiled tremendously. "I can only imagine some of the war stories from over there. It takes a really strong person to endure all of that. It's very impressive."

"It's definitely not easy." I felt more comfortable with her. "There's always the risk that you won't make it back home. But I love my country, and I do the best I can to keep beautiful women like yourself safe and out of harm's way."

"Aren't you just a charmer, Mr. Tyler?" Lucinda gently caressed my freshly shaved face, and I felt on fire, and passion ran through my body like never before.

We had hit it off and were inseparable for the next few months. It came time for me to ship off, and it was harder to leave because of her. We promised to stay in touch and did just that.

Lucinda waited eight months for my return, and when I got home, I proposed on the spot. Two months later, we were married, and the twins were soon to follow. I moved the family to the army base that I was stationed at. Things were good for a while, and then they took a turn for the worse.

4

Nova: Survivin'

I wish I could say that life was all peachy and great without Phillip in the picture, but that would be a damn lie. He accepted the college offer and did great things at Stanford. As much as I resented him, I was proud of him and wanted to see him shine. I, on the other hand, had a son to feed and bills to pay. I was still at the grocery store, but that was barely making ends meet.

Jacques was about to graduate high school with a few college scholarships, so I was glad that his school career would be paid for without my help. Daddy drank a lot less after Markus was born. That helped me tremendously because I had a babysitter and opportunity to get more hours at the job. I just felt like my life was at a dead-end and everyone around me was doing so much better.

"Nova." I heard my coworker and friend Mia call my name. "Girl, what are you thinking about over there?"

"Damn, my bad." I frowned and remembered where I was. "I guess I was just daydreaming."

"I can understand that." Mia smiled. "Like I was saying, do you think you can get one of the other cashiers to cover me on Saturday night?"

"I'm sure I can." I glanced over the work schedule for the following week. "What you got to do that day?"

"On the real, I'm trying to hit up a few clubs. Plus, my homegirl is one of the new strippers at Uriah's. You know that new place downtown? She said she be making a grip of cash every night!" Mia smacked her glossy lips.

"I heard a little bit about it." I crossed out Mia's name and replaced it with someone else's. "One of my old classmates works there. She said the same thing about the money flow. I wish I had that kind of confidence. I don't think I could take my clothes off for money."

"Shit," Mia chuckled. "I was thinking about going to an audition, on the real. I mean, think about it, how long have you been working here?"

"Girl"—I rolled my eyes—"too damn long to mention!"

"And how are your pockets feelin' right about now?" Mia continued.

"Still empty as fuck," I admitted. "I do get help with Markus, but kids aren't cheap, and he's always needing more and more."

"Exactly my point." Mia patted me on the back. "So, you need to do two things: contact that big-shot baby daddy of yours and come with me to that club this weekend. You can use the break, girl. You're too young to be stressin' the way that you do."

"I ain't really spoke to Phillip that much in the past few years," I sighed and thought back to our blowup before Markus was born. "He probably doesn't want to hear from me anyways."

"Fuck all of that," Mia replied. "Y'all got a kid together, and you didn't make him by yourself. You better get in touch with that nigga, girl! So, are you down to ride with me this weekend or what?"

"Well," I said, giving a sly grin, "I am off this weekend. I will see if Daddy or my brother can watch Markus."

"That's the spirit!" Mia gave me a high five. "And if we get too fucked up, you can always crash at my place."

"Sounds good to me," I laughed.

It had been a while since I let loose. I hadn't had the time or the desire to get out and do much of anything. I finished the rest of that work night and thought long and hard on what Mia and I had discussed that day. Perhaps it was time for me to reach out to Phillip. What was I so afraid of? Once upon a time, we were the best of friends. We had a bond, and I shouldn't feel so scared to give him a call.

I looked up Stanford's directory on my phone and talked to one of the receptionists at the university. After a long wait, I was finally connected to his room number. His voice was on the answering machine, and I nervously left my number for him to call me back. The ball was in his court, but I hoped to hear back from my friend.

"I'm so glad you reached out to me, Nova," Phillip laughed on the other end. "I have missed your voice and just everything about you. Seems like old times with us on the phone."

"Yeah." I grinned and placed him on speakerphone while I bathed our son. "I really do apologize for all that shit I said to you back then."

"No need to mention any of that," Phillip cut me off. "I know you were just being emotional and all that jazz. We are cool, believe me. So, when can I see Markus? I bet he's so big now."

"He's definitely a handful." I smiled, and Markus splashed me with a few suds in the tub. "How often do you come to town?"

"Well," Phillip began, "I try to make it home for all the usual holidays. Summertime is always hard to predict because of my practice schedule, but I will do the best I can to be home more often now that we are back talking."

"Sounds good to me." I hesitated because I didn't want to just blurt out about some cash, but it was on my mind.

"So, how are you doing? Financially I mean." Phillip brought it up before I got the chance to mention it.

"Shit's tough," I confessed. "Working at the grocery store barely makes ends meet, and Daddy, well, you know how he is!"

"Yeah, I remember," Phillip sighed. "Is he still drinking like he was when we were kids?"

"He's cut back some since I had Markus," I admitted. "But he has his relapses every now and then."

"I know that can't be easy on you. How's your brother doing? Still the bookworm?"

"Yeah." I dried off Markus and put his pajamas on. "He graduates this year and plans on going to State with a scholarship."

"That's great news," Phillip continued. "You know all you gotta do is ask and I will send you some ends. I been saving up a lot of my funds for the past two years. I figured you would come around in your own time. I always told you that I would support our son, and none of that has changed."

"That's wassup." I felt relieved. "You don't know how happy I am to hear that. I have been wanting to get our own place. A fresh start is what me and Markus really need, and I wouldn't be able to do that on my own."

"Consider it handled," Phillip stated. "I will be home next month, and we can get that squared away when I get there."

"I love you, Phillip," I blurted out and felt a tear roll down my eye. "Thank you so much."

"I love you too, girl," Phillip joked. "I can't wait to see the both of you."

I felt so inspired and in a better place after I finished my conversation with Phillip. I decided not to tell anyone about my moving situation until I knew for sure that it was real. Phillip was a good guy, but things could always change, and I didn't want to jinx myself. Daddy agreed to babysit, and I spent an additional hour getting dressed for the club that night.

I was applying the rest of my makeup and heard my phone ring on my dresser.

"Hello?" I replied and finished with my eyeliner.

"Are you ready, bihh?" Mia clowned on the other end.

"Ready as I'm going to be." I gave myself one last look over. I purchased a red minidress with black four-inch pumps to give me a height of five foot nine. I curled my mid-length hair and used my gray contacts for the night.

"A'ight then," Mia replied. "I will come get you in twenty minutes."

"I'll be ready." I finished our conversation and relaxed on my bed while I waited on my friend to arrive.

Strip clubs were out of my realm of comfort. I had seen a few movies with strip clubs in them but never actually went inside of one. I had just turned 21, so this was all new for me. Mia had been sneaking into clubs for a few years now. She was the vet, and I was the rookie.

"I hope we can find some good seats." Mia pulled into the packed parking lot. "This is hip-hop Saturday, and the ballers always come out to play. Be sure to check out the VIP area. You never know who you might see in here."

"Damn, girl." I felt like a kid in a candy store. "This shit is on swole!"

"Girl, I told you!" Mia came to a stop and reapplied her lip gloss before exiting her ride. "This is the place to be. We over there at the store making chump change. Just imagine, one week of this could change our whole life!"

"You might be right if the parking lot stays this packed," I thought out loud but felt the butterflies churn in the pit of my stomach. "But I don't know if I could do the dancing thing. Not in front of all these people."

"You trippin'!" Mia laughed as we paid our entrance fee for the club.

The place was decked out with big lights and a huge DJ booth. The records were spinning, the bar was packed, and the girls were doing their thing on the stage.

"She's basically naked." I pointed to the dark-skinned vixen who did the splits on stage. "That G-string ain't coverin' up shit!"

"And did you see all that paper she just picked up?" Mia pointed. The girl had two arms full of cash. "That bitch just covered my bills for two months in thirty minutes or less. Girl, I don't know about you, but I'm with it. I will definitely be here for the auditions on Monday night. And if you knew what was best for you and yours, you would have your ass in here with me. Shit, I will come pick you up. So, what do you say?"

I felt as though I was at a standstill. I had some great news from Phillip, but I couldn't bank on that just yet. Words meant nothing without the action behind it. There were so many things that could go wrong, and then I would still be stuck at a dead-end job. Could I really dance naked for money? Was I cool with guys lusting over my body and me dancing for them? Would they have to touch me? Was I expected to touch them?

"Nova!" Mia tapped me on my shoulder and escorted me to our open booth. "Are you still with me? Did you hear what I said? Are you coming with me on Monday?"

"Yeah." I nodded nervously. "I'll get someone to cover me that night. What time do I need to be ready?"

5

Montezz:

That's Tha Way Love Goes

"Do you love me, Tezz?" Kyomo asked after one of our many hump sessions.

That night of the dance was the beginning of our sexually dominated relationship. She was hooked on my dick. She wanted it every day and everywhere. I will never forget the time she asked me about sucking a dick. There was no way I could teach her, so I had a bitch over to suck me off, and she watched from the closet of my room.

"Yeah." I stumbled over my words and washed up in her bathroom, "I . . . I love you. What made you ask me that?"

"Because I have something big to tell you." Kyomo seemed upset.

I headed back to her bed and placed my arms around her. I could tell she had been crying, and I felt concerned and worried about her.

"What is it?" I searched her face. "I hope it's not about the head. I told you last time that you are getting better at it. Some chicks are just better than others, but the sex is really good."

"It's not about that, Tezz!" She pushed me away and stood. "Is that all you think of me? Just to have sex? I have made a big mistake. Very big mistake!"

"What are you talking about, Ky?" I stood in the bathroom door and watched my sexy Asian climb into the shower. I felt my young joint rise and immediately planned on getting naked once more. "You are doing better with your English. You breeze through all the classes, too. Hell, this is our sophomore year approaching and you are already signed up for junior classes. What mistake could you have made?"

"All this sex with you, Tezz!" Kyomo sobbed, and the suds were washed away from her petite frame.

She was almost inconsolable, but I got her cleaned up and wrapped in a towel after I cleaned up the restroom. I combed and dried her jet-black hair as she sat on her bed almost in a trance. I was worried and wondered why she felt so down.

"Do you feel better now?" I sat beside her and grabbed her petite hand in mine. "You know, whatever it is, you can tell me. Please, tell me what's wrong."

"I no bleed." Kyomo grabbed her tight stomach. "Not in two months now. I worry that I might be pregnant!"

"Pregnant?" I felt like blowing chunks. I ran to the bathroom and hurled into the toilet bowl.

Fuck, we were only 15 years old. There was no way we could take care of a damn baby. My parents were gonna kick my ass.

"I told you." Kyomo rubbed my back and offered me a washcloth to wash my face. "It is bad, very bad."

"First things first." I gathered my thoughts and chugged the rest of my orange soda. "We gotta go to the store and get you a pregnancy test."

"How are we going to buy one?" Kyomo shrugged her shoulders. "They will not sell to me. I am too young, Tezz!"

"Don't you worry about none of that." I held her close and felt her shiver at my touch. "I will get one for you, and we can take it after school tomorrow."

"I worry," Kyomo sobbed. "And I am scared."

"I am too." I kissed her softly on the cheek. "But we don't know for sure yet. So, let's just try to keep cool, and we will see how things go, okay?"

She blew her nose and relaxed a bit. I stayed for another hour and decided to head home. My heart and stomach were so heavy as I entered the house. I spoke to everyone and tried to remain normal, but I was more stressed than I could ever imagine. If Kyomo was pregnant, my life would forever be changed. I was just a damn kid, never lived or been much of anywhere. And now there was a possibility that I had a child to take care of.

"Hey, bruh." My older sister, Koran, peeked into my doorway. "Do you have a few mechanical pencils I can borrow until tomorrow? Are you okay?"

I could hear her footsteps getting closer, but I kept my head buried in my pillow.

"Tezz." Koran plopped down on my bed. "Wassup with you? You know you can talk to me."

"I don't know if I should talk to anyone about this right now," I sighed and wiped the loose tears from my eyes before I sat up next to her.

"Damn, it's like that?" Koran frowned but kept on. "I always thought we were the closest of the siblings. I ride on you like the other sisters, but we always kept one another's secrets. Talk to me, Tezz."

"It's Ky." I brought my voice down to a whisper and lightly closed my bedroom door.

"Your little girlfriend from across the street?" Koran snickered, but I motioned for her to keep it down. "Why? What's going on with her?"

"She said she's missed her period for two months!" I looked away from my sister's horrified stare.

"Tezz, no!" Koran placed her hands over her mouth. "So, you have been smashin' my boss's niece and didn't have sense enough to strap it up?"

"Fuck that she's your boss's niece," I popped back. "Y'all were the ones who pushed her on me in the first place. I hadn't thought any more about her, but everyone wanted me to be her friend and show her around."

"Exactly." Koran rolled her eyes. "Befriend her, not knock her up!"

"Fuck, sis!" I shook my worried head. "This is just too much for me. I can't believe this is happenin'."

"Me either." Koran rubbed my back in comfort. "Damn, bruh, you are only fifteen. And Momma and Daddy, oh, are they gonna be pissed. Not to mention, Ms. Sue will probably blow a damn gasket!"

"I know all of that." I lay back on my bed. "We did use condoms some of the time, but not all. I know we should have used one each time. We just weren't thinkin' it through, but I never expected this shit to happen."

"No one ever does, bruh." Koran stood and headed to the doorway. "So, what's the next move?"

"I gotta cop her a pregnancy test tomorrow," I whispered. "I was just gonna steal one. Ain't no way anyone would sell me one."

"I can get it for you." Koran nodded. "I will stop by the store after school today. Try to keep it relaxed. I pray her period is just thrown off or something like that."

"That makes two of us." I gave her a thumbs-up before she walked out. "Thanks, sis."

I wish I could say that Kyomo's period was just late, but I can't say that shit. She was definitely pregnant, and life as we knew it was over. I told Kyomo that Koran knew about us. She was mad at first but came around to the idea. At least we had an ally and someone to run to for advice. Kyomo was scared to face her aunt, and I felt the same about my parents. I thought about telling them at least a hundred times a day, but I always chickened out. Days turned to weeks and weeks into months. I wasn't sure how far Kyomo was, but we had made it past Christmas break and still hadn't shared our baby news.

"You comin' over later?" Kyomo snickered to me on the phone. She had been in better spirits lately, and that baby made her hornier than ever. I was scared to even breathe around her because that might cause her to jump my bones.

"Yes, boo." I smiled and combed down my fade. "What time does your aunt leave for out of town?"

"She leaves this morning," Kyomo told me. "I just do a lot of sleeping and eating today."

"How long will she be gone this time?" I raised an eyebrow.

Her aunt would be gone several times a month and always for three or more days at a time. It was very easy to fuck without interruptions, but our folks were very trusting people.

"She say four days this time, but could be longer," Kyomo giggled. "You spend the night like last time?"

"Yeah, of course I will." I licked my lips. Kyomo had graduated to a professional dick sucker. I never had to ask for it. She loved to do it on her own. I had it made in the shade. Not many 15-year-old boys could ever say that shit.

We finished our conversation and I ventured to my parents' room to lie about where I was going for the weekend. My homeboy Tommy lived two blocks from me. His mom was home less than Kyomo's aunt, so I never worried about getting caught up over there. I would walk up the two blocks and then cut through a yard, climb Kyomo's fence, and enter through her back door. We had our routine down to a science.

"The baby kick a lot today." Kyomo lay on her bed with only a T-shirt and panties on. "You want to feel?"

I placed my hand on top of hers and felt a foot or something through her skin. I yanked my hand away and felt shocked by it.

"Damn." I shook my head. "Does that hurt you? What does it feel like?"

"Sometimes it does hurt." Kyomo positioned herself against the headboard. "Hard to explain, but it's okay."

"I can't believe we have made it this far and still not told our families about the baby." I rubbed her belly and felt another kick. "I am worried about your health though. I read in health class that women are supposed to take vitamins and have checkups."

"Your sister bring me the vitamins a few months ago." Kyomo pointed to the pill bottle on her nightstand. "I take them, and I feel okay, Tezz. I still scared to talk to my aunt. She will say I shamed the family."

"I know how you feel, Ky." I kissed her on the cheek and grabbed her hand. "But you still have to deliver the baby. They will know about it eventually anyways. I don't want you to risk your health or the baby's any more than you have already. We need to tell them before it's too late. And what do you mean shamed your family?"

"Chinese stuff. You would not understand in America." Kyomo looked away from me and tapped her foot on the carpet. "I am a teenager, unwed, and pregnant. That brings shame to my family because we are not married."

"We are too young to be married," I pointed out.

"All the more reason that we should not have sex," Kyomo answered and felt another kick from her tummy. "I don't know how my aunt will react or what she will do to me."

"She will be mad." I gave a nervous grin. "I know my parents are gonna be furious. But what else can they do? The damage is done. They will just have to help us until we are old enough to get jobs and provide for the baby."

"I guess we will see." Kyomo kissed me softly and rose to her feet. "You are lucky, Tezz! You have a nice family. They love you and will be here for you and the baby. My family will never understand any of this. But there's nothing I can do about it now."

Ky and I shared a few nice days together, and I went home to ponder telling my parents the truth. They had been so proud of my academics that year. I was no longer the slacker they knew me to be. Hanging out with Kyomo had definitely improved my grades for the semester. I made my way to their bedroom door, and they smiled right at me.

"Hey there, son," Pops laughed and focused on their big-screen TV.

"Wassup, honey." Momma blew me a kiss and joked with Dad about one of their television shows.

"Nothing much," I lied and fiddled with my shirttail. "I needed to talk to you guys about something, but if you want to watch your show, I can tell you about it later."

"It's fine, Tezz." Pops motioned for me to sit down. "We are never too busy for one of you kids and you know that. What's going on? What's on your mind?"

"I really don't know how to say this." I looked away and sat on the far end of their bed. "I know that I have really let y'all down, and that was not my intention."

"What are you talking about, Tezz?" Momma became worried. "Your grades reflect how well you are doing. Why would you ever think that you have disappointed us?"

"It's not about grades or school," I replied and studied both of their faces. I felt the tears swell up in my eyes. I tried to remain strong, but my emotions were all over the place. I knew my parents were shocked because, even as a kid, I hardly ever cried.

"You are really concerning me, son." Pops cut off the TV. "What is this all about? Whatever it is, I promise we can talk about it."

"It's Kyomo!" I blurted out.

"Your friend from across the street?" Momma answered. "Such a sweet little girl."

"Yeah." I paused. "Well, we have been dating for over a year now, and we have sex a lot. Now she's pregnant!"

6

Marvin: In the Line of Fire

"Marv," Lucinda sobbed after she hung up the phone in the kitchen. "Baby, we need to talk!"

"What's wrong, love?" I frowned as I rocked one of our twin daughters to sleep in my arms. "Who was that on the phone?"

"That was my mother." She motioned for me to put the baby down and follow her into our bedroom. I did just that, and she closed the door behind her.

"What's going on with your mom?" I kept my voice low and offered her my handkerchief.

"It's my dad," Lucinda cried out. "Momma said she had gone out with friends, and when she came home, she found him unresponsive on the couch. She's at the hospital with him now. He had a massive heart attack."

"Oh God, no!" I comforted my wife, and we sobbed together momentarily.

After a few minutes, Lucinda blew her nose and headed to the master bath to wash up. She came back with a more stern and focused disposition.

"I have to fly home as soon as possible," she relayed to me. "I'm not sure how long we will be there, but I know that my mom needs me and the rest of the kids. You understand, don't you?"

"Of course I do, honey." I kissed her passionately. "This is a family emergency. There's no way that I couldn't understand."

"Good, I figured you would understand."

Lucinda pulled out her phone and immediately tracked and booked a flight. It was only a one-way ticket for the time being. We made the most of that day and night together. I knew I would miss my family, but it was for the best.

Lucinda called me the moment she landed and promised to keep me posted on any changes with her dad. I had my work cut out for me on the base. Although I was not directly in combat anymore, I was in charge of a platoon of soldiers. It was up to me to get them ready for combat and strengthen their cognitive skills. I had fewer and fewer nightmares about my old demons and tried to stay focused on the positive things in life.

My nightly routine consisted of an hour of video chat with my wife and kids, but after two weeks away, the video chats were not as regular anymore. Tonight was one of those nights that I was unable to reach Lucinda, and that worried me. I called her phone several times and the house phone as well. I decided to leave a few voice messages, took my pills, and passed out on the couch.

My father-in-law had succumbed to his heart attack, and my heart went out to Lucinda and her family. I was approved for three days of leave, just enough time for the funeral and time with family. I tried to console my wife, but she was in such denial and cold to my touch.

"Do you want me to help you with that?" I asked my wife in her mother's kitchen. The family had congregated at the house after the graveside services. Food was decked out and Lucinda was scrubbing a few pots and pans.

"Uh, sure." Lucinda blew out some steam and stepped away from the sink. "I should probably go and check on Momma. She said she needed to lie down and take a nap."

"Why don't you let her rest and slow down for a second?" I dried my hands on the wash towel and sat at the kitchen table with her. "I know you are worried about your mom, we all are, but I'm just as worried about you. You have been nonstop around here."

"I know." Lucinda's eyes filled with tears. "I just have the need to stay as busy as possible, so I can't think about . . ."

She collapsed into my arms, and I held her close to my chest. She had finally broken down, and I'm glad I was there to catch her. I regretted having to get back to the army base that following day. I contacted my superiors, but there was no way for them to give me more time off. Lucinda agreed to stay a few additional days with her mom and finalize things with the family. I was sorry to leave and boarded the plane rather solemnly.

I had anticipated the return of my family that Monday morning, but Lucinda didn't show up empty-handed. She said she felt guilty about leaving her mom in that house alone and decided to move her in with us. I was against that shit from jump but tried my best to hide it. I figured it wouldn't be forever and maybe my mother-in-law would do better around a new place. However, I spent less and less time with my wife after that. She had her mom as a new project and no real time for me. I spent most of my nights jacking off in a warm towel or in the shower.

"Marv." Lucinda tapped on the bathroom door after I just came in the washcloth. "Are you about finished in there? I need to pee, and Momma is in the other bathroom."

"I'll be out in just a minute, my love!" I breathed and cleaned up my mess.

I unlocked the door. She rolled her eyes at me and shut the door behind me. Where had my sexy goddess gone? Why was I the target of her aggression these days? Confused and hurt, I walked into our kitchen and heated up the meal from that night. I checked on the twins while the oven heated. They were into everything and the apples of my eye. I entered the kitchen, and my mother-in-law sat at the table beside me.

"Good evening, Marvin." Momma James gave a weak smile and drank her cup of coffee.

"Hey, Momma James." I gave her a comforting smile. "How are you tonight? Is there anything I can get for you?"

"Today has been an all right day for me." She sniffled. "There are times when I don't know whether I'm coming or going. I really appreciate you opening up your home to me. I'm sure that wasn't easy for you. If I'm intruding, just let me know."

"Don't be silly," I chuckled nervously and checked on my food. "I'm happy that you are here and so is Lucinda. You are always welcome in our home, so don't think anything of it."

"You are the best son-in-law." Momma James blew her nose into a tissue. "My Lucinda really picked a good man, and my husband really respected you, fellow army man and all. I was just concerned. I have heard you and my daughter argue through the night. I'm no fool. I know she's been spending a lot of her time with me and not much time being a wife."

"That's not for you to worry about." I stirred my potatoes and gravy before placing it back in the oven. "We will work everything out. It's really not a big deal."

"You don't have to talk to me like I'm naive, Marvin," Momma James continued. "I will talk to my daughter tomorrow about all of this. You are a good man, and you have gone out of your way to provide for your family. You should expect quality time and all that it involves. Don't try to talk me out of it. I know exactly what to say to her. Don't worry, she won't snap at you about it."

"Snap about what, Momma?" Lucinda peeped her head into the kitchen and gave her mom a hug. "What are you two in here talking about?"

"Oh, nothing, dear." Momma James finished her coffee and placed the mug in the sink. "I was just thanking Marvin again for letting me move in here. Not every man would be so understanding in a situation like this one. You have a very good husband, daughter. Well, I'm off to bed. I will see the both of you in the morning."

We said good night to her, and a silence fell through the kitchen. We commenced with small talk but nothing too major. I finished my meal alone, cleaned up the kitchen, and headed for the bedroom. I was unsurprised to find my wife asleep and unconcerned with her horny husband. I shook my head, grabbed my pajamas, and headed for a nice, hot bath. I tried to remember that Lucinda was grieving, but it hurt me that she seemed to forget about me. I dried off and got into our bed, my back facing her.

"Marv," I heard Lucinda whisper as she placed her arm around my waist.

"Yes, Lucinda?" I seemed uninterested with my back to her.

"I do appreciate that you are cool with Momma being here." She kissed my lower back. "And I'm sorry for all the distance between us. I know this can't be easy for you."

"You're right, Lucinda." I turned to face her and placed her palms on my rock-hard dick. "It's not been easy for the both of us, but I try to remember that you are grieving and everything. I just miss our quality time together, you feel me?"

"So I see." Lucinda licked her lips and disappeared under the covers.

She sucked on me until I came in her mouth, but she didn't end it there. She got me hard once more and allowed me to nut in her face. I wanted to feel her pussy walls, but she claimed she wasn't up to all of that. I didn't argue with her because her mouth had given me the attention I had longed for these past months. I held her close to me and slept better than I had for a while. I forgot about my pills and my normal routine. The orgasm was my medicine. If only things had kept up that way. If only.

7

Nova: In Transition

"Let's do this shit, bihh! Are you ready?" Mia was hype on our ride to the club auditions that Monday night. I, on the other hand, was on the verge of blowing chunks on her dashboard. "You all right over there, girl?"

"Fuck no!" I felt anxious. "I don't think I can go through with this shit. I will come and support you, but I don't think I can strip in front of people. I don't want anyone to know I'm working in a strip club."

"It's nothing to be ashamed of, girl!" Mia cut off her car and grabbed both of my shoulders. "This is a legit establishment, and you are not breaking any laws inside of there. You said you don't want anyone to see your face, right? Here you go!"

Mia threw me one of those Mardi Gras face masks, the type that covers your eyes and nose area. I gave her a puzzled look.

"I thought about using this with my act, but maybe you need it more than I do," Mia laughed. "That way, no one will know who you are, and you can focus on dancing."

"You might have a great idea." I smiled and grew more confident with my audition.

I had always been a great and flexible dancer. Never thought I would be shaking it for cash, but after a few drinks, I would loosen up nicely. There were quite a few girls at the audition, at least ten to twelve of us.

"Hello, ladies!" A tall, dark brown, middle-aged man graced us with a smile. He wore an expensive black suit with a red silk shirt underneath and shiny black shoes. He had gold caps on both of his incisors, and there was a sprinkle of gray in his curly hair.

"Welcome to Uriah's. I'm the owner and boss man. You can call me Mr. Marvin. To my left is the house manager, Wilson Daniels. In charge of dancers is Candy Phillips, and the baddest DJ in all the land is DJ Fab. We will be your judges tonight. We are lookin' for sex on a stage. Excite us and leave us wantin' more. Understood? Okay, first up, Mia Andrews!"

"I can't believe I'm the first one," Mia whispered in my ear and handed me her raincoat.

She wore blue tight lingerie and stood in four-inch black pumps. If she was nervous, she didn't show it. Mia made eye contact with all the judges individually, and when the music began to play, she owned every beat. Mia's body was immaculate and the color of hot cocoa. She gave the decked-out DJ a lap dance and later rubbed her pussy print in Mr. Marvin's face. As the music ended, Mia ended her routine in a set of splits on the marble floor.

The judges whispered with one another as Mia walked off the stage and headed in my direction. I smiled and graced her with a big hug. I was very impressed by her.

"Damn, bihh!" I gave her a playful nudge while I whispered. "You owned that shit!"

"I was about my business," Mia breathed and patted herself on the back. "There are a lot of girls here. I had to make sure I stood out in the crowd, you feel me?"

"Looks like you did that," I snickered, and Mr. Marvin called the next girl's name.

I started to feel rather lightheaded and motioned for Mia to follow me into the dressing room behind us.

"Wassup?" Mia gave me a look of concern.

"I just feel so anxious and nervous." I placed my head between my knees, and Mia fanned me with a sheet of paper. "I don't think I can go through with this. What if I get up there and make a damn fool of myself? No, I think I will just sit this shit out."

"Nova, you are really trippin' right now!" Mia reached down into her raincoat pocket and pulled out a glass vile. "Here, take a few lines. And I got a couple shots of Henny in my other pocket. I thought I would be the one to freak out, but clearly you need this shit."

"Coke?" I felt my voice raise, and I calmed it down. "Are you crazy right now? I've never done that shit before. I don't know how it will make me feel. I will take the Henny though!"

Mia fixed a few lines and shook her head at me. "Girl, it's not gonna do shit but take the edge off. I do it sometimes when I'm feeling stressed the fuck out. It makes me feel more sexual, and my pussy gets super wet. Trust me, it's not gonna do anything fucked up to you. If it makes you feel better, I will do a few lines with you, okay?"

I was hesitant at first. Mia walked over to the dressing room door and left a small crack in it. She snorted a few lines and motioned for me to join her. That first line stung the inside of my virgin nostril. I felt my nose grow more numb by the line, and finally I sneezed a few times.

"Here." Mia handed me a Kleenex. "Look in that mirror and clean up your nose, and then take these two shots of Hen. You ought to be good after that. I haven't heard them call your name yet, so just try to relax and let those drugs do their job. Do you have that mask?"

"Yeah," I replied and took a few deep breaths for comfort. "Okay, you are right. I can do this!"

With a new sense of confidence, we rejoined the crowd of dancers, and I had to admit that I felt a lot better.

There was a lot of talent in the group of girls. All were beautiful and fit and had a glow all their own. I thought more about a routine and a judge to single out of the group. If I could own one, maybe the rest of them would become aroused by it. The owner was okay on the eyes. Older than I would ever fuck, but not a total waste. Not to mention, he looked fit and seemed to have a nice amount of money from the look of his clothes.

"Ja'Nova Jacobs!" I heard Mr. Marvin recite my name, and I gave my thin jacket to my homegirl.

I had on a black and sheer two-piece bikini. I grabbed the red sequined mask and placed it on my face. The red was a close match to my red heeled pumps. I allowed myself to get into character. For this song, I was a woman of the night in search of a man to dry hump, seduce, and take home with me.

"Hello, big daddy!" I climbed on top of Mr. Marvin and whispered sweetly in his ear. I caressed him gently and gyrated my hips to the motion of lovemaking. I stared deep into his eyes and knew that I had him under my spell.

"Uh . . ." The house manager snapped us out of our moment we had shared. "Marv, are you ready to tally up your votes, or are you going to keep the girl on your lap for another song?"

Mr. Marvin gave a short chuckle, licked his lips, and released my thick hips from his grasp. I climbed off his lap, took a short bow, and strutted off the stage.

"Mm-hmm," Mr. Marvin proclaimed, and they commenced with their deliberations.

"And you were worried about makin' a fool outta yourself." Mia winked and laughed with me. "My bihh brought that shit!"

"Yeah," I joked. "Thanks to you!"

The group of us hung out in the stuffy dressing room while we waited for the judges' decisions. I learned that most of the girls were in their early twenties like me and some of them had stripped in clubs before. A few of them had kids and bills to pay, same as me. I thought back on the promises that Phillip had made, but I wanted money that was my own. I had to grow up faster than most. I couldn't rely on word of mouth. If I wanted anything, I had to go out and get it.

"We are ready for you, ladies!" the manager for the dancers, Candy Phillips, hollered to us.

I was a little on edge but decided that, either way, I would make a way for my son. They called off a few names that were not surprising to me, but Mia and I were both selected to be new dancers. I was so thrilled and couldn't help but notice that the owner hadn't taken his eyes off me.

"We appreciate all of you comin' out for auditions this evening." Mr. Marvin briefly looked away from me and addressed the crowd. "We only need the seven girls we named at this time, but we will keep everyone else on file because things are always subject to change. Can the seven selected please stick around for an additional conversation with us?"

The two managers and owner had individual conver-sations with each of the dancers, mostly explaining the rules and fees that the club provided and that whole thing. When it came to my turn, Mr. Marvin motioned me over to the bar.

"Ja'Nova." Mr. Marvin smiled and showed his gold caps. "You made quite the impression on this old man."

"Thank you, Mr. Marvin!" I gave a playful smile and decided to stay in character with him. "And I believe that you are as old as you feel."

"Is that right?" He gave a chuckle. "I'm glad you auditioned here tonight. I look forward to seeing a lot more of you, my dear."

"On or off the stage?" I playfully rubbed the top of his hand with mine.

"Aren't you a fresh one?" Mr. Marvin blushed. "Let me try to remain professional here, okay?"

"As you wish." I sat back on the barstool, but he lowered his left hand by my voluptuous booty.

"I did say I would try, little lady." Mr. Marvin winked at me and gave my butt a grab before he walked away.

So, that's the kind of game he wants to play? I laughed to myself and shook my head. *He looks like the type who ain't gettin' any at home. I saw that tired wedding band on his finger. He probably gets his nut off seein' us pop our coochies. Maybe if I play my cards right, I can get some real cash outta his ass.*

"You ready to go, girl?" I heard Mia approach me from behind. "I'm starvin' like hell. Where did you wanna get something to eat?"

"Yeah, I'm ready." I smiled big and proud. "You can pick the place. I could eat just about anything right now."

8

Montezz: Playtime Is Ova'

"Damn, bruh!" my homie James exclaimed over the phone after I told him my secret. "I kinda thought Ky was on tha plump side, but I never thought she was pregnant. I can't believe you kept that shit from me. I thought we were boys."

"Man," I sighed and peered through my curtain window to see if I saw my parents' headlights emerge in our driveway. "We kept that shit from everybody. I wanted to say something from the jump, but Ky kept talkin' me out of it."

"I know your parents shit a brick," James snickered in a boyish fashion.

"That's puttin' it lightly." I shook my head and sulked in my bedroom window. "I think the hardest thing I ever had to do was tell them about the baby. And they made me call Ky's aunt and tell her, too. She flew back home and beat the brakes off Ky. My mom had to go over there and separate the two of them."

"I guess that was to be expected," James said dryly. "I mean, y'all are only fifteen years old. How can y'all take care of a baby? I wouldn't want to be in your shoes, bruh."

"Thanks a lot," I huffed and puffed.

"It's awful quiet over there," James noticed.

"Yeah." I sighed once more. "My older sisters are at work, younger sis is at a friend's, and my parents went to the ER with Ms. Sue and Ky. They tryin'a figure out how far along she is and all that jazz. I wanted to go, but Ms. Sue said she couldn't stand the sight of me right now."

"That's fucked up, man," James breathed out. "So, what were y'all thinkin'? I mean, eventually someone would notice Ky giving birth, you know what I mean?"

"We were just scared." I stuck to my story. "There were so many times that I wanted to say something to someone, but I just didn't know how to do it. It's a shame though. I really managed to pull my grades up this year. But now, like my pops said earlier, playtime is ova'."

"A daddy at the age of fifteen," James replied. "Shit's just sad every time I think about it. Are y'all gonna keep the baby?"

"I mean, yeah." I watched a few cars ride by nervously. "I never thought of any other options."

"How are the two of you gonna provide for a kid right now?" James made a valid point. "Y'all can't really get jobs right now."

"I figured our parents would come around and help us for now." I shrugged my shoulders. "I would get a job as soon as I could, and Ky could get one too."

"She's not even from here, man," James pointed out. "Who's to say her aunt won't ship her and the baby back to China?"

I started to rebut but saw the headlights of my parents' minivan in the driveway. I ended my call with James but promised to call him back as soon as I could. My parents entered the house with loud words and a slam of the front door.

"Montezz!" Pops hollered for me, and I emerged from my bedroom.

I entered the family room and saw Ky huddled on the couch with a few luggage bags beside her.

"What's going on?" I looked stunned at both of my parents. "What's with the luggage bags?"

"Kyomo will be staying here with us for the duration of her pregnancy." Momma looked away from me and fired up a cigarette in the kitchen. "Ms. Sue doesn't trust herself around her and said something about disgracing the family or some crap. We will make room for her in Koran's room for now. We are not happy about this, but it's the least we can do given the situation you put us in."

"Oh, wow!" I sat down beside Kyomo. I moved closer to her, but she pushed me away from her. "What did they say about the baby?"

"Surprisingly," Momma began, "she's all the way into her third trimester, about seven months right now. I don't know how, but the baby is fine. She's very healthy considering she's had no prenatal care."

"She?" I blurted out and looked at Kyomo's belly. "So, it's a girl?"

"Yes." Momma had tears forming in her eyes. "I just don't know what else to say. I am very disappointed in the two of you. I thought you would have been smarter than this. In this day and time, there are ways to protect yourself from pregnancies. But you are kids, and kids never seem to think about the consequences of anything."

Pops said nothing but headed to his bedroom and shut the door behind him. I knew I had let them down, but there was nothing I could do about it now. Our daughter would be here in the next few months. I only hoped that we could find some way of dealing with this together.

"Tezz?" Momma wiped her weary eyes. "Can you show Kyomo where she will be staying and help her get un-packed?"

"Why can't she just stay in my room, Momma?" I frowned. "The damage is done. No point in puttin' her in the room with Koran. I got plenty of room for her things. I mean, what else can we do?"

"I guess you are right about something." Momma stood up and paused in the hallway. "We will discuss this more tomorrow. But for now, we are all exhausted. I suggest the two of you talk about things and try to get some sleep."

I did as Momma had asked and made room for Kyomo's things in my room. She moved at a gracious pace and plopped down on my bed disgusted with herself. I tried to talk to her, but her responses were short and very distant.

I ran my hand across her back to soothe her. "Ky, please talk to me! We are both going through this shit together. Please don't shut me out."

"That hurts so bad." Kyomo made a face while I rubbed her back.

She revealed all the bruises on her body, and I felt enraged and guilty for them. I went in the kitchen and grabbed a bag of frozen peas. I had gotten in a few fights over time, and Momma always gave me a bag of frozen peas for bruises or swelling.

"I can't believe your aunt beat you like this!" I frowned and applied the frozen veggies to her back and shoulder. "The fact that you are pregnant must not have crossed her mind at all."

"I deserve it," Kyomo cried out and collapsed into my arms. "I have shamed my family and my whole way of life, Tezz! What we did was so wrong! I'm lucky she didn't kill me!"

"No." I raised her teary face to mine and dried a few tears. "You are just having a baby. That's not the end of the world, and it gives no one the right to abuse you. I don't know how things work in China, but that type of shit don't work over here in America. I'm surprised they didn't try to press charges against your aunt at the hospital."

"They probably would have." Ky blew her nose on some tissue. "I just told the doctors I fell and was clumsy. I didn't want to make things worse than they already are. I can handle this."

"Well, you are not alone." I kissed my girl on the cheek and held her close to me. "I'm here with you. I won't let anyone hurt you again. We will figure something out."

We stayed up until the daylight just talking and thinking of names for our baby girl. It seems rather naive now that I think of it, but at that time, a teenager would never know the sacrifices linked to raising a child. We had a million plans and ideas for her future but no real way to see them through. I knew from that moment that it was up to me to protect Ky from herself and her wicked aunt. I would sacrifice whatever I had to. I had to grow up fast and take responsibility for the life I helped create with her.

"How much longer is she gonna be in there?" I paced the maternity floor nonstop on that rainy April day.

Kyomo's water had broken right before school, and I had to get Koran to bring us to the hospital. We called Momma immediately, and she went in the delivery room with Ky. I wanted to be in there, but Ky felt more comfortable with her instead of me.

"I don't know." Koran bit her fingernails nervously and tapped her right foot on the linoleum floor. "I still can't believe my baby brother is about to be a daddy. This is all so unreal to me."

"Tell me about it," I sighed. "I must admit, I'm excited to meet my little girl. We already have a name picked out and everything."

"A name picked out, really?" Koran rolled her eyes at me. "You are such a kid. You two are focused on a name and haven't given any thought to the lives you have changed. Ms. Sue fired me yesterday. Apparently, she found out that I knew about the baby all this time, and now she's forbidden me from coming to the shop. Well, me, you, and Kyomo. I'll just get another job, but it was fucked up the way she went about it!"

"Damn, sis." I felt like I was the one to blame. "I'm sorry about your job. I never meant for any of this to happen. You gotta believe me."

"I'm sure you didn't." Koran softened her glare. "I'm sorry for coming down on you like that. I just don't like to see everyone stressed out like this. I will love my niece no matter what, and you, of course."

We embraced for a short while and saw Momma run in our direction from the delivery room.

"Ky and the baby are doing fine." Momma was out of breath. "She was a breach baby. Which means she was upside down. So, it took a little longer than expected, but they are both fine. She's absolutely beautiful and a gift from God!"

"When can I see her?" I raised an eyebrow.

"Soon, I'm sure," Momma replied and glanced at the nursery. "I gave our last name, so they should place the baby here in a few minutes or so."

"So . . ." I peered nervously at the baby pods and thought about the fact that my life would be forever changed after today. I was now responsible for another human being and my life hadn't even begun yet. I felt scared but determined to see things through the best I could. "What happens now, Momma? I'm only fifteen. Are they gonna just give us the baby, or what is gonna happen?"

"Oh, son!" Momma burst into tears and held me close to her bosom. "Your father and I looked into all of that weeks ago. Ms. Sue said she has wiped her hands of the baby and Kyomo. Such a sad scene, but maybe she will come around one day. The baby is an American citizen, so she had every right to be here. Your father and I will be legal custodians of her until you are eighteen and able to provide for her yourself."

"And what about Kyomo?" I wiped a stray tear from my tired eyes and looked away from my mother. "Will she be able to stay here with us?"

"I don't know that for sure, son." Momma started to cry all over again, and my sister grabbed on to her for support. "I just don't know."

Kyomo spent an additional two days in the hospital with the baby. My parents alerted the school that I would be absent the rest of that week. They already knew about Ky's pregnancy. Our friends came by the hospital and shared in our moment of happiness. Up until that moment, I realized that my life was plain and ordinary. Myesha Danielle Alexander changed all of that. She was my reflection and the first girl I ever loved instantaneously. Her smile warmed my heart, and her cries made me want to try harder to erase them.

Kyomo seemed kind of distant from the baby, almost as if she didn't want to see her at all. I asked the doctors about it, but they said that was normal for some mothers. I hoped her feelings would change and that she would see the beautiful creature we had created.

"It's almost time for us to get out of here." I grabbed a few baby things and folded them into a duffel bag. "I bet you will be glad to get home and take a real bath or shower!"

Kyomo looked away from me and changed the TV channel. Something had changed in her, and I didn't know how to react to it.

"Did you hear me?" I stood in front of her, and she simply turned her head from me. "What's the matter, Ky? You have been acting so different lately."

"I don't want to talk about it," she said rather quietly. "Can I just have a moment alone, please? And take the baby with you."

I did as she asked and bundled up our daughter before I shut the room door. I saw Momma and Pops by the vending machines on the maternity floor. Happy to see some normal faces, I walked over with my bundle of joy.

"Hey, grandparents," I joked with them but noticed their looks were rather stern and hurt. "What's up?"

"Tezz," Pops began but then was at a loss for words.

"Yeah?" I sat in a waiting room seat and rocked my fussy baby.

"It's about Kyomo." My momma picked up where my father left off. "She won't be coming with us."

"Won't be coming with us? Why would you say that? Where is she going?" I tightened my grip on the baby, and she let out a small cry. I loosened my grasp and handed her to my dad while I waited on my mother's response.

"She contacted her family in China, and they want her to return home immediately," Momma continued. "Her flight leaves this afternoon."

"What tha fuck?" I let the curse word slip, but my parents didn't seem bothered by it. "How can that be? I mean, we just had a baby, and they expect her to just leave her here?"

"Son," Momma said, patting me on my leg, "Kyomo contacted them, not the other way around. From what I was told, she can still right her wrongs with her family if she goes back and gets married. She was supposed to be given away in an arranged marriage. That's her family's custom."

"No." I jumped up and waved my arms around. "This can't be true. There's no way she would do me like that. There's no way she could just leave."

I took off for Kyomo's hospital room, but my pops grabbed my arm. He gave the baby to Momma and held on to me. I collapsed to the ground and shed a few tears. My heart was so crushed, and I felt like a real sucker. The first chick I ever loved suckered me in, took my heart, had my baby, and now planned on leaving the both of us. It was that easy for her to walk out on us? I just couldn't understand it. I knew after that moment that my heart and my feelings would never be the same.

9

Marvin: Fightin' a Losin' Battle

"I'm so sick and tired of arguin' back and forth with you on this, Marvin!" Lucinda screamed at me and threw a shirt at me from across our bedroom. "Why do you have to bring this shit up every single night?"

"It's not every night, Lucinda!" I fired back and motioned for her to lower her voice. I made sure our bedroom door was closed and hoped her loud mouth hadn't disturbed our girls down the hall. "Why must you be so damn loud? Do you want to wake up your daughters with this mess?"

"This mess?" She placed her hands on her voluptuous hips, and I felt my dick harden immediately. "You are the one always harpin' on me about giving you some pussy. Damn, am I a fuckin' machine or a person?"

"It's nothing like that." I tried to move closer to her but stayed cautious. "I love you, woman. I don't see what's so wrong with me wanting to express my love to you in a sexual way."

"But that's all you talk about anymore!" Lucinda plopped down on the bed, and I sat beside her. "I feel so exhausted most days. I clean the house, feed my family, support my mother, grocery shop, run errands, and that's all before four o'clock. I have literally no time for me anymore!"

"Oh, baby." I fell to my knees and crawled in between her fat thighs. "I'm so sorry if you feel neglected in any way. We all appreciate you and everything that you do. I'm sorry if I haven't been more supportive of you. I start my retirement soon, and that should free up a lot of my time. I had a good life in the military, but now I'm thirty-six. I want to spend my time with my family. So, you can have more me time, and I can tend to the girls. Is that cool?"

"Yes, baby." Lucinda wrapped her legs around my neck and pulled my face closer to her forbidden fruit. "You know what? All of a sudden, I feel more in the mood than I have in months."

"Is that right?" I raised her nightgown and was happy to find no panties underneath. I tickled her pussy lips with the tip of my tongue and tasted her pre-cum on my lips. "I'm awfully hungry right now, baby. Can I take a bite of you?"

Lucinda pushed my face into her crotch, and I pleased my face with all of my might. Those were the moments I dreamed of every night. I thought that my retirement would bring us closer, and that maybe she would have fewer excuses for turning my dick down. I could have pursued my career for a few more years, but truthfully, I had gotten tired of it.

The months away from my wife and girls almost felt too normal at times. And there was always that awkwardness I'd feel when I finally came home. Like I had to adjust to civilian life all over again. There was at least a week I wasted trying to readjust. And my girls, who by this time were almost 10 years old, were growing up to be little ladies without me. I had missed so many events and activities, and they were used to that. I wanted to be more involved and less of a visitor to them.

The first few months home from the military were the hardest for me. I had been accustomed to a certain routine, and being at home was like unearthed territory to me. I spent two hours a day at the local VA medical center. Therapy had helped in the past with my anxiety, and I needed my sleeping pills most nights. One of my therapists told me to have positive hobbies or things that allowed me to pass my time constructively. The military was always in my blood from an early age, but I always loved music and watching females dance erotically.

I would never forget a conversation I shared with my older brother one day in the summer. I was bored and feeling anxious, so I gave him a call. He came and got me, and we posted up in a local bar for some drinks. The scene was chill with a small crowd, and that was definitely my speed. The crowd was in their thirties and forties. It was a laid-back scene indeed.

"I agree with that shrink, baby bruh." My brother, Rodney, stuffed some peanuts into his mouth while he spoke. *"You need some hobbies to keep yo' ass busy. I wish I had more time to do the shit I wanna do, but I gotta maintain my job at the plant."*

"It wasn't necessarily a shrink, bruh." I felt a little self-conscious but finished my beer. I signaled for the waiter to bring us another round from the bar. *"But yeah, I do need to find something to do during the day. The girls are at summer camp, and Lucinda has her daily routines. Oh, yeah, she's pregnant again."*

"Congrats, bruh!" Rodney dapped me up. "That baby will keep y'all busy for sure! But on the flip side, what are you into?"

"I always liked music and watching women dance." I shrugged my shoulders and watched my brother think.

"You said you liked music and watching women dance?" My brother repeated my words. "Sounds like

an easy answer to me. You need to open a strip club. You got the best of both worlds with that. Shit, I'd be a faithful customer and you know it."

"A strip club?" I laughed at him. "I don't know the first thing about any of that. I need to know about costs, liquor licenses, the whole nine. I wouldn't know where to begin."

"So, you are curious about it?" Rodney smiled. "You ain't said nothing but a word, baby bruh. I can look into the legality of it, but you would still need a good location for the business."

"Wait a minute." I sat back in my seat. "Don't you think you are jumpin' the gun a little bit here? I just showed some interest, and you are already talkin' about finding a place?"

"You gotta live in the moment, baby bruh!" My brother finished his beer and started a new one. "It's not like you don't have the money to do it. And you would be making a legitimate profit from it. How can you lose? I know a few bitches who might be down to dance for you. Hell, we can come up with the prices and fees for everything. Aren't you friends with a few attorney types?"

"Yeah." I nodded. "I have a few army buddies who pursued law or have family members in that type of work. Why you ask that?"

"You need contracts and agreements for the business." My brother laughed at my stupidity. "You don't want a lawsuit or to possibly lose your business. You remember my homie Steve from around the way?"

"Your high school buddy?" I scratched my head. "The one with the younger sister Susan?"

"Yeah, I figured you would remember big-booty Sue!" Rodney winked. "But that's the one. He used to have a bar by the old neighborhood but never got the correct permits and shit he needed. He was a cheap-ass nigga but was making money hand over fist. Anyway, he had a kitchen fire that injured an employee's hand. Dude got sued, fined, and had to close down!"

"Oh, word?" I gasped.

"Yeah, man," Rodney replied. "He had to get his job back at the plant because he couldn't afford the lifestyle he used to be in. He's a'ight now, but shit, he would've been straight if he just went about things the right way. I don't wanna see that happen to you, bruh. Shit, I would even be an investor in it. I got two or three thousand that I can invest with you."

"That's wassup, bruh," I said with a smile.

I woke up that morning with no expectations of anything out of the ordinary for that day. But here I was with a valid goal ahead of me. I thought long and hard about the pros and cons, and surprisingly, there wasn't much for me to lose. I was more motivated than I had been in years. The club idea could really work. I had a new life to think about, and perhaps the extra money would allow Lucinda to spend more on herself and be happier.

"What are you complaining about now, Lucinda?" I hollered over the phone from my Lincoln Navigator and turned into my strip club. "Money is great right now, so what's the problem?"

"You know damn well what the problem is, Marvin!" Lucinda hissed back at me. "You spend too much damn time in that hellhole of a club you got. Are you fuckin' some of those girls in there? Is that what it is, Marvin? Is that why you don't have any time for your girls anymore?"

"You are talkin' so crazy right now, Cinda!"

I played in the pussy of a dancer in the passenger seat. Damn right I was fuckin' some of the dancers at the club. I was damn near 40 years old, and I was tired of beggin' my damn wife to fuck me. I paid all the bills and supported everyone, but I couldn't get my dick sucked in my own house. What the fuck was I supposed to do?

"You know that you are my favorite girl. Always have been and always will be. Everything I do is for you and the girls, so why are you coming at me like that?"

I put the phone on speaker and motioned for the dancer to remain quiet. Lucinda ranted some more, and I leaned back in my seat and unfastened my pants. The dancer caught on fast and leaned over the seat to swallow my dick. I felt my toes curl and fingered her in her tight bootyhole.

"Do you hear what I'm saying, Marv?" Lucinda continued. "I want us to have a family night, just the five of us. And maybe the two of us can plan a weekend together? I know it's been a few months, but I've just been so tired lately. Kelsey is almost three and into everything, and the twins are in all the sports."

"I feel you." I tried not to moan and bit my bottom lip. I played in the dancer's long hair and fingered her pussy deeply. I wanted to cum down her throat, and she knew I would pay her for it. There was no shame in my game!

I tried for years to do right by my wife, but three kids later and in the same boring-ass marriage, I was still miserable. The dancers made me feel young and still attractive. I knew most of them were just trying to get in my pockets, but hell, I had the money to spend. I didn't mind paying to play in some pussy. It was a win-win situation for everyone involved. But there were times that I felt guilty about lying to Lucinda. However, if she did better, I wouldn't have to lie in the first place.

"So," Lucinda babbled on as I held my orgasm a little longer, "how's business going? Are you still hiring some new girls? What's happening with that?"

"Uh, yeah," I mustered up and tugged on the stripper's head once more. I dropped my load down her throat and fingered her pussy after my nectar was spent. "We had some prospects come through the other night. You know what? I'm getting a call from DJ Fab. I really need to call you back."

"Oh, all right," Lucinda replied rather dryly. "Well, I guess I can get started on dinner. What time will you be home?"

"Let me hit you back, love," I pleaded and parted the stripper's legs from the back seat. We had climbed to the back and stayed quiet enough that Lucinda hadn't noticed. "I will let you know. I love you!"

"Okay, I love you too!"

My wife finally hung up, and I strapped on a condom before I tackled the pussy in front of me. Most times I could picture my wife's face on the dancers. I imagined giving her the pleasure I gave to them, and sometimes I just thought about the thrill of getting caught.

"Fuck me, daddy!" the honey-complexioned stripper Cristol moaned in my right earlobe. "I love the way this cock is hittin' my pussy!"

"You love it, huh?" I pounded her harder and raised her legs above her head. "Are you still givin' my lovin' away to that no-good nigga Chauncey?"

"No, daddy!" she moaned and clawed into my back. "I put his ass out last week. I promise he's gone now!"

"He better be." I pounded her until she creamed on my dick once more.

Her legs shook uncontrollably, and I found pleasure in the pain I caused her pussy. I ran my fingers up and down her six-pack stomach. I admired how fit the dancers remained and was turned on again. I licked all over her and allowed her to skeet in my beard and moustache.

"Damn, daddy!" Cristol grabbed her clothes and used one of my baby wipes to clean herself off. "You gon' make me late for my shift tonight. I'm feeling kinda drained right now."

"My bad, beautiful," I chuckled and got myself together before I climbed back into the driver's seat. "Sometimes I just can't control myself around you. I don't know why you do me like that. But I'm glad you gave that nigga his walkin' papers. Do you need anything, money-wise?"

"Rent is coming up, and I need some new wigs for my performances." Cristol batted her sexy lashes, and I readjusted my dick in my pants.

"I figured all that. Here." I handed her a stack, and she placed the hundreds in her bosom. Those perky size Ds sat up so nice, and I loved to suck on them. I fondled her a few minutes and made myself stop. "Get on out of here before I take you to a hotel suite."

"That could be arranged, daddy!" She tongued me down before she hopped out of my truck. "Do you have anything else for me?"

"Oh, yeah." I reached into my glove compartment and handed her the gram of coke I had scored earlier that day. I didn't want my girls on the heavy shit, but I allowed coke from time to time. They seemed to be more seductive, and Cristol sucked a mean dick when she had her coke.

"Me and you tonight, daddy!" Cristol licked her perfectly glossed lips and waited for my response.

"I will see what I can do about that." I smiled and fired up a smoke. "I gotta go home at some point or another, baby."

"But you know you have more fun with me." She winked and slowly walked toward the club doors. Her hourglass shape and vivacious curves had me hypnotized in every way. She was my number two for the moment and had been for the past year. Every now and then, I would switch up on the girls. Sometimes I would have to fire them when it got out of hand, but Cristol had been easy to love. We shared a 3-month-old son together, and she agreed to keep it under wraps. So far so good with that. Her stupid ex, Chauncey, was on our son's birth certificate. I was against it at first but thought it was the best answer since I was still married.

"I said I would see what I could do, woman." I gave her a devilish grin and climbed out of my truck.

Cristol laughed and entered the club. I walked around the back and entered through my office door. I had a decked-out office with all the perks. Money was rollin' in, and with the right DJ on my team, I had all the major rappers every weekend. It was nothin' for us to make $10,000 on a weekend. And with the extra dancers we just hired, money could double.

I washed my face and brushed my teeth in my office bathroom. My beard was still flawless, and I gave myself a quick look over. I could see a few gray hairs, but that brought more distinction and character to me. My mind drifted back to that new girl, Ja'Nova. She was really something to look at. Maybe she could be my new project if she played her cards right, just maybe.

10

Nova: More Dollars and Sense

"Hey, girl." Mia's bubbly voice vibrated on the other end of my phone. "What are you doing today? I'm over here bored to death!"

"Oh, wow!" I stretched and yawned while I looked at my alarm clock. I noticed it was ten in the morning but remembered that Markus was with Phillip for the week. I loved having him back in town, and Phillip was establishing a bond with our son. I loved the new townhouse, and with the income from the club for the past few months, I was able to get myself a car. Nothing too fancy, a used Lexus, but it got me where I needed to go. I was tired of bumming rides or catching the damn bus.

"I guess I'm just now wakin' up over here."

"Well, unlock the front door, bihh!" Mia laughed. "I'm at your front door looking real silly with food in my hands."

I hung up the phone and mustered my way out of my queen-sized bed. I longed to have a man on the other side of me, but maybe that would come in time. I did enjoy the company of Phillip from time to time when he was here. He assured me that his sexual curiosity was only that. Not to mention he was the best lover I had ever known.

"'Bout time!" Mia staggered into my front room and placed the bags on the kitchen table. "I thought you would never answer your phone. I hope this food isn't cold because of you!"

"I'm sorry." I let out another yawn. "You act like I knew you was stoppin' by or some shit. I'm still kinda tired from last night. The club was really poppin' all night."

"I'll say." Mia pulled out her stack of twenties from her pocketbook. "I'ma go ahead and pay up my bills and do some much-needed shopping. I'm so glad we got those jobs. Now I can relax and not stress as much."

"I know what you mean, girl!" I smiled and put on a pot of coffee. "Life is definitely a lot sweeter these days."

We waited for the coffee to brew, and when it was done, we started eating. "Did you tell Phillip about the club, or did you decide against it?" Mia asked while she placed some ketchup on her hash browns.

"I just don't see the point in saying anything to him right now, you know what I'm saying?" I brought over the two mugs of coffee and unwrapped my breakfast burrito. "I mean, if he asks me about my ends, I have no problem telling him about it. I do wear a mask, so it's not like people see my face or anything."

"Exactly, girl." Mia sipped her hot coffee. "And it's all legit in there. So, Phillip shouldn't have anything to say about it."

"Right." I tried to sound convincing but shook it off and enjoyed my breakfast. "So, what's up with you and the DJ? The two of you seem rather friendly here lately."

"What?" Mia blushed then looked away from me and to her phone. "I don't know what you are talkin' about, Ms. Thang. We are just cool and that's it. Nothing to really tell. And what about you and Mr. Marvin? Don't try to make this all about me. I notice the way he gives you extra compliments and more alone time in his office."

"Oh." I gave her a shocked look. "So, now you keepin' tabs on me, is that it? Well, there's nothing to talk about there, just like there's nothing to say about you and the DJ. How about that?"

Mia finished a spoonful of her eggs. "So how long have the two of you been fucking?"

"Oh, my." I blushed and almost choked on my strip of bacon. "You are really too much this morning. So, that's it? You and DJ Fab are fucking?"

"Hell yeah, we are!" Mia rocked her hips and stuck out her tongue at me. "I just left from his condo before I brought this food over here. Girl, he is the absolute best! At first, I thought he just wanted to fuck because of my dance skills. But now, like, we really get along with each other, you know what I'm saying? Like, it's more than just fucking!"

"That's great, friend." I gave her a comforting smile but remembered all the times that I saw the whorish DJ give other girls the same attention when she wasn't around.

"Yeah," Mia continued. "I'm supposed to meet his family this weekend. They are having a family reunion or some shit like that. He asked if I would come with him, and of course I said yes. I'm so excited, girl!"

"I'm happy for you, boo!" I smiled and decided to keep my doubts to myself. I didn't want to see my friend hurt, but I knew that most women took offense when a friend would try to check their men. I didn't want to lose her because of his sleazy ass. I figured in time she would learn for herself.

"Thanks, girl." Mia finished her meal and threw her trash in the garbage bin. "So, you avoided my question from earlier. What's the deal with you and Mr. Marvin? Spill it, bihh!"

"I'm telling you." I turned away from my friend and picked up a napkin from the kitchen floor. "There's nothing to tell."

"So, the two of you are not messin' around?" She raised an eyebrow in disbelief.

"No." I kept a straight face. "We're not. I'm sure that he wants to, but I'm not trying to get involved with him like that. I'm sure he fucks other girls at the club, so why would I want to be another number, you get me?"

"To get that bread, why else?" Mia rolled her eyes at me. "I mean, yeah, he probably has other bitches he fucks, but so what? What's that got to do with you? If it don't make dollars, then it don't make sense, you feel me?"

"So, that's what you got going on with the DJ?" I inquired and changed the topic from myself.

"Something like that," Mia agreed. "Don't get me wrong, I do like Fab a lot, but I don't see anything wrong with him paying some bills for me. I mean, I'm fucking him, and he loves my pussy, so what's the big deal? A lot of girls fuck all their customers for extra money. I'm not doing all of that, but I'm not judging them."

"True that." I thought of a few girls who told us who they fucked in the club. "You have a point there. I didn't mean anything by it. I was just asking. I hope you didn't take what I said the wrong way, girl."

"No, not at all." Mia gave a warm smile and sent a text on her phone. "See what I mean, girl? He just can't get enough of me. I just saw him an hour ago and he's already askin' me what I'm doing."

"You puttin' that pussy down, aren't you?" I winked at her.

"For him?" Mia snapped her neck. "You better believe it. He got a damn python, bihh, and he knows how to use it. And his sex drive is so crazy. As soon as he goes down, he gets it right back up. He fucks like a high school boy."

"How old is he?" I asked out of curiosity.

"Fab is thirty-eight." Mia sent a few more texts to her boo. "Almost as old as Marvin."

"Why you always gotta throw Marvin into the conversation?" I rolled my eyes and threw away my trash before I returned to the table with my friend.

"No real reason." Mia gave me a sly grin. "Just that Fab had said Marvin likes you a lot. Apparently, he discusses you quite often with my boo."

"Oh, yeah?" I thought aloud. "And what does he say about me?"

"Somebody is interested now, huh?" Mia teased me, and I hated when she did that. I folded my arms and pouted for a few minutes. Yeah, I wanted to know what he had to say about me. Why wouldn't I?

"Why do you keep playin' with me like this, little lady?"

Marvin came up for air, and I forced his face back in my pussy lips. Marvin's old ass knew how to please, and right now that was all I wanted from him. I got great dick from Phillip, but the head game was no comparison between the two.

"Stop talkin' so much," I moaned and ran my fingers through his scalp. "I'm about to cum."

"Oh, are you now?" Marvin raised his head once more and fingered my pussy with his free hand. "I want to feel that pussy around my dick. You been playin' cat and mouse with me for over a month now. I can't stand much more of this. Look at what you are doing."

I glanced over at his veiny, swollen member and licked my lips a little bit. He pulled out a rubber and placed the Magnum over his dickhead.

"I just wanna put the head in." Marvin released his wet fingers from my throbbing cooch and positioned himself between my legs. "I promise you are gonna love it."

I was a little hesitant at first but caved in and allowed him to proceed. Marvin had been good to me since

I'd been working for him. He never made me pay the monthly booth fee, and he allowed me to keep 100 percent of my tips. I guessed I owed him that much for the time being.

"Oh, shit!" I moaned in ecstasy. "It's so big."

"Take it, baby." He held me close and placed my panties into my mouth. He picked me up, and I wrapped my legs around his waist while he posted my back against his office wall.

"Do you love this dick, baby?" he whispered in my ear.

I gave a muffled response and dug my fingers into the pit of his back. That seemed to make him go harder, and I felt my body explode from the inside out. After we both succumbed to our rhythm, he laid me on the cold leather loveseat in his office. I turned on the air and allowed it to cool my hot body.

I admired the man who had just given me pleasure. He was fit for his age. Marvin had a chiseled dark brown chest, great legs, and a butt that could crack a walnut. He had a little peppery chest hair, but overall, I would rate him as a nine or better.

"You all right over there, baby girl?" Marvin called out to me from his office bathroom. He ran the hot water and took a ho bath in the sink. "C'mon in here and wash up, girl!"

"I'm comin'!" I staggered to my feet and almost lost my balance a time or two.

"Damn." Marvin licked his lips as I stood before him totally naked. "You are so damn beautiful in every way. You got me wanting some more of you right now."

"You move pretty good for an old man," I teased him and ran my hands down his fit stomach to his bulging member. "I had no idea you were working with all of this."

"And you still wouldn't know if I left things up to you." He laughed and allowed me to touch all over him. "You were gonna send me home with blue balls again, girl. Why were you playing with me like that? I thought I was looking out for you. I let you get away with a lot at this club, and I don't make a dime off you."

"And how many other girls get that same courtesy?" I kissed his collarbone and massaged his balls. "Huh?"

"Why you worried about all of that?" He moved my hand to his shaft, and I stroked him up and down. "You don't need to worry about any of that. Just keep doing what you're doing and I got you. Okay?"

"You got me?" I rubbed his hard dick over my pussy lips and teased him. "How you got me? Tell me!"

"If you need something or whatever it is," Marvin moaned, and I kissed his dickhead lightly, "you just let me know."

"I may need a few things." I climbed on top of his dick and rode him slowly. He felt so good, but I tried to remain calm and in control of the situation. I knew just how to handle a man like him.

"Oh, yeah?" Marvin placed his hands on my hips and placed all nine inches inside of me. "And what do you need, love? You tell daddy."

"Oh," I let out a cry and bit my bottom lip to stay quiet. "I will let you know. You can believe that, big daddy."

Although Marvin had a big dick, he never seemed to last longer than ten minutes or so. I tried to appear unbothered by it, but I wondered why he came so fast. Was my pussy that good to him or could he not hang with me? I tried not to seem bothered, but as a young lady in her twenties, I wanted that hour-long lovemaking! Phillip would be headed back to Cali before too long, and I needed a new sex toy to play with. I also needed to get some work done to my back bumper. Maybe I could get Marvin to put it in the shop for me.

11

Montezz:

Happy but Wanting More

"What it do, bruh?" I answered my cell phone during my thirty-minute lunch break at the shop. Things had changed dramatically since Kyomo up and left me with our daughter eleven years ago. I was blessed to have my family support, and Myesha never missed a beat or cried a tear over her negligent momma. Of course, there were times that she wondered about her, but I always kept it one hundred with her. I didn't know where her momma was. I never saw her again after we left the hospital that day.

I was able to finish high school thanks to my parents watching my daughter as much as possible. I made the necessary sacrifices but was able to hang out with my fellas from time to time. Women came and went for me. I vowed years ago that I would never give my heart to another bitch! Some things just weren't worth reliving in my eyes. I would give a chick just enough to keep her happy, no more and no less. My baby girl was the only one to ever get my full heart, or at least for the time being.

Pops suffered a bad stroke a few years back, and I happily took over at his auto shop. It allowed me to show my own independence and make steady pay to support my baby and myself. Pops would still come by and chill from time to time, but I ran the shop with the help of my receptionists, baby sis Carol, and Myesha.

"Hey, bruh!" Fab responded on the other end. "You busy at the shop right now?"

"Shit." I smirked and finished my ham sandwich. "We stay that way. What's good though?"

"Need a favor from you, brother-in-law," he began.

"Aw shit." I shook my head.

"C'mon now," he laughed. "Nothing too serious, but one of the dancers needs some work on her ride. You know I always refer you to the boss man. We family and all, you feel me?"

"Yeah," I huffed and sipped my soda. "Must be one of his favorites or some shit. So, how long has Marvin been fuckin' this one?"

"You wild, bruh," Fab chuckled. "As far as I know, he ain't hit this one yet, but he wants to get in them thongs. She young as fuck. Still got milk on her breath, you feel me? Hell, I'm knockin' down her homegirl though!"

"You and them young girls," I thought out loud. "I see why you and Marv are so tight. Y'all got the same MO!"

"I'm just enjoying my life." Fab got on the defensive. "You should try it sometimes."

"I'm good ova' here," I rebutted. "Business is good, and I got a daughter to think about. I can't be runnin' around chasin' skirts like y'all fools. Speaking of, whatever happened to that one dancer Giselle? I ain't seen her around in a while."

"Aw, man," Fab sighed. "She was a fine bitch, but Marv had to cancel her ass. She got on them drugs too heavy. She was doing more fuckin' for drugs and less dancin' in the club. Man, that shit was tragic on the real. Last I heard, she in a rehab place upstate."

"Damn." I frowned and thought about some of our sex sessions. "She was tight on tha real. I knew I hadn't seen her around for a few months."

"Yeah, man," Fab continued. "But we got a new breed of them now. You need to come down here this weekend. I'll put you on the VIP list, no worries."

"I might." I gave a slight smirk. "So, what's the status on the new fish, and what time was she tryin'a come up here?"

"Nova is her name," Fab relayed to me. "She's about twenty-two, I think. Got a son, but she flies pretty straight, or at least she does for now. Boss man been tryin'a fuck, but according to her homegirl, she thinks he's too old or some shit."

I smiled. "So she's a dancer with standards. Now that's something to work with."

"There you go," Fab joked. "But she should be there before three o'clock. She drives a fully loaded silver Lexus."

"And what was her name again?" I wiped off my freshly trimmed beard and walked into my office to examine my appointment book for the day.

"Nova Jacobs," Fab repeated. "So, you gon' come down to the club this weekend or not?"

"I might swing through." I jotted down Nova's name and car description. "Koran and Darrell were supposed to come by the crib for dinner this weekend. I haven't seen much of them since their wedding, so I wanted to get some family time in, you feel me?"

"I heard that," he responded. "Your sister got my li'l bruh so whipped. Hell, if you can, bring him with you."

"Now you tryin'a get my ass cussed out!" I laughed uncontrollably. "I'll see what I can do."

"A'ight," he replied. "And good looking out."

"One," I ended the call and walked to the reception desk to look for my sister Carol. Fab was quite the character. I always thought he was the sneaky type but gave him a pass because his brother married my sister. I had to admit, it was nice having new brothers in a houseful of sisters!

"Hey, Daddy." Myesha smiled and showed her deep dimples as I gave her a big bear hug. "Are you looking for Auntie Carol?"

"Yes, baby." I beamed from ear to ear. "Where did she run off to? I have a new client coming in today and wanted to make sure I would be available around three."

"She said she had a few errands to run, so I will fill in for her. Don't worry, Daddy, I got your back." My baby gave me a wink with her almond-shaped gray eyes.

Myesha was my joy and everything else. As resentful as I was toward her momma, I wouldn't trade my baby for anything in this world. She gave me purpose and motivated me to do my very best every day. Myesha was a star student, a sixth grader but already taking mostly seventh-grade classes in school.

"Thanks, Bookie!" I kissed her on the cheek, and she began to blush.

"Ugh," She rolled her eyes. "I hate when you call me that in public. Geez, you are so embarrassing at times."

"I'm your dad and that's my job." I teased her further but headed to my workstation and examined the finished Dodge Durango in the garage.

I had a stable crew of workers. Most of them had been with my Pops for years, and of course, I added a few friends of mine.

"Wassup, Tezz, or should I say boss man!" James wiped some engine oil on his work pants and dapped me up. "We have been so busy this Saturday morning. How many more appointments do you have on the schedule for today?"

"You must have some plans or something." I raised my eyebrow because I knew my best friend like no one else. "What chick are you tryin'a go see?"

"See, there you go," James laughed. "I do have a date around six thirty. A new one. She came in here with the fender bender on Wednesday."

"You talkin' bout the black Benz on eighteens?" I thought back and recalled the caramel diva with the phat ass.

"Yes, Lawd." James licked his lips. "I got her number and been hittin' her up ever since. She finally agreed to give a nigga some play. So, I really need to be outta here by four o'clock."

"I guess that will be cool." I shrugged my broad shoulders and watched my friend's charismatic expression. "Fab got one of them dancers coming by at three, and then we just have two oil changes left to do. I was gonna let you go around four o'clock anyway, so you good."

"A stripper, huh?" James seemed interested.

"Yeah, nigga." I shook my head. "Calm down. You got plans, remember?"

"Look at you," James joked. "No worries, friend. I was just curious. Don't get mad at me or nothing like that."

"What you saying?" I frowned.

"I wasn't tryin'a step on your toes," James teased. "I just wanna see how she looks, that's all. You know, options in case li'l shawty don't pan out tonight."

I inspected the Durango and checked off the work that was done to it. "Like I said, she works at Uriah's, so if you really wanna see her, you know where to find her. Fab asked me to come through and said he would put me on the VIP list."

"Hell yeah." James smiled once more. "I'd be down for that if you don't mind me rollin' with you."

"I don't know." I handed the keys to one of my workers and waited for the next client to arrive in the workstation. "I don't really be feeling the stripper scene. A bunch of niggas droolin' ova' bitches who are just after a damn buck? But shit, I'll let you know if I decide to go."

It was almost three o'clock, and my two o'clock appointment cancelled and rescheduled for the following week. James kept hinting the need to run a few errands, so I let him go earlier than expected. With nothing to do for the moment, I messaged a few of my regular chicks because I was a li'l horny. I always kept my options open when it came to the ladies. If they tried to hit me with the L word, I gave them walking papers. I didn't have time to get my heart broken again. They could ride this dick, suck this dick, and get the fuck on.

"Daddy!" Myesha walked down to the workstation with a sexy vixen behind her. "Your three o'clock is here."

Myesha folded her arms and rolled her eyes at the customer before she returned to the reception desk. She assumed all the women wanted her good-looking daddy, and she was right for the most part. I had my ways, and I guessed my baby was always on the lookout for me.

"Thanks, baby girl." I sent another text to one of my freaks and stood to greet the young lady.

"You have quite the receptionist here." The new customer gave a nervous grin after she examined me from head to toe.

"My daughter." I smiled and glanced at the silver Lexus in the garage. "So, you must be Nova."

"Yes, that's me." Nova extended her freshly manicured French tips, and I shook her hand. "Thanks for squeezing me in on such short notice. I heard this is the best shop in town and usually pretty busy."

"Yeah." I licked my lips and felt my nature rise from the shawty in front of me. Her curves were immaculate, and her D-cup titties sat up perfectly and jiggled when she laughed nervously. "We do all right ova' here, miss. So, you need some work done on that back fender, correct? Did you need me to service anything else for you this afternoon?"

"Umm." She blushed slightly and looked over to her vehicle. "Other services like what exactly?"

"We do tune-ups, oil changes, and things of that nature." I walked with her and smelled her sweet perfume. "I had an appointment that cancelled, so I'm available for a bit."

"That's very nice of you." She showed her dimples and bit her full lip slightly.

"And where are my manners?" I playfully nudged past her and directed Nova to the lounge. "Please, have a seat. We have a snack machine just around the hall. And here's the TV remote while you are waiting."

She gave me a gorgeous smile. Our hands touched once more, and I was pleased with that. I forgot momentarily that I had a job to do. She was such a beautiful lady. I excused myself and went on to the job. It looked as though someone backed into her fender. I could suction this out in a few minutes' time. I wasn't ready for her to leave just yet. I had to keep her around. There was just something about her that made me want to know her better.

12

Nova: Tired of the Same Ol' Same

"You know I got you, boo." Marvin tapped me on my juicy ass while I got dressed in his office.

I finally caved in and gave his horny ass a taste. I knew I had Marvin in the palm of my hand from my audition dance with him. I locked my eyes on to his ass like a mighty lioness to her prey. There wasn't much he could do to fight those feelings I saw flow through his eyes. I enjoyed all the perks that came with that hypnotizing dance. I kept it from Mia and never gave a hint that Marvin and I were on an intimate tip.

He promised not to tell his friends or anyone about us. Marvin confided in me about his side chick, Cristol, and the baby they had together. A married man and a side bitch is a cocktail for disaster. He claimed I was easy to talk to and not like the average stripper in his club. I never was the type of bitch to follow a crowd. Then again, I never had the time to do so. I had to drop out of school and help raise my brother and a child of my own. I missed out on a lot of the moronic crap kids my age were on.

"What end of town is the auto-body shop on?" I splashed some warm water on my face and blotted it with a bath towel.

"On the north side." Marvin fired up a cigarette and leaned back in his office chair. "Fab's brother-in-law owns the place. Alexander Auto Body. It's the best place in Birmingham. I send all the girls there."

"All the girls, huh?" I gave him a heated stare. I truthfully didn't give a fuck, but I wanted him to think I was bothered by it. I knew that would make him think that I cared for him, and ultimately, more ends would come my way.

"Aww, look at my boo." Marvin pouted his lips and flicked some ashes in the ashtray. "Don't get all in your feelings. He just cuts the business a huge deal. Kinda like a wholesale type of deal. Don't you worry, you will always be VIP with me. You just keep doing what you are doing, and you will never have to worry about being replaced."

"Keep doing what I do?" I placed my manicured tips on my luscious hips and tapped my yellow stiletto on his carpeted floor. "What's that all about?"

"Aw, c'mere, girl!" Marvin motioned me closer and stood up.

I dramatically flowed over to him and allowed his old hands to molest me. He kissed the gap of my neckline and ran his fingers over the outline of my nipples.

"Uh-huh." I swayed my hair across his face. I tried to seem uninterested in his vibe. "And what did you want? You know I need to get going. I have some things to do before I head to the auto-body shop."

"Always so damn sassy," Marvin laughed and gave me a kiss on the forehead. "Well, don't let me keep you, baby girl. You need anything? You got any bills that are about due or something?"

"Yeah," I lied because Phillip had already paid the rent that month. "I need to buy more clothes for Markus. He's growing like a damn weed these days. And I was thinking about remodeling my living room suite."

"I hear ya, momma." Marvin pulled out his wallet and dropped two stacks in the palm of my hand. "That ought to help a little bit, don't you think?"

"I guess so," I pouted, and he added more to it. "I can work with that, poppa."

He shooed me away from his lap and desk. "Now get your fine ass outta my sight before I make you late for everything and miss my office meeting. Don't forget, you need to be at the shop at three o'clock."

"Thanks again, poppa." I blew him a kiss and stood in his doorway. "I will be there."

"Call me later." He winked, and I exited the office.

I made it through the club hallways and talked to a few of the girls who had to work that night. Marvin gave me the night off. I told him I needed to spend some time with my son for a change. I had him wrapped around my pinky, so of course he bought my story. Phillip would be flying back to Cali for his season practices. I wanted to get in some QT before he was out of our lives for a few months.

I would sometimes envision a life of a football star's wife and all the luxuries that came with it. I wouldn't have to work, and Markus would be set for life, but would that be enough for me? A nigga that was constantly on the road and tempted by strange ass? I snapped out of my trance and searched the radio station for a song of mellow thought.

Jagged Edge blasted through my speakers. I thought of that and wanted it more than anything, but who was I fooling? I didn't have any real prospects and didn't have the time to start a real relationship. But there was no doubt about it. I wanted that more than anything. I sang along with the radio and pulled into my father's garage. I noticed the red Ford Taurus and knew Jacques was there. I climbed out of my car and unlocked the front door with my spare key.

"Hello, family," I almost sang as I walked through the family room of my dad's home. "Where is everyone?"

"In the kitchen, Momma!" Markus yelled at me.

"Hey there, sis!" My baby brother walked over and gave me a big hug. "Long time no see! How have you been?"

"Really, Ques?" I joked with him. "Didn't I see you the other week?"

"I know, but that seems like forever ago." Jacques walked back over to the stove and stirred a big pot. "I know I have been busy with my studies and you are working where you work, but I think we should take some time out and hang out like the old days. I miss our talks and things like that."

"We just miss having you around, daughter." Daddy smiled and seasoned some chicken breasts before placing them in the oven. "Do you have to work tonight?"

"Actually," I said, and dramatically held their gazes for a few seconds more, "I'm off tonight, so maybe we could play some board games, rent some movies, or just hang out. Old-day style!"

"Yay!" Markus jumped up and down before planting a wet kiss on my cheek. "My momma doesn't have to work tonight. Yay!"

"That's wassup!" Jacques tasted his collard greens and added more salt to them. "Well, we plan on having a nice feast, and I can definitely pick up some movies from Redbox."

I appreciated the good family moments and just kicking back, spending time with the ones I loved. I spent a good part of the afternoon at my daddy's house not doing shit at all, just eating and catching up with everyone. I guessed time had escaped me, but I felt my phone vibrate and saw it was a message from Marvin.

Marvin: Hey there, sexy! Had you on my mind and my dick. LOL. I hope you were able to get the things you needed. Don't forget about your car appointment, and call me later, babes.

I rolled my eyes and stood up when I saw it was a quarter after two. "Damn!" I blurted out and searched the living room couch for my purse and keys.

"What's going on?" My brother raised an eyebrow when he saw me panic.

"I got an appointment for my fender bender." I found my belongings and planted kisses on everyone's forehead. "I almost forgot about it. It's way across town, and I don't want to be stuck in a lot of traffic."

"Yeah, I can understand that." Daddy nodded and sipped his iced tea. "These fools can't drive worth a damn these days. You need to give yourself an extra ten minutes because you don't want to get road rage."

"Are you coming back when you get done, Momma?" Markus frowned as I approached the front door.

"Of course I am, baby boy!" I gave him one last hug before I jetted to my car.

Traffic was moderate and to be expected for a sunny Saturday afternoon in Birmingham. I reached the auto-body shop and was happy to see few cars in the parking lot. I glanced at the time on my radio, and it was ten of three. I always liked to be early for appointments, and I barely made it to this one.

"Pull into the carport, ma'am!" one of the attendants hollered from the garage, and I did as I was asked. I handed him the keys and walked into the office doors. I was surprised to find a beautifully tanned china doll behind the desk. She couldn't have been over 12 years old with long, flowing jet-black ponytails and gray slanted eyes.

"Good afternoon." The young girl gave a smile. "Welcome to Alexander Auto Body. How can I help you today?"

"Hello." I smiled back at her from the other side of the desk. "I have a three o'clock appointment today."

The young girl scanned over the appointment book and scratched off the three o'clock spot before looking up at me. "Nova with the silver Lexus?" she asked, and I nodded. "Okay, right this way please."

She walked me through the hall of accolades that showed the success of the business. There were various newspaper articles that raved about their success and professionalism. I was very impressed that it was also a black-owned business.

"Daddy!" the young girl addressed the handsome milk-chocolate man in a work suit under a car hood. "Your three o'clock appointment is here."

The once-smiling face became stern and rolled her slits at me before she walked back to the office desk. I guessed she noticed my gaze and felt protective of her father's honor. I couldn't blame her on that tip, but damn, he was fine as fuck. He appeared to be around my age, and I tried to remain calm as he approached me.

"So, you must be Nova." The handsome man gave me a pearly white smile. He wiped the grease from his hands and extended one to me for a handshake. I felt my palms sweat but did not turn away from his gray eyes for a second.

"Thanks for squeezing me in on such short notice." I licked my lips and pictured his fine-ass muscles with much less clothing on.

"So, you need some work done on that back fender, correct? Did you need me to service anything else for you this afternoon?"

"Umm," I stuttered and fantasized about the sexy stranger before I gave a response. "Other services like what exactly?"

"We do tune-ups, oil changes, and things of that nature." He casually wiped a few beads of sweat from his taught neckline and chocolatey forehead.

"That's very nice of you." I felt at a loss for words. I could think of a few things I was interested in, and none of them were the things that he had mentioned.

"And where are my manners?" He chuckled and walked past me, touching my shape ever so effortlessly. "Please, have a seat. We have a snack machine just around the hall. And here's the TV remote while you are waiting."

I simply nodded and marveled over the chocolate specimen. I wondered if he was single and if he had ever seen me dance in the club. He went to work on my car, and I flipped through a few TV channels. Bored but curious about the new stranger, I pulled out my phone and gave my girl Mia a call.

"What up, bihh!" she replied on the other end.

"Not much." I applied some gloss to my full lips. "I'm at Fab's brother-in-law's auto-body shop, and, girl, he's fine as fuck!"

"You must be talkin' about Tezz!" She snickered. "Yeah, I heard he's a fine one. Fab's brother is married to one of Tezz's sisters."

"Does he come to the club?" I wondered. "I can't remember ever seeing him there."

"Not that I know of," Mia answered. "From what I know, he's not really into the stripper scene, but all the bitches think he's fine as hell. I think a few of them purposely fuck up their rides just to catch a glimpse of him. You must like him or something."

"What's not to like?" I kept my voice low but watched him work from the corner of my eye. "I wonder what his story is."

Mia smacked her lips. "From what I know, he took over the business after his dad got sick. He's a single parent and has a daughter. Don't really know much else about him. I guess he stays under the grid."

"Hmm," I breathed out.

"Seems like you want to know more," Mia cackled. "You there in his presence, bihh. Talk to him and get to know him. He's clearly successful and that's always a plus."

"True," I replied nervously. "He looks about our age, and his daughter is like twelve or something. I guess he started out pretty young."

"I think he's about twenty-five or twenty-six, not that age matters. Fuck all of that. If you see something that you like, jump on it," Mia coached me. "Stop being so afraid all the damn time. You was like that about the club, but you got over that like a champ."

"You're right." I sucked up my pride and stood to my feet. "I do tend to be on the shy side at first. But a nigga that damn fine, I'm gonna shoot my shot for sure."

13

Montezz: She Got Me Curious

"Good Lawd," one of my handymen, Sean, exclaimed. "Them dancers just get finer by the minute, huh, boss man?"

"I can't front on that." I shook my head and admired our fast work on the dent. "She definitely caught my interest, I can't lie."

"She looks like she stays clean, you know what I mean?" Sean rubbed the bottom of his nose, and I nodded in agreement. "She probably ain't been workin' there too long. I hope she keeps her head above water."

"True that," I agreed. "From what my brother tells me, she's all about her business. It's hard to read a lot of those dancers. Some of them just like to dance or fuck, and then there are some who use the money to better themselves and retire."

Sean cleared his throat and wiped off a smudge of dirt from the bumper. "So are you gonna shoot your shot or let your boy get in?"

"Look at you," I chuckled. "Didn't you just get married a few months ago, nigga?"

"Yeah, man." Sean glanced down at his wedding ring. "But you can't blame a man for trying. Married life ain't all that it's hyped up to be. I think I loved her more when we were just dating and fuckin' around. Now she acts like she controls a nigga or some shit."

"Y'all niggas are a trip." I shook my head and glanced over at Nova. "That's why I keep my feelings at a distance. I don't have time for all that drama. My baby girl will always be my number one. Women, nowadays, are more of a headache than anything else."

"But it seems like you are thinkin' about your other head right now," Sean chuckled as I walked away from him.

I saw that Nova was on the phone, and I watched her movements without her noticing me. She laughed a few more times and ended her call as I walked over to her.

"That was really quick." She smiled and placed her phone back in her Gucci bag.

"Yeah, we have a new suction joint. Clears up most bumps in a manner of minutes." I smiled and sat across from her in the waiting room. "So, is there anything else I can do for you today?"

"Well, actually . . ." she stammered and looked away from me a time or two. "I hate to come off a little bold, but umm, I would like to get your number. If that's all right with you?"

"Nice." I smiled and showed my pearly whites. "I'm not really used to women making the first move with me, but I like your style, young lady. I was actually thinkin' about gettin' your digits anyways."

"Oh, really?" She breathed easier. "That's a relief. I don't feel so bad now."

"There's nothing wrong with going after what you want." I moved closer to her and entered my number into her phone. "So, what are your plans for this weekend? Are you working at the club or what?"

"No," she replied bashfully. "Mr. Marvin had enough slots filled for the night, so he gave a couple of us the night off. I was just gonna hang out with my son and the rest of my family. I don't usually see much of them on the weekends, so it will be a nice change for me."

"I'm glad to see that you have your priorities in order."
I found some loose change and purchased a soda from
the drink machine. "You would be surprised how many
chicks work at those joints and get burnt out on coke or
worse. It's a real waste if you ask me."

"Yeah," she agreed. "I have seen a couple go from bad
to worse, and I haven't been working there that long. It's
not like that for me. I'm about stackin' my paper and
securing the bag for my son. All that fuckin' for extra
bucks doesn't excite me."

"So," I continued, "do you have a man or a nigga you
fuckin'? Excuse me if that's too personal for you."

"Oh!" She seemed startled but played it off very well.
"No, no man on my end. I don't really have the time for
that. I guess if the right one came along, I would make the
time for him. It's just hard to know when a guy is being
serious with me. Being a dancer, you get a lot of creeps
who seem interested in you for all the wrong reasons."

"Well," I sighed and placed my phone back in my
pocket, "I'm glad that you are one of the few who has her
head on straight. Now, when can I expect to hear from
you?"

"I was just about to ask you about that." She smiled
again, and I stayed focused on her perky breasts. I
wanted to caress them and put them in my watery mouth.
"Are you open on Sundays or are you free?"

"Sundays are mostly family day for me and my baby
girl." I shrugged my shoulders. "But I'm sure I could
make some arrangements for you. What time were you
talkin' about kickin' it?"

"I have a steady babysitter," she assured me. "So, I will
send you a call, you lock me in, and let me know."

"I can do that, lovely." I bit my bottom lip and wondered how sweet hers would be. "Did you want an oil
change or tune-up on the house?"

"On the house, huh?" She snickered. "Aren't you so nice?"

"I have my moments." I blushed before her. "I like to show my customers appreciation from time to time, and I have the extra time."

"Are you sure that you just don't want to keep me around?" she replied playfully.

"Oh, shit!" Nova mumbled through the G-string panties I stuffed in her mouth.

Passion got the best of us, and we ended up on top of my office desk. All of my papers were thrown savagely on the floor, and I was mounted on top of the vivacious vixen. Her body called out to me, and curiosity had gotten the best of me.

"Quiet down," I whispered in her ear and wrapped her legs around my waist. I posted her against the wall and continued to pound her with every stroke I could muster. She was so wet, and her pussy wrapped effortlessly around my shaft. "Damn, girl, you feel so damn good."

"I feel like such a fast ass," she huffed and dug her fingers deeper into my back.

"Don't feel that way." I gripped her soft ass and looked deep into her wanton eyes. "We both wanted this, and I'm glad we acted on it."

I turned her caramel body around, and she poked her butt out for my easy access. I was glad she couldn't see my facial expressions because I felt my eyes roll into the back of my head.

"Shit," she moaned. "I think I'm about to cum."

"Me too." I pumped harder and faster before I reached my peak. I hadn't worn a rubber, which was a definite no for me. When I felt my juices about to bust, I exited her pussy and released my juices on her back. "Goddamn it, girl!"

We lay there motionless for a few moments. I soaked up the last thirty minutes of our fuck fest and found all of my clothes throughout the office. We took turns leaving the office and washing up in the employee bathroom.

"Well," she breathed heavily and wiped some sweat from her brow. "This was definitely spontaneous and not expected."

"Definitely." I licked my lips and sat on the edge of my desk. "I hope I didn't scare you away from our meetup tomorrow."

"Oh, no." She batted her long eyelashes. "I hope I didn't make you think I was that damn easy. I usually take my time gettin' to know a guy. I don't know what came over me just now. Definitely not the norm for me."

"I hear ya, shawty." I blushed a bit. "We are both grown, so there's no need to explain yourself. I wanted you, and I guess it's safe to say that you felt the same way. I do still wanna see you tomorrow, if that's all right?"

14

Marvin: Fightin' a Losin' Battle

"Dammit, Marvin!" Lucinda hollered at me on the phone. "I get so sick and tired of arguing with you about your late nights at that whorehouse you call a club. Time and time again, you miss out on important things the kids have going on, and I'm tired of covering for you and giving our girls all these lame excuses."

"Baby," I whined as I pulled up to a red light. My wife was really on my last nerve, but I couldn't afford to let her leave me. My dumb ass never signed a prenup, and with all the dirt under my fingernails, she would leave me bankrupt for sure. "You know that I'm working hard to provide the best life for you and the girls. That hard work comes with sacrifices. Why do you stay so mad at me?"

"Don't you lay that crap on me, Marvin!" She continued to spit more venom. "Jasmine had a soccer game, and she expected you to be there. The rest of the kids always have both of their parents in the stands, but you never have the time to show up. And Justice did such a great job at her piano recital yesterday. She got a standing ovation from the crowd. I know it broke her heart not to see you there."

"And I have apologized a thousand times for all of that." I fired up a cig and took a few deep breaths. More than ever, I wanted to get an apartment for myself. Just

a chill spot to run to when Lucinda had me on the verge
of ringing her damn neck. "We can watch the videos of
the girls together as a family. You know that I love you all
very much. The last thing I want is for any of you to feel
that I take your accomplishments for granted."

"Yeah, yeah." She smacked her lips. "Always such the
smooth talker. I see why you do so well at that whore den
that you own. I bet those tramps are all in love with you."

"That's crazy talk, babe." I gave a sly grin and thought
about the head I received from Cristol that morning. "I'm
an old married man, and those girls have a sea of men to
choose from. Ain't none of them are worried about my
ass. They just work for me."

"Yeah, I bet," she replied with a deep breath.

"So, what are your plans for the rest of the day? I
finished my business meetings earlier than expected, and
I'm headed to the house right now. Did you or the girls
need anything while I'm out?"

"No, we are good!" she blurted out. "Just get your ass
here, okay? The girls would be thrilled to spend some
quality time with their father."

"And what about you, Lucinda?" I questioned. "Are you
looking forward to spending some quality time with me?"

"Maybe," she snickered and ended the call.

I made it through another one of our heated argu-
ments and decided to stop at a floral shop before I made
it home. Women always seemed to love flowers, and I
was a regular at Dawn's Boutique. All of my special girls
got regular arrangements every week, and the owner
seemed to cut me a sweet deal. I had several businesses
that I worked with on the regular. It just became routine
with me.

I loaded up the back seat with the floral arrangements
I purchased for my girls at home. I had given a lot of
thought about the secret apartment, and maybe it wasn't

the worst idea that had run across my mind. I had my hands on plenty of cash due to the success at my club. I just had to make sure that money didn't leave a paper trail back to my nosy-ass wife.

My radio jam session was interrupted by yet another call from Lucinda. I was under ten minutes away from the house and grew more and more irritated with her complaints and demands.

"Yes, sweetheart?" I mustered up some compassion for the woman who bore my three daughters. "I'm almost home right now."

"Uh-huh." She smacked her lips. "I was just checkin'. I never know if you're really comin' home. For all I know, one of them hoes at the club could've broken a damn nail. And like the old pervert I'm sure you are, you would have to run in behind one of them."

I huffed at the red light ahead of me. "Why would you say such a thing like that, Cinda? Have I ever given you any reason to doubt my love and devotion to you and our family?"

"Don't give me any of that crap, Marvin!" She proceeded to argue, and I turned on our street. "Just because I can't prove anything doesn't mean you're not out there doing wrong,"

"I just pulled into the driveway." I turned off my Suburban and leaned back in the driver's seat. "Can we continue this conversation later?"

"Fine!" she blurted out and hung up the call.

There was a part of me that wanted to rev up my engine, place my ride in reverse, and peel off on her stubborn ass. Hell, I had paid my dues and done everything that was expected of me as a husband. She never had to lift a manicured finger or bat one of her fake eyelashes, but she always gave me nothing but grief. And where was the thanks that I deserved? Shit, I couldn't even get some pussy in my own house.

"Daddy!" My teenage daughter ran up to me and gave me a big hug. "I can't believe you are home this early on the weekend. What's up with all the flowers?"

"Hello, baby girl." I gave a huge smile and kissed my princess on her forehead. "I got finished with things a lot earlier than I expected, and I missed my girls. Some of these flowers are for you."

"For me?" She giggled and helped me place the bouquets in some vases with water. "So, what's really up with all of this, Daddy? Let me guess, Momma is giving you a hard time again?"

"It's that obvious?" I shook my head and felt embarrassed that my own daughter was hip to my old tricks.

"Yeah." She giggled and smelled the sweet bouquets in front of her. "I've heard the two of you on the phone more than I'd like to remember. Always arguing about the same old thing. Plus, she calls her friends and family, and they always have something foul to say about you and the club."

"I'm sorry you have to hear all of that, baby," I sighed and felt my blood begin to boil. "None of this concerns you or your sisters. Just know that your daddy is doing everything he can to secure a great life for you all. I put in a lot of hours, but this is all for you. You can understand that, right?"

"Yeah, Daddy." Jasmine gave me a wayward smile. "I mean, it would be nice to see you more often at my events or around the house a lot more. But we are used to you being gone, and we know that you work hard for us."

"What are the two of you in here yappin' about?" Lucinda waltzed in wearing her pink bathrobe and curlers in her hair. She was once so flawless and always dressed to impress, but over the years, she stopped trying to look good for me.

"Nothing, Momma." Jasmine walked toward her with a bouquet of lilies, her favorite. "I was just telling Daddy that he did a great job picking out these flowers. Lilies, your favorite."

"Uh-huh." My wife sucked her teeth and set the vase on the kitchen table. "Always with the expensive gifts. I'm sure there's a good reason behind that."

"Do we have to do this now, Lucinda?" I squinted my eyes at her and glanced over to our daughter.

"Jasmine, why don't you take those flowers to your room and let your sisters know that dinner will be ready in another hour? I think your father and I need to have a talk." Lucinda kept her eyes on me with every word.

"Yes, ma'am." Jasmine gave a slight smile and did as she was told.

"Let's continue this in our bedroom." She motioned for me to follow her, and I did just that. I had hoped for some real quality time, but Lucinda made sure I knew that suggestion was off the table.

"What is it now?" I plopped down on our custom-made king-sized bed and waited for my wife to answer me.

She poured herself a glass of wine, drank it, and lit a cigarette. The anticipation was enough to drive me crazy, but I said nothing while I waited on her.

"I'm so sick and tired of your ass!" Lucinda flared her brown eyes at me. "All these gifts and bullshit that you try to give, I know it's all to cover up your bullshit! Why don't you just be honest with yourself or try to be honest with me! I know you're not happy here anymore!"

"Where is all this coming from, my love?" I played along with her.

"Would you just cut the damn crap!" She blew out some smoke and took another pull from her cigarette. "I know you are sleeping with someone else! Just admit the shit to me, and we can try to move forward from there!"

"Why would I admit to something like that?" I frowned and felt my palms begin to sweat. "If anything, I could say the same shit about you. It's been over four months and you won't let me touch you. Not a blow job, kiss, or any damn thing physical in four months!"

"Don't you dare raise your voice to me in my house!" Lucinda stood directly in front of me and attempted to slap me, but I swatted her hand away.

"And don't you dare raise your hands to me in our house!" I lowered my tone and grabbed both of her hands as she attempted to free herself from my grasp. "I have provided this life for you. I have been doing that from day one, and don't you forget that. If anything, you are the one who must have a dude on the side. Someone or something clearly has your attention, and it's not me!"

"Something or someone?" Lucinda mocked my words. "Yeah, you got that right! Try three growing girls with school and activities. They're who have all my attention. They are supposed to have two parents who give a damn about their lives, but one of them only has time for a damn titty bar. I, on the other hand, spend all of my days devoted to my kids. Can you say the same?"

"I wake up early every damn morning and support my kids and my unappreciative wife." I let go of her hands, and she backed away from me. "Where are you getting the money for activities, cars, food, accessories, and whatnot? I don't remember your ass bringing in a paycheck around here. And would it kill you to dress up a little bit? You know, make yourself look appealing for your husband? Is that asking for too damn much?"

"Fuck you, Marvin!" Lucinda pounced on me once more. I allowed her to give me a few whacks across my head. And as much as I wanted to, I would not raise my hand to hit her. I didn't need the police called or a new reason for Lucinda to divorce my ass. I had my secrets to keep, and I wasn't about to slip up now.

"Calm down, baby! Please calm down." I held her tightly while she attempted to punch me on my sides. "I love you and only you. I don't know why you won't believe that. Tell me what I gotta do to prove that to you. Why do you continue to shut me out?"

"Let go of me," she huffed, and I released my grasp. "I don't care what you say. You are foul, and I can smell the deception seeping out of your pores. Women's intuition is never wrong, and don't you forget that."

"Let me make love to you, baby." I dropped to my knees and crawled over to her. "I'm down on my knees in a five-thousand-dollar suit. I miss us, and I want that back. Can we please try to get our intimacy back in our relationship?"

"I just . . ." She paused, and I saw that her eyes were welled up with tears. This was definitely not the reaction I had hoped for, but any kind of emotion was better than rage or vengeance.

"Oh, baby." I placed my head on her stomach and wrapped my arms around her chubby waistline. "Please, don't cry! You know I can't bear to see you upset."

She sobbed and took her time to respond. "I just feel like you're not attracted to me anymore. I know I push you away, and I feel so guilty about the shit. But I'm not the same young girl I was when we met. I've had three babies, and I can't maintain my weight the way I used to. I just feel so tired and hopeless all of the time. I don't have the energy to be sexy and look the way that you want me to."

"I'm sorry, baby." I lightly pushed my wife against the bed and slowly began to undress her from the waist down. "I was wrong to make you feel like anything but the queen you are. I know you are a great mother and you work hard at keeping the girls in line."

"And you are sure that you are satisfied with me, Marvin?" She sobbed some more, and I lightly kissed her inner thigh.

"You are all that I ever needed." I inhaled her sweet pussy scent and played with her spur tongue. "Please let me show you, baby. It's been so long. I want you so badly."

Lucinda dropped her guard down and allowed me to fuck her with my thick tongue. She squirted a few times and got me harder than Chinese arithmetic. I felt my swollen member throb in my boxers as Lucinda massaged my scalp with her fingertips.

"Oh, my God!" she whimpered in delight. "I have missed this more than I'd like to admit."

"That's what I like to hear." I wiped her juices from my chin, and she pulled down my boxers to stroke my cock. "I don't think I can last too long, but my round two will be monumental."

"Let me handle this first round all by myself." She gave me a wink and deep throated me with ease.

I felt my eyes roll to the back of my head and allowed her to do the damn thing. I wanted to fill her throat with my creamy goodies, but right before I could bless her, I heard my phone go off on the dresser.

"I'm about to cum, baby," I moaned with delight but also wondered about the string of calls on my cell.

Lucinda picked up the pace and almost gagged while I released my soldiers down her throat. She swallowed all of it and lay back on the bed.

"I think you better check your phone." She fired up a smoke but seemed satisfied with me for a change. "I hope everything is all right."

I nodded and scrolled through my missed calls. Cristol had called three times and left a voicemail. There must be some bullshit on the agenda because she knew not to call me when I was at home. Was there something wrong with our son? Did her ex come by her house with some drama? I wasn't sure, but I knew I needed to come up with a fast lie before my wife started to ask too many questions.

15

Nova: Caught in the Middle

"Girl, it was the best I ever had." I smiled from ear to ear as I relayed to Mia my slutty experience with Montezz. "I was afraid he would've thought I was too easy, but he said that we both wanted it."

"It's about damn time you met a man to unleash the beast inside of you," Mia joked as I poured her another glass of red wine. "So, is he as fine as all the girls say he is?"

"Fine?" I took a deep breath and thought back to his lovemaking techniques. "Now that is definitely an under-statement. I just wish I could've damaged my car much sooner, girl. And his daughter, now she's a real pistol. She looks like a caramel-colored china doll."

"Yeah." Mia smiled. "I heard a few stories about that whole scene. Fab won't go into too many details, but apparently the girl's mother walked out on them right after she had the baby."

"Damn." I frowned with disgust. "Are you serious?"

"Yes." Mia nodded and sipped her drink. "From what Fab said, the chick was an exchange student who stayed across the street from Tezz, and they fell in love. Then they hid the pregnancy up until she was almost due, but when the girl's aunt found out about it, she threatened to disown the girl because she was unwed and pregnant."

"Oh, wow," I thought out loud. "Well, you know there are some people who will never be understanding of unplanned pregnancies. I know my dad was upset with me but never to the point of disowning me. That had to be tough on the girl."

"Not to mention," Mia chirped on, "she was fifteen at the time and an exchange student. I guess Chinese custom is very strict on that issue and the girl had shamed the family or whatever."

"That couldn't have been easy on Montezz either." I sighed and thought highly of the man who sacrificed his childhood to care for his daughter. He reminded me so much of myself at that moment.

"I know, right?" Mia agreed. "You had your son as a teen too, so you all definitely have that in common. Sounds like the two of you can relate on a lot of issues."

"Girl, yes." I smiled and checked my phone for any messages. "He said that he wanted to meet up with me today."

"Sounds good." Mia winked at me. "So what time are the two of you meeting up, and what's on the agenda?"

"I don't really know." I shyly placed my phone on the kitchen table. "Do you think I should call him, or wait for him to make a move? I mean, I don't want to come on too forward. I was the one who asked him for his digits."

"What have I always told you time and time again?" Mia grew impatient and grabbed my phone. "Go for it!"

I heard my phone ringing, and when I grabbed it from my friend, I saw that she had dialed Montezz's number. A part of me wanted to hang it up, but he picked up on the third ring. I guessed I had no choice but to talk with him, and I was upset that Mia made that choice for me.

"Hey there, beautiful," Montezz answered with his sexy baritone voice. "I definitely had you on my mind all morning."

"Is that right?" I gave a nervous snicker, and Mia stuck her tongue out at me. "I have been thinking about you too."

"I'm glad to hear that." Montezz let out a light chuckle. "So, wassup with ya?"

"Nothing much." I finished my glass of wine and took a few deep breaths. Being the forward one was never my style, but since I was put on the spot, I had no choice but to react. "I was just calling to see if you still wanted to link up later."

"Most definitely," Montezz answered.

Mia mouthed, "I told you so."

He said, "I was gonna call you a little later and see what your schedule was looking like. So, what would be a good time for you?"

"Oh . . ." I thought about it. "Well, I don't have any plans this afternoon. I was headed over to my dad's for brunch with the family, and then I should be free. What's your schedule looking like?"

"Well," he began, "my sister and brother-in-law are supposed to come by my place for dinner around five o'clock. They are newlyweds, and I haven't seen much of them since the big day. Remember I had told you that Fab was my brother-in-law? Well, my sister is married to his younger brother."

"Oh, yes, I do remember you telling me that," I replied, and Mia raised her eyebrow with curiosity.

"Would you like to come over around four o'clock?" he asked. "I can text you my address, and we can catch up before my family gets here."

"Sounds good to me." I smiled, and Mia jokingly applauded in the background. "Just shoot me a text."

"Sounds like a plan, beautiful." He chuckled. "Now that I think about it, I might want you to come by a little sooner than that. You know, pick up where we left off from yesterday."

"Hmm." I felt my face blush with desire. "We could definitely do that, too."

"All right then," Montezz continued. "I will shoot you a text, and you let me know when you can come on over."

"Will do," I answered and ended the call.

I felt as if I were floating on air as I placed my phone on the charger. I guessed I had missed my friend's words because she seemed upset with my faint and blank expression.

"Girl?" Mia tapped me on my shoulder abruptly. "Are you listening to me or what?"

"Huh?" I shook my head at her.

"That damn Tezz must have really put it on you," she teased and helped me clean some dirty dishes. "I was saying that this would be a great opportunity for you to do some diggin' for me."

"Do some digging?" I blurted out and dried a few dishes in the sink.

"Yeah, girl." Mia dried her hands and plopped down at the kitchen table. "Since you will be meeting Fab's brother, I just thought you could ask a few questions about him and tell me what he has to say. You know, see if he has mentioned me to anyone or whatnot."

"But didn't you say that you went to the family barbecue?" I questioned her. I didn't want to get involved in their relationship at all.

"I was supposed to go." Mia paused. "Fab had some engagement that came up at the last minute. We did link up later that night if you know what I mean."

"Girl, really?" I rolled my eyes at her. "Spare me the slutty details, okay?"

"I'm just saying," Mia continued, "do you think you could just look out for your girl? I really like him, and I just want to know if he's really feeling me too. Can you do it or not?"

"I gotcha, girl," I reluctantly replied. I felt uneasy about snooping into the situation with Mia, but she had proven herself to be a good friend to me. I never would have become a stripper and bettered myself if it weren't for her. The least I could do was ask a few harmless questions.

We chatted for another hour or so and said our goodbyes for the day. I selected a casual sundress with matching sandals for my date with Tezz. I still had to go by my dad's and chill with the fam, but in the back of my mind, I felt nothing but butterflies for the new man who had entered my life.

"You really have a nice home." I applauded the cleanliness of Tezz's three-bedroom pad. There was a matching dining room and living room set. Modernized TV screens and family pictures decorated the walls.

"I'm glad everything is to your liking, beautiful." Montezz smiled, and I felt hypnotized by his gorgeous gray eyes. "Please, make yourself comfortable. Would you like something to drink?"

"Sure." I hesitated but made my way to his cozy leather sofa. "What's on the menu, bartender?"

"I have cognac, vodka, Crown, and some Bud Lights," Tezz replied from behind his bar. "What would you prefer?"

"Surprise me." I gave him a playful wink.

He laughed and got busy behind the bar. I tried to remain calm, but for some reason, I wanted to jump his damn bones. I also felt uneasy about snooping into his brother-in-law's business. The last thing I wanted to do was make a bad impression on a new love interest who had me wide open.

"I brought us both cognac with Coke." Montezz sat close to me on the sofa, and I slowly sipped my drink.

"Are you all right, Nova? You seem a little tense about something. What's on your mind?"

"Oh, I'm good," I lied. "Just enjoying the company I'm with. I'm sure a few of these drinks will relax me a bit."

"Oh, yeah?" Tezz wrapped his muscular arm around my shoulder, and I inhaled the smell of his sweet cologne. "Or maybe there is something that I could do to relax you even better?"

"I'm definitely open to your suggestions." I casually set my drink on a coaster by the lamp.

"Just lie back," he commanded while he removed his white tee. "Relax and come out of those panties. I promise I got the rest."

I did just that, and he mounted me like I was his prey. He knew just how to touch me and how to caress the simple yet delicate parts of my body. I felt my pussy cream from just the thought of his member or mouth on me.

"Damn, love." Montezz laid his head on my tight stomach. "You are like a drug to me. From the moment we locked eyes on one another, I haven't been able to think about anyone else but you. I don't know how to feel about all of this, but I want you so badly right now."

"Take me, Tezz," I whispered. "Please."

"I just want to please you right now." He lightly kissed the outline of my inner thighs and shaved pussy lips. "This can be an appetizer for an evening of passionate sex. Plus, I don't want my family to be knocking on the door in an hour and interrupt us."

I allowed him to caress my body ever so softly and devour my treasure with his wanton mouth. I bit my bottom lip several times and moaned with such ecstasy while he made my body cream with delight.

"You taste so damn good." He came up for some air, and I shoved his face back into my love box. He gripped my butt cheeks with such vigor that I cried out to the gods above and thanked them for allowing our paths to meet.

"Are you gonna cum for me, baby?" Montezz fingered my pussy, and I vibrated my hips back and forth. "I want you to skeet all over my face."

"I want to cum," I moaned.

"Let me taste it." His tongue vibrated vigorously against my clit, and I tried my best to hold out for another second or two. "Stop trying to fight it."

"Fuck!" I hollered and felt my love juices explode all over his face and the sofa beneath me.

"Oh, yes." Montezz continued to tease me more and more. "I love a squirter. That shit turns me on. Damn, I wish we had more time to continue with this."

"When is your family coming?" I panted and tried to gather my thoughts as I watched the sexy specimen stand up.

"Let me wash up and check my phone, beautiful." He smiled and slapped me playfully on my inner thigh.

My first instinct was to call Mia and tell her about this great feeling that I was involved in, but I knew that she would only want to know about Fab and his family business. I found my black thong and made my way to the guest bathroom. I splashed some cool water across my face and overheard Tezz on the phone with someone.

"Here you go, beautiful." He smiled and handed me a washcloth. "I hope that can tide you over until later on tonight."

"I think I can hang on until then." I smiled and freshened myself up.

"All right then," Tezz said, continuing with his phone conversation. "Yeah, I'm just waitin' on y'all to pull up. Oh, yeah? That's cool. A'ight, in a minute."

"Are your folks on the way?" I sat back on the sofa and finished my drink from earlier.

"Yeah." He smiled and made his way to the kitchen. "Join me in here. I just need to warm up a few things that I had prepared earlier. I hope you like fried chicken, mac and cheese, and green beans."

"What kind of black person would I be if I didn't?" I joked and watched the sexy man work in his kitchen. "I have to admit, I'm very impressed with you. I don't know too many men who know their way around the kitchen. Then again, I don't have a lot of experience with many men. Let me shut up. I'm probably talkin' too damn much."

"Thanks, sexy." Tezz gave me a sly grin and placed the chicken in the oven. "Becoming a dad at an early age made me learn things that I never imagined I'd need to know. But it allowed me to be more independent, so I'm thankful for it."

"Where's your daughter?" I asked while I continued to watch him. "She's so beautiful."

"Thank you." He stirred his mac and cheese a few times and found some dinner rolls. "She's at my parents' house for the night. Myesha, that's my everything right there. Being a dad kept me out of a lot of bullshit because I had to make her my priority. I just don't understand niggas who step out on their kids. Women either for that matter."

I could see a little rage in his face as he finished that sentence. I thought back to the story Mia had told me about his baby momma. He obviously saw my stare and replaced his look with another smile.

"Well," I tried to continue with our talk, "your daughter is very lucky to have a daddy like you. A very fine one at that. I could tell that she wasn't happy with the way I was looking at you."

"Yeah," Tezz chuckled. "She's always been protective of me. She just doesn't want me to get hurt or have anyone take her place. My baby is a piece of work."

I blushed. "Well, I can't blame her for that one bit."

Tezz received another phone call and stepped away from the kitchen momentarily. I felt more relaxed and waited for his return.

"Nice to see you in the flesh, my brother," I heard a familiar voice say in the living room.

"No doubt," Tezz replied. "I'm glad you decided to kick it with us today."

"Fa sho," the familiar voice replied. "Where do you want us to chill at?"

"Y'all can go in the living room. Let me get my li'l baby. She's in the kitchen," Tezz replied and graced me with a smile. "Nova, you can join Fab and his chick in the living room. Unless you want to kick it in here with me."

"Fab is in there?" I felt more at ease. I guessed he decided to show off Mia after all. I was more at ease because I wouldn't have to do any snooping after all. "Cool. He's been kickin' it with my friend for a while now. I'm glad he brought her because—"

I walked into the living room and saw Fab snuggled up with a blond Puerto Rican, definitely not my friend Mia. *Oh, shit, what the fuck did she get me into?*

16

Montezz: It's a Family Affair

"What it do, bruh?" I welcomed Fab and his sexy *mamasita* into my house. Fab always kept a few freaks in his corner, and this one was definitely hot and young.

"You know me." Fab gave his chick a kiss on the cheek and dapped me up. "Just livin' life and makin' this paper. I'm glad I could make it over here today. What time is my baby bruh comin' through?"

"They should be here any minute," I replied and showed them to the living room. "You know your way around in here. Fix you and your boo a drink or something. Let me go back in the kitchen and holla at li'l momma."

"Oh, you got you one?" Fab winked at me.

"Yeah." I nodded with his approval. "Nova from the club. We hit it off after I fixed that fender bender of hers."

"I bet you got all the kinks out, huh, bruh?" Fab joked and kissed his girl on her cheek.

"You a real fool," I joked, rejoined Nova in the kitchen, and then walked with her back to the living room. She looked as if she saw a ghost when I presented her to Fab and his *mamasita*.

I put my arm around Nova. "Fab, I'm sure you know this fine lady right here, and I guess this is her homegirl she was speaking of."

"Oh . . ." She tried to stop me in my tracks. "You know what? I was probably mistaken about that. Fab is just a great DJ, and I see him around a lot of people from time to time. Hey, Fab!"

"What it do, shawty?" Fab gave a nervous grin and wrapped his arms firmly around Marisol. "Nice to see you outside of the club. I see you have caught my brother's attention."

"Uh, yeah." She fumbled over her words and sat across from them in my loveseat. "He's a really great guy from what I see. But how well do you ever know somebody, you know what I'm saying?"

"Hey . . ." I gave a puzzled look to both of them. There was definitely something going on between them, and I was curious to find out the info on that. "What was that about?"

"Oh, nothin'." Nova cleared her throat and walked over to the bar to freshen her drink. "I was just sayin' that in most cases, you may think you know a person, but most people aren't the way they seem to be."

"I can assure you," I said, massaging her shoulders, "what you see is what you get with me."

"Well, that's good to know." She gave me a worried smile and poured a double shot of the cognac in her glass.

I looked back over to my bruh. "Why don't you and your girl find us some good tunes on my music player?"

"No doubt, bruh." Fab relaxed and escorted his chick to my music system by the TV set. "You know I can find something for us to vibe to."

"Nova?" I looked deep into her weary eyes. "Do you mind helping me set the table for dinner?"

"Uh, sure." She nodded nervously. "I can do that."

"Great," I breathed and continued to feel the tension in the room. "Answer the door for me, bruh!"

Fab nodded, and I walked back into the kitchen with Nova. There was a definite silence that had fallen over us, and I wanted to know the deal.

"Is everything all right, sweetheart?" I asked her as we set the dinner table. "I can tell that something is on your mind."

"It's fine, really," she huffed and placed the plates vigorously on my table. She never maintained eye contact with me, and I knew she was hiding something from me.

"I know that we are new to one another, but I want you to feel comfortable around me." I walked over to her, and she turned away from my gaze. "If I had to take a wild guess, I would say that Fab showed up with a chick who's not your friend. Am I right?"

She nodded and took a few deep breaths. "This whole situation is making me feel out of my zone, Tezz." I saw her eyes begin to well with tears, and I took a step back from her. "Mia has been a really good friend to me. She wanted me to ask Fab's brother a few questions tonight. Nothing too major, but just to see if Fab was really feeling her, you know?"

"I get it," I sighed and walked over to comfort her. "And Fab showing up with Marisol kinda put a hold on that process, huh?"

"You could definitely say that," she confessed. "I knew that he was a big player in the club. I mean, he's always in some chick's face when Mia isn't around. But I didn't want to be a snake and hate on my friend's happiness. I mean, you should hear the way she raves about his lowlife ass!"

"Fab has always had a wandering eye," I confessed. "He wouldn't know the meaning of commitment if it slapped him dead in his face. So, what's your next move?"

"I really don't know what to do." She shook her head and tapped her foot nervously on the linoleum. "If I tell her, she will be crushed by it. And if I say nothing and she finds out, she will probably hate me for it."

"Yeah." I patted my fade nervously. "They got you between a rock and a hard place right now. I wouldn't want to be in your shoes at all. And I could never blame you for the decision you decide to make with all of this. Either way you go, your friend is gonna be hurt."

"Exactly!" she cried out. "I just hate his fuckin' ass! I mean, he doesn't seem bothered by the shit in the slightest bit. I don't know how I'm gonna get through dinner watching him snuggled up with that chick knowing my friend is gonna be devastated by all of this."

"Can I make a suggestion?" I replied and looked deep into her weary eyes.

"Sure," she sighed and wiped her loose tears from her eyes. "I'll take any advice that I can get right now."

"I wouldn't say shit about it to her." I shrugged my shoulders. "In fact, I would just say that the family dinner never happened. You feel me? Did you tell her that me and you were linkin' up today?"

"Yeah, I did." She listened earnestly to my every word.

"Okay." I nodded. "You stick to that script and just say that my family had to reschedule their plans. For all that she knows, just the two of us kicked it. That way you don't have to say anything about Fab or his brother, you get me?"

"I don't know." She hesitated. "Mia is really good at smellin' my bullshit a mile away. I'm not the best at lying because I hate liars."

"I really think that's the best option for you, sexy," I pled my case. "Deny everything or admit it all. Fab definitely won't confess to anything, and if I know him like I know I do, he will show his true colors to her."

"And you really think that will work?" She seemed so unsure, but I liked the fact that she had a problem with liars. I knew from personal experience that lies only led to self-destruction.

"I got your back." I held her tightly and caressed her beautiful body. "I promise, when everyone leaves, I will do my best to make you forget about all of this."

"Such the smooth talker, Mr. Alexander," she snickered and relaxed in my arms.

"I aim to please, sweetheart." I smiled and tapped her on the ass.

"Well," she sighed and recomposed herself, "I know one thing, If I'm gonna get through this dinner, I'm gonna need way more liquor to drink!"

"You know where the bar is at," I chuckled and continued to get the table set.

"We should definitely do this more often, you guys," my sister Koran giggled and held her hubby's hand at the dinner table. "I'm having such a great time. I missed catchin' up with my favorite brother."

"Your only brother," I jabbed at her.

"Not anymore, fam." Fab gave me a wink and smacked on his chicken leg. "You know I'm another brother who needs her help and guidance."

"I'll drink to that," Nova snickered, and I could tell she was more than tipsy.

"What was that, dear?" Koran smiled at her with a curious expression.

"Oh, nothing." I steered the convo back to myself. "But yeah, what are you guys doing next weekend?"

"No real plans." Darrell wiped his mouth and sipped on his beer. "Why, what's up?"

"Hey, Koran," Fab replied with his arm around Marisol, "do you think Darrell could come kick it with the fellas one good time?"

"Are you really asking me?" Koran seemed surprised, but that was all for show.

"Well, yeah," Fab laughed. "You know he won't join us unless you're cool with it."

"I trust my husband." Koran rolled her neck. "If he wants to hang out with the fellas, he knows that I'm cool with it. Hell, I might want to have a ladies' night for myself."

"That's good to know." Fab glanced over at his younger brother. "Seems that you have the green light, Darrell. So, are you down to kick it?"

"What did you have in mind?" Darrell asked and kissed Koran's hand gently.

"One of your favorite rappers, Boss Hog, will be performing at the club next weekend." Fab waited for Darrell's look of amazement. "You know I got the hookup for the VIP treatment. I could arrange for you to meet up and kick it with him after his set. I mean, if you are interested."

"Oh, word?" Darrell smiled and looked to his wife for approval. "I mean, yeah, I guess I could do that. Are you kickin' it with us too, Tezz?"

"Me?" I blurted out. "Who said anything about me going?"

"Tezz has a lot of static about swingin' by the club," Fab confessed. "Clearly, he doesn't have a problem kickin' it with a dancer, but he doesn't like going to the club to see them dance."

"I know he didn't," Nova whispered loudly in my ear and drew the attention back to herself.

"I never said anything like that," I spat out and comforted my drunk li'l missy. "I just said I'm not that big on clubbin'. But if it makes Darrell feel better, I can come through. Fab, can you put my boy James on the list with me?"

"You know I can, bruh." Fab smiled and finished his meal. "I'm lovin' this right here. It's been forever since we all kicked it. This will be like old times."

"Not entirely, Fab!" Koran corrected him. "None of them chicks better end up on my husband's lap. I don't play that crap!"

"I got your back, sista!" Nova raised her glass to Koran. "I will be there next weekend, and I can assure you no one will be gettin' a lap dance!"

"Well, thank you, Nova!" Koran applauded her. "You know we girls have to stick together."

"So," I responded before Nova had the chance to, "I guess that settles that. Next Saturday it is!"

"But, *papi*," Marisol whined with her thick accent, "I thought we were goin' out of town next weekend. *Tu comprendes?*"

"Don't you worry about that, love." Fab held her closely and whispered something into her ear. She giggled from whatever he told her, and I felt Nova's leg and foot tap on the floor below us.

"I don't know how much of this bullshit I can stand, Tezz," Nova whispered in my ear. I kept a smile on my face to hide the severity of her statements from my nosy family.

"You are handling it like a champ." I kissed the nape of her neck. "Why don't you excuse yourself from the table and go relax in my bedroom? I can clear out this static, and we can pick up where we left off earlier today."

She did as I suggested, and I entertained my family for another hour or so. The crowd started to lessen, and we said our goodbyes to the happily married couple. I did want to speak with Fab before he left my house.

"I really had a great time tonight." Fab dapped me up and grabbed his jacket and keys. "We gotta do this shit more often, for real."

"No doubt." I kept my smile and softened my voice a bit. "Do you think I can holla at you for a minute?"

"Fa sho, bruh." Fab nodded. "Hey, baby, why don't you go on out to the car? I will be out there in a few minutes, okay?"

"Okay, *papi*." Marisol smiled as she made her way to my front door. "It was *mucho* nice to meet you, Tezz!"

"Same here, love," I said graciously and waited for her to close the front door behind her.

"Wassup, bruh?" Fab said nonchalantly and waited for my response.

"I think you know the answer to that." I frowned. "So, you runnin' game on Nova's homegirl? When are you gonna stop your shit?"

"I didn't think you would be the one to judge me." Fab got on the defensive. "I never question any of the shit that you do."

"That's because I'm upfront with mine," I fired back. "I let these bitches know the deal upfront, but you are playin' with fire right now. Not to mention you dragged Nova smack in the middle of it!"

"Nova ain't got shit to do with this, man." Fab shook his head. "Yeah, I fuck Mia and shit, but we never said that we were exclusive. So, what's the real problem?"

"The problem is . . ." I paused. "Mia is really feelin' you. She wanted Nova to bring her up at dinner tonight. Clearly she couldn't do that since you brought a bitch with you tonight!"

"Oh, word?" Fab seemed pleased with himself. "Yeah, I do be punishin' that tight little pussy. But you know how it goes, bruh. Shit, I can't just be tied down with one bitch. Variety is the spice of life, you feel me?"

"I hear you." I shook my head with disgust. "But just be careful. I told Nova to deny the family gathering. She said that she would, so that should buy you some extra time to break things off with Mia."

"Break things off with Mia?" Fab frowned. "Now, why would I want to do that? That young bitch tosses my salad, sucks my dick from the back, and some more shit. I would never give her up, not for nothing. You are buggin'!"

"You are somethin' serious, bruh." I shook my head and dapped him up before he headed to the door. "Well, don't say that I didn't warn you."

"I got this," Fab assured me. "But thanks for lookin' out."

I locked the front door and cleaned up the dining room and kitchen areas. Fab made me think about my own routine with the ladies. I was told that I could be the heartbreaker, but at least I was an honest one. I never came across like I was monogamous with any of them. If they caught feelings, that was a choice these women made on their own. But Fab seemed to find enjoyment out of breaking these young girls' hearts. I only hoped Nova was able to stay out of the crosshairs.

I had almost forgotten that she was chillin' in my bedroom. I felt a slight erection in my boxers, finished the dishes, and hurried to my bedroom for another great love session.

17

Marvin: A Double-edged Sword

"Is everything all right, honey?" Lucinda sighed and headed for our master bathroom.

"Just some shit at the club, love," I lied to her and immediately sent Cristol a text after Lucinda closed the bathroom door. "I'm sure I can get it handled."

Me: What is the deal? This had better be an emergency. You know the rules when I'm at home with my wife and kids!

I wrote Cristol and kept an eye on the bathroom door.

"Do you think you will be out very long?" Cinda replied with the bathroom door closed. "I was just about to get dinner started, and the girls would love to have you home for that."

"I'm not sure how long this will take!" I hollered back at her and waited impatiently for Cristol to respond. "But I will try to be back home as soon as possible, I can promise you that. From here on out, I will be more attentive to my girls."

"That's all that I ever wanted." Lucinda emerged from our bathroom and planted a juicy kiss on my lips. "I want things to be better between us."

I nodded and felt my phone vibrate. I tried to give my wife my undivided attention, but I was more interested in what Cristol had to tell me.

"I promise," I replied with a fake smile. "I will do my best to make you feel appreciated, my queen."

"I think you really mean it this time." Lucinda headed to the bedroom door. "Well, go ahead and handle your business. Let me get dinner started and check on the girls. Those flowers were very beautiful, though."

"I'm glad you liked them, beautiful." I maintained eye contact with her until she headed down the hallway.

I took a few deep breaths and unlocked my iPhone. The picture I saw only made my blood boil to my core. Cristol had sent a few pictures with bruises and scratches all over her body.

Me: WTF?

Cristol: Chauncey came over here trippin'. Said I was keepin' him from our son and that I needed to give him another chance. When I told him no, he blew up and hit me a few times. I'm so scared!

Me: Did you call the cops on his ass?

I searched the room for my wallet and keys.

Cristol: Yeah, but he ran out of here when he heard me on the phone with the cops. He's been callin' from unknown numbers and threatenin' me. I'm just so scared right now!

Me: Just take the baby and head to the club parking lot. You know where I keep my spare office key. Sit tight, I'm on my way!

Cristol: Okay.

I said my goodbyes to my family, raced to the garage, and peeled out of my driveway. I wanted to ring that fool Chauncey's neck. Although I had only met him a time or two at the club, Cristol put me on game about his abusive and childish ways. She did her thing at the club and had a lot of regulars, but her inner spirit drew me to her, and before long, we were fucking like rabbits. There were a few times that I slipped up and forgot to wear a rubber, and our son was conceived. But I knew that Cristol was the loyal type, hell, I made sure she was straight, and she had no reason to ever turn on me. I was scared when she first told me about the pregnancy. I was a married man with obligations and shit. We knew the best bet was to pin the baby on Chauncey and hope that the fool became a better man. From the pictures I was just sent, there was no way to ever see him as anything but a straight clown.

I gave my boo a call and she picked up after the first ring.

"Where are you now?" I asked angrily.

"I just pulled up at the club like you told me to," she replied.

"Good," I sighed with relief. "Do you think that fool followed you there? How's the baby doing?"

"He knows better not to come here," she reassured me. "I took Jamel to my sister's house after I sent you the last text message. I just wanted us to talk alone."

"All right, sweet thang," I babied her. "I will be there in a few minutes. I want to kill that fool nigga."

"I know, baby," she sobbed.

"Just hold tight for me," I replied and ended the call.

A million thoughts were running across my mind as I made my way to the club parking lot. There appeared to be a nice crowd, and the regulars were parked in the first three rows of the lot. I pulled around the back and saw Cristol's gray Highlander next to my privileged parking space. I exited my vehicle, turned the lock on the door, and headed to my office. Cristol was a complete mess, and her bruises had begun to blacken her face.

"Look at what he did to me, baby."

I ran over and embraced her gently.

"I'm just so scared." She sobbed on my chest and collapsed into my arms. "I just don't know what to do. What if he comes back to beat me again? I'm just so tired of this shit. I wish he would just disappear and leave us alone."

"I hate this shit!" I pounded my fist on my desk and knocked a few documents to the floor below. "I think we need to get you and Jamel into a new location. Somewhere that Chauncey knows nothing about."

"But what about my lease?" Cristol wiped her tears with a Kleenex. "I just renewed it, and they will make me pay a grip if I leave right now."

"Since when are you worried about paying for anything?" I questioned her eyes. "Do you want that fool to keep beating you or some shit? Do you want him to come over there and do something to the baby? Our baby!"

"You know that's not what I meant at all." She hugged me tightly.

"So, what's the problem?" I continued.

"I'm just so tired of runnin'," she sobbed. "All my life, I've had to fight off one nigga or another. As a child and now again as an adult. Why can't I just be left alone and live my life?"

"So, what do you want me to do, Cristol?" I wiped her fresh tears with my hand and waited for her to calm down a bit. "I'm trying to give you a better option. I mean, what is it that you want me to do?"

"Can't you just . . ." She paused and lowered her voice. "Get rid of him?"

"That's easier said than done." I stepped away from her and sat in my comfortable chair behind my desk. I rocked back and forth to steady my thinking. "Not to mention I have more at stake than you do. If any of that gets traced back to me, well, you know what it is."

"I'm sure we could find someone around here to do the job for us," she said, continuing with her idea. She plopped her sexy ass in front of me on the desk. "Chauncey owes a lot of people, and it's not too farfetched to think that any one of them could want him dead and gone."

"So, what are you sayin'?" I massaged her juicy pussy and pulled her panties off.

"I'm sayin'," she breathed deeply and spread her caramel legs apart to invite me inside of them, "you let me do some diggin' of my own, and we can come up with a plan to get rid of him together."

"I don't know about this, love." I sucked on her inner thigh and played in her pussy with my right hand. "Seems really risky to me."

"Come on, baby." She scooted closer to the edge of the desk and lay back on it. She wrapped her legs around my neck, and I succumbed to her sweet nectar. "For the safety of me and our son, don't you think him being gone is worth it? Don't you?"

I let my actions speak for themselves and ate on her pussy like it was my last meal. I couldn't deny the fact that I loved Cristol deeply. She was a weakness and had my heart when she bore my only son. As a man, I had to protect the both of them. I would please her right now and erase all of her doubts. She was right. Chauncey was a menace and had a lot of enemies in the streets. I did my search on that fool, but finding someone willing to take him out was another subject altogether.

"Allow me to prove my loyalty to you, baby." Cristol pushed my chair away from the desk and got down on her knees in front of me. She unfastened my belt and pulled out my bulging member before me. "I'm going to suck this dick until all of your doubt is removed from your mind. I don't care how long that takes, but I'm not going to stop until you agree to do this with me."

Cristol was the best at giving head. If I weren't already paying her bills, I would double what I gave to her. I squirmed and tried to hold my nut, but she made me bust before I could bat my eye.

"Are you feeling me yet, baby?" she breathed and swallowed my cum before my eyes. She knew I loved to watch her swallow my shit. Damn, I felt so weak to her. "I can't hear you."

She got me hard once more, and I moaned and played in her hair tracks.

"Dammit, girl," I sighed with such pleasure. "Why do you have to drive me so damn crazy? Fuck!"

"I'll stop when you give me the answer I wanna hear." She paused and deep throated me again and again. The sound of her gaggin' on my shit almost made me nut once more.

"I can't take this torture anymore!" I pushed her head back, turned her body around, and punished that pussy from the back. "Shit, you feel so damn good!"

"You know this belongs to you," she moaned and played in her pussy while I punished it. "Isn't that right, daddy?"

"Oh, yes!" I moaned and smacked her on her plump ass. "Shit, I can't hold it much longer, girl!"

"I wanna catch it." She pushed my dick outside of her and wrapped her lips back around my veiny member. "Just tell me, what's it gonna be?"

"Shit!" I hollered as I let my babies erupt down her throat. "Yes, we will end that fuck nigga!"

18

Nova: Back to Reality

"Hello, sexy," I answered a call from Tezz that morning.

"Hey back at cha," he snickered with pure delight.

The two of us had really hit it off since my trip to his shop two weeks ago. Every day I wanted him more than the day before, and he really seemed to be feelin' me the same way. I had my doubts as any woman would, but for the most part, I felt safe with him.

"Wassup witcha?" he asked with his sexy baritone voice.

"Just waking up," I yawned and sat up in my bed. "How about you?"

"You know me," he replied. "At the shop, but I took a break to call you."

"Aww," I said seductively. "Isn't that the sweetest thing?"

"No, baby," he laughed. "What's in between your legs is the sweetest."

"There you go." I blushed and made my way into the bathroom. "Don't get me started while you are way across town!"

"That's the great part about being the boss," he replied. "I can always leave when I get good and ready. So, wassup?"

"You ain't sayin' nothin' but a word to me," I hinted back at him.

"Okay then." He laughed. "Let me finish up the job and I will hit you back. And you better be ready when daddy gets over there."

"You already know." I smiled through the phone and ended the call.

I hopped into the shower and imagined Tezz's hands caressing me as I masturbated to the thought of him. Then I wrapped a towel around my wet body. As I searched my closet for something to slip into, I heard a loud knock at my door. I checked my phone and thought that Tezz had made his way here sooner rather than later. I made my way to the door and stood in a sexy pose while I unlocked it.

"I guess you couldn't wait any longer." I had my back turned to the door, but when I got no response, I felt uneasy as I turned around. "Mia?"

I could tell that she had been crying, and immediately I got out of horny mode and into friend mode with her.

"Girl." I hugged her closely and walked with her into my kitchen. "What's going on? Talk to me."

"It's Fab!" She continued to sob, and I handed her a few Kleenex. "He's definitely steppin' out on me. Oh, I feel like such an idiot!"

"Oh, wow!" I tried my best to appear shocked and amazed by the hurtful news. "That's so fucked up, girl. Why do you think he's steppin' out on you?"

"I went through his phone last night!" Mia broke all the way down, and I ran over to console her. "I normally don't do that kind of thing, but when a woman's intuition takes over, you just seem to go with it, you know?"

"Yeah," I said sympathetically. "I feel you. So, what did you find in there?"

"He's been hookin' up with some Hispanic bitch named Marisol. Can you believe that shit?" She blew her nose a few times, and I remained quiet. "That time he said he was too busy to take me to the family barbecue, come to find out he took that bitch with him. Ugh, I feel so sick to my stomach!"

"What a damn dog!" I frowned and hated him more than ever.

"I just feel so damn stupid." Mia cried even more than before. "I should have listened to you. You told me not to trust the damn DJ, but did I listen? Oh, hell no!"

"Don't beat yourself up too badly about his ass," I comforted my friend. "At least you know the truth now, and you can be done with his ass for good. No harm, no foul, right?"

"Well . . ." She paused. "I don't know about all of that."

"What do you mean?" I raised an eyebrow. "Don't tell me you got knocked up by that fool!"

"Okay, fine." She blew her nose once more. "I won't tell you that I got knocked up!"

"Mia, no!" I held her tightly and rocked her back and forth. "How could you let that shit happen? You saw how fucked up my life was. Why would you want to go that route?"

"It's not like I planned on it." She dried her tears. "We do a lot of fuckin', and sometimes I would forget to take my damn pill. But I always doubled up the very next day. I just thought I was covering my shit, you know?"

I tried to remain calm and not spill the tea that I knew about Marisol all that time. "What's your next move? Are you going to tell him about the baby or what?"

"Hell no!" She shook her head vigorously. "Not now. There's no way! I want this baby out of me as soon as possible! I can't deal with this shit right now!"

"Okay," I sighed and heard another knock at my door. I was sure that was Tezz and looked away from my friend.

"Was you expecting some company?" She raised her eyebrow. I nodded and let Tezz in the front door.

"I thought I told your ass to be ready for me." He pouted but erased his expression when he saw Mia sitting at my kitchen table. "Oh, hello, Mia!"

"Hello." Mia mustered up a wayward smile. "Nice to see you again, Tezz. I can tell that the two of you are really hittin' it off. I'm glad someone's life is headed in the right direction."

"How's that?" Tezz looked at me for a suggestion.

"Umm . . ." I hesitated, and Mia wiped her tears once more.

"It's fine, Nova," Mia sighed and ran her fingers through her messed-up hair. "I don't care that he knows because I'm gonna take care of this problem. My dumb ass got knocked up by your no-count brother Fab!"

"Oh, wow." Tezz was taken aback and stood there in shock.

"Yeah, I know." Mia blew her nose once more. "That may have been the best news. But after I snooped through that ho's phone, I found out that he's been creepin' with a foreign bitch. Has he ever mentioned someone named Marisol to you?"

"Marisol?" Tezz kept his poker face and scratched his temple. "Nope, that name doesn't sound familiar at all. It's hard to keep up with that dude, for real. So, were the two of you exclusive?"

"As far as I knew," Mia spat out. "I don't see how he found the time to fuck that bitch as much as I was on his dick. I'm talking daily or every other day! Niggas just don't know when they have it good. I mean, the things that we shared together . . . I'm not gonna bore the two of you with all of that."

"Please," I interjected, "spare us the details."

"Oh, hush." Mia let out a laugh. "You act like you never do any freaky shit. Tezz, can you please unlock the freak in this one? I'm talkin' blow her damn back out a time or two. It'll be good for her."

"I'm definitely up for the challenge." Tezz winked and gave me a slight nudge.

"Enough with all of that," I interrupted their fun. "So, what do you want to do, friend? You know I got your back."

"Yeah," Tezz chimed in. "A baby is nothin' to play about. It has a way of devastating some people, and if I know Fab, he's not daddy material in the slightest bit. He's managed to go thirty-eight years without a kid under his belt. Do you think that's by accident?"

"You know," Mia said, looking over at him, "I guess I never really thought about it like that. But yeah, he's definitely not the father-figure type. I think an abortion is the best route for me."

"Abortion?" Tezz gave her a look of disgust. "Really? That's what you want to do?"

"I'm only twenty-two years old." Mia placed her hand over her chest. "I have way too much livin' left to do. There's no way that I want to have a baby right now. And I sure as hell don't want to be tied to Fab for the rest of my life. I mean, look at what he's doing right now. A baby isn't gonna make him any better. I'm sure he couldn't care less if I get rid of it."

"Get rid of it?" Tezz shook his head. I could tell this was a salty subject for him. "That's good. Think of the baby as an 'it' and not a person!"

"I didn't mean any harm." Mia wanted to take back her last statement, but the damage was already done. "That's just the way I feel."

"No need to apologize to me, little lady." Tezz plastered on a fake smile. "It's your body, do what you want, but it couldn't be me. There's no way a chick would ever abort my seed. Are you gonna tell Fab about the baby?"

"Naw," Mia blurted out carelessly. "I don't see the point, and I hate his ass right now!"

"I hate to get in your business . . ." Tezz paused and glanced over at me. "But if you don't feel comfortable tellin' him, I could if you would like. Only if you want me to."

"Really?" Mia gave a huge smile. "You really wouldn't mind?"

"I don't think that's a good idea." I shook my head in objection. "If Mia wants to keep it under wraps, I think she should do that. The last thing she needs is Fab comforting her out of pity or obligation. If he can't do right by her now, what's the whole point?"

"Because it's his baby too!" Tezz stood his ground. "You know how I feel about people not steppin' up and being there for their kids, Nova!"

"Hey." Mia tapped on the kitchen table. "Calm down, you two, okay? Fine, if it makes you feel better, Tezz, I will tell Fab about my pregnancy. Matter of fact, I can call his bitch ass right now."

"You go right ahead and make that call, Mia." I tried to remain supportive of my friend. "Tezz, can I speak to you in my room for just a moment, please?"

"All right." Mia dialed Fab's number on her phone. "But if the two of you are about to fuck, I can just leave."

"You're good, girl." I rolled my eyes, guided Tezz to my bedroom, and shut the door behind us. "What the fuck was that all about?"

"What do you mean?" He frowned and folded his arms in front of his chest.

"Why would you volunteer to tell Fab about the baby?" I gave him a disturbed look. "Weren't you the one who told me to stay out of their business in the first place?"

"I know." He sighed. "But the game changed when she said she was knocked up by him. It's one thing to mess around, but when it involves a baby, the game has really changed. We both know how serious that is, c'mon now!"

"That's still not our place to get involved," I pointed out.

"How soon you forget." Tezz shook his head in disbelief. "We are already involved!"

19

Mia: Played by a Real Playa

I really appreciated the love and concern that Tezz and Nova gave me with my baby news. I was a little scared and unsure about calling Fab, but fuck it, what did I have to lose? I mean, I planned on getting an abortion anyway, so where was the harm in telling him about the baby?

I waited until Nova and Tezz shut her bedroom door, and I called Fab's number. I almost chickened out and hung up the call, but that bitch answered after the fourth ring.

"Yo," he replied nonchalantly. "Where did you run off to?"

"Just shut the fuck up, nigga!" I found some courage deep inside of myself. "Look, I could beat around the bush, but that's just not my damn style!"

"What is all of this about, baby?" Fab played the innocent role with me. I couldn't believe that I fell for all his lies and crap for this long. "I'm just worried about my boo. I was just about to blow your phone up and see where you had run off to. Tell me, what's up?"

"I'm over at Nova's place!" I blurted out.

"Aw, okay." Fab seemed satisfied with my answer. "You could've sent me a text or left a note saying you was going over there. I mean, damn, why would you want to make me worry about you for no reason?"

"Can you just stop with all the games and lies, Fab!" I
stood to my feet and paced the floor. "I mean it. You are
way too old to be playin' as many games as you play!"

"What the fuck?" Fab yelled. "Where is all of this shit
comin' from, girl? And don't be over at your homegirl's
house showin' out on me! We really don't have to go
there! You could've talked to me face-to-face about all of
that!"

"I'm alone," I assured him. "Video call me if you think
I'm joking. Tezz and Nova aren't in here with me. This is
a conversation for just the two of us."

"Tezz?" Fab blurted out and gave a wicked laugh. "So,
now you're tellin' me that my own brother is in on this
bullshit too?"

"No one is in on shit." I became confused. "I'm going to
video call you. Hang up, crazy nigga!"

Several thoughts went across my mind as I thought
about why Fab was so upset when I brought up my friend
and his brother. I appreciated the both of them. They had
been more supportive and real than his bitch ass.

"There's my baby!" Fab replied with a stupid grin on his
face.

"Yeah, right." I rolled my eyes at him and walked
throughout Nova's apartment. "As you can see, there is
no one in here with me. I have no reason to stunt. That's
not me at all."

"Okay then." Fab nodded his head. "So, what's all of
this about, and why did you sneak out of the house while
I was asleep?"

"Okay." I took a deep breath and looked away from him.
"I'm gonna be all-the-way real with you right now. I went
through your phone last night, nigga!"

"You did what?" Fab squinted his eyes and seemed
offended by my statement. "Why in the hell would you
do that bullshit? See, that's what I'm talkin' about right

there. No trust! What did we say about having boundaries in this shit?"

"Nigga, fuck all of that," I cut him off and felt the tears forming back in my eyes. "I did trust you, but my woman's intuition never fails me. I felt like there was something foul going on, and it just turns out that I was right about it. So, is there anything that you want to confess to before I continue with what I gotta say?"

"Confess to anything like what?" Fab continued with his dummy role. "You went through my phone, so you tell me!"

"Okay." I nodded and wiped my eyes. "Who the fuck is Marisol, and how long have the two of you been fuckin'? Better yet, when do you have the time and energy to fuck her? Seein' how much you always end up in my bed!"

"Marisol is just a damn friend." He shrugged his shoulders. "No more and no less. You saw the texts! It's not like I ever said I loved her, and it's not like the two of us are exclusive. So, why the fuck did you really go in my damn phone? You know I hate that sneaky shit! That's why I had to cancel the last bitch!"

"Cancel the last bitch?" I raised my voice and stared deep into his eyes. "So, now I'm just some useless bitch to you, is that it? All the talks and secrets we shared with each other and the only word you could think of was bitch?"

"Wait a damn minute, Mia." Fab tried to correct himself, and he should have because all the borderline gay shit he had me do would bury his ass for good. "I never called you a bitch. I said the last chick I was with was a bitch. There you go, twisting my words around like you always do. Can't you just come home and we can talk about this? I don't like everyone in our business."

"Nova is my best homegirl," I assured him. "She's always known how much I dug your ass! And even when she told me to steer clear of the DJ, I chose to do otherwise. Ugh, I wish I had just listened to her in the first place and never fucked you!"

"Oh, I see." Fab grew angrier by the second. "So, now Nova is givin' you advice on me?"

"Anyways," I cut him off, "don't make this about Nova, okay? It's not her fault that you forgot to lock up your phone last night. She and Tezz were both shocked when I dropped my bit of news on them today!"

"News, huh?" Fab continued to toy with me. "Well, are you gonna bless me with it, or do I need to holla at your great friends about it?"

"I'm only tellin' you this because Tezz seemed to think you ought to know," I pointed out and jabbed him even further.

"Man, if you don't tell me what the fuck is goin' on right now . . ." He pointed his finger at me through the phone.

"I'm fuckin' pregnant, nigga!" I blurted out. "Yeah, that's right! I found out two days ago, and I planned on tellin' you about it. But when I went through your phone and saw that you were untrue, I just wanted to abort the baby and be through with it! I mean, I still plan on havin' an abortion, but I wasn't gonna tell you shit. Tezz thought I should let you know since you were the father, okay? So now you know!"

"So, now you think that Tezz and Nova are such great friends to you, right?" Fab chuckled, and I grew madder by the second.

"Yeah, they are!" I spat out. "What the fuck is that supposed to mean? I mean, you are the one hidin' bitches and then lyin' in the bed with me at night! So, you really think that makes you daddy material?"

"I never said I wanted to be a daddy," Fab replied. "But since you wanna talk about hidin' bitches, we can go there! You're right, I was wrong to fuck off with Marisol.

I met her a few weeks ago at a party I DJ'd. I had been drinkin', she looked good, and the rest is history. I didn't tell you about it because I didn't think it would ever be that serious. I mean, she got a dude at home, so we just kick it every now and then. But as for your 'friends,' they met Marisol two weeks ago. Did they tell you about that?"

"Two weeks ago?" I felt flushed and sick to my stomach. "What are you talking about?"

"Yeah." Fab laughed at my stupidity once more. "Tezz had a family get-together, and I brought Marisol with me. Nova was there. I was really surprised she kept that from you all this time. But then again, Tezz gave me the heads-up. Said he convinced Nova to stay quiet about Marisol until hopefully I could decide which chick was more important to me."

"You're fuckin' lying!" I yelled at the top of my lungs. "I don't believe anything you're saying right now! Fuck you, Fab!"

"Oh, yeah?" Fab fired back. "I can prove it to you."

"And how are you going to do that?" I fumed at him.

"Head on home, baby." Fab looked deep into my eyes on the phone. "I will message Marisol right now. All I gotta do is bring up the family dinner. I will send you a screenshot of our conversation. And we can talk about the baby. Just come home, please!"

I was so furious with everyone right now. I didn't dare tell Nova that I was leaving, but please believe I would make Nova and her nigga pay if I found them to be salty in this shit.

I quietly exited Nova's apartment, made my way to my car, and revved up the engine. I didn't even play the radio as I normally would. I wanted to make sure I heard my notifications if Fab was being one hundred with his version of the story. It never dawned on me that Nova would betray me like that. I had been nothing but good to her. Hell, she would still be at the damn grocery store if it weren't for me.

Ding! Ding! I heard my notification go off and pulled into a gas station by the next light. I read the messages and let out a hurt and pained yell. There it was in front of my face. Marisol talked about the fun time at Tezz's dinner gathering and how drunk Nova appeared to be. But she lied and told me the dinner was cancelled.

Game on, bitches, I thought as I drove like a bat out of hell to Fab's studio apartment. *I see these bitches ain't loyal no more, so I'll have to make them all pay!*

20

Nova: A Man of My Own

"Oh, my God!" I screamed at the top of my lungs. "Oh, yes, baby, do it to me harder!"

Tezz flipped me on to my back and mounted me like a purebred stallion. He wrapped his manly bronzed arms around my taut torso and immersed his gorged member inside of my tight womb.

"Tell me how much you love it, baby." He pumped harder and harder. I felt my body burst from the inside out. "I can't hear you, dammit!"

"Oh, shit, baby!" I sounded like an injured puppy. "I love this dick. You know that I do!"

"How much do you love it, baby?" Tezz handled my body with ease and placed both of my legs above his shoulders. "Let me see you cum on daddy's dick!"

We played our sex games and succumbed to our passionate end with me on top of him. I laid my body against his hairy chest and felt his heartbeat against mine. He ran his fingers up and down my spine, and I felt my body tingle in erotic delight.

"Dammit, girl," Tezz breathed heavily and raised my face in front of his own. "You know I still have to go to work this morning! Are you trying to tire me out before I even get started?"

"Don't you blame this all on me!" I winked, kissed him softly on his lips, and climbed off of him. "I'd like to think that you met me halfway in all of this."

"Where are you going, sexy?" Tezz rubbed on his semi-hard python and watched me enter the bathroom.

"I'm about to take a hot shower," I replied seductively and rubbed on my pussy lips. "I gotta get Markus ready for his first day of kindergarten."

"If you keep doing all of that right there," Tezz said, walking over to the doorway and parting my legs before him, "my man Markus will be late for his first day of school. But I'm a little hungry, baby. Let's hop in this shower, and let me munch on that pussy for you."

Tezz and I went crazy on each other one last time and finally managed to put on some clothes and start our day. The past couple of months had been some of the best in my whole life. I could practically say that we were living together and basically spending equal time in each other's homes. On this particular day, I had spent the night at Tezz's house. He had even cleared out a dresser drawer and closet space for me.

Myesha was a little more open with me compared to our first real encounter. I could say that she was a very observant 11-year-old, but that would be an insult. My-My spent plenty of time asking me why I liked her dad and what my intentions were for him. She also let me know that if I broke his heart, she would track me down and whoop my ass! Yes, that's right. Myesha don't play about him! I loved their tight and understanding relationship, and I only hoped that Markus and I shared the same compassion when he got to be her age.

"What time do you have to be at the shop, boo?" I chomped on a piece of cinnamon toast and took a sip of my orange juice.

"I'm supposed to be there at ten o'clock." Tezz sipped on his coffee and winked his gray eye at me. "Today should be a rather busy day. You know how the middle of the month can be. But I can't complain about the money."

"I know that's right, baby," I laughed and thought about my days at the club. "I appreciate the dollars I receive! That shit pays the bills, and we all have those to consider."

"Do we really have to talk about that club shit?" Tezz finished his coffee and placed the mug in the kitchen sink. "You know how I feel about that place."

"Can we not go there today, please?" For the past month or so, we had been arguing about my job at the club. Tezz and I didn't like to label our relationship, but it was well known that we fucked with each other on the regular. He wanted me to quit shaking my ass at that club and get a "real job."

Tezz frowned and walked over to kiss my face and neck. "Baby, you know how I feel about you, right?"

"I know how you feel." I playfully pushed him away. "Even though you never want to say the words out loud!"

"Oh, I see." Tezz backed away from me and grabbed his lunch pail on the kitchen counter. "Now you want to turn this thing around on me. This is not about me, Nova! This is about you feelin' like you still gotta shake your ass on the dance floor! That shit might have been cool in the past, but I would like to think that you have something more concrete to stand on now!"

"And like I have said to you before," I said, pointing my index finger at him and placing my other hand firmly on my hip, "I was working there when you met me, so why is it such a problem for you now?"

"Who do you lie up with every damn night, Nova?" Tezz yelled and pushed my finger away. "Who is here for you day in and day out? Shows his affection, spends time with Markus, and would buy you the damn world if he could? Huh, who is that? Is it tha muthafuckin' club?"

"Baby," I pouted and wrapped my arms around his waist. He tried his best to fight me off, but I would not budge from my grasp of him. "I know that you got me, babe. And I appreciate all the things that you do. I just don't want you to feel like you have to take care of me. You know that I'm not used to that! I've been taking care of people all my life! I'm so used to working and being a provider!"

"That's the very reason that I want to give you so much." Tezz ran his fingers through my hair and tongued me down by the kitchen door. "Because you give so much and don't expect anything in return for that. You are the type of woman all women should strive to be! I love that about you, and I just want to see you in a better environment. I told you I can find you a job at the shop, or maybe you could go to college and get a degree in something."

"I hear all of that, baby." I kissed him softly on the cheek and felt my heart melt for him once again. "And I promise I will give this some serious thought."

"That's all that I can ask for." Tezz hugged me. "You know, if there's anything that you need, I will try my best to be that."

"Anything?" I raised an eyebrow playfully.

"Just name it." Tezz licked his lips and sucked on my neck.

"Are you sure about that?" I gave him a devilish smirk, and he seemed concerned with it.

"Shoot your shot, beautiful." He looked me up and down.

"Will you say those three little words for me?" I stepped away from him and saw the beads of sweat line his brow. "Do you think you can make that happen?"

"See?" Tezz gave a puzzled look and played it off. "Why you always gotta play so much, girl? I will call you when I get to the shop, all right? Lock the door when you leave, crazy girl!"

"Uh-huh." I headed to the kitchen sink and started on the rest of the dishes. "I love you too, boo!"

He made his getaway out the door, and I shook my head with amazement. I knew in my heart that Tezz loved me, but I couldn't for the life of me get him to say those three words. I blamed his bitch of a baby's momma for that shit! She crippled a part of him that he would never let me see. Even though he beat the odds, raised a little girl, and became a success, there was still a part of him that felt so incomplete and so very jaded.

I had almost lost all track of time, and then I heard my phone ringing beside me. I sucked my teeth and answered the call.

"Hey there, sexy!" Mr. Marvin replied on the other end. "Where are you at, love?"

"I'm at my nigga's crib." I rolled my eyes and found my keys and Gucci purse. "Why do you ask?"

"Damn, baby." Marvin gave that annoying whine that made my flesh crawl. "Why you gotta come at me like that? But you know that everything you do turns me on! Shit, got my dick hard as a rock right now."

"Yeah, yeah." I continued to show disinterest and made sure to lock the door before I left. "Spare me all the details, okay?"

"I'm just gonna ignore all of that," He laughed and took a deep breath. "So, what time will you be here for our appointment? You know, we have a few things to discuss. Might take an hour or two if you know what I mean!"

"More like thirty minutes or so," I whispered to the side of the phone and cranked up my ride.

"What was that, love?" Marvin replied in his seductive but pathetic voice.

"I said, what are we gonna discuss today?" I wanted to gag as I left the street of Tezz's residence and approached a stop sign ahead.

"You know," Marvin continued, "a little bit of this and a little bit of that. I still would like to have a time so I can mark you on my schedule book."

"I have to get Markus signed up for kindergarten today," I relayed to him.

"And what time do you have to be there for that? It's been a while since I've had a kid that age," he asked me.

"Noon today," I answered and made a left turn at the light.

"All right then." He cleared his throat. "So, you are just getting him dressed and dropping him off for a few hours, right?"

"Yeah," I breathed. "I have to pick him up at three thirty. With it being toward the end of the week, they are only going for half days until Monday morning."

"Sounds cool," Marvin chuckled. "So, I can put you down for about twelve forty-five or so, right? That should give you enough time to get here, and you will be free before three thirty."

"Yeah," I huffed and came to a complete stop.

"All right then, sexy," Marvin said, wrapping up the convo. "I will see you in my office around twelve for-ty-five. And please, forget your panties!"

"Bye!" I replied and ended the call.

I'm sure you are wondering why I still kept up a sexual relationship with that old man, especially since I was gettin' punished on a regular by Montezz. But the answer was a simple one: it was for the perks and extra money! It wasn't like I had to fuck with him that often! Marvin had his hands full with the club, his homelife, and his other baby momma! I guessed he found a type of normalcy with me because I wasn't pressurin' him all the time! It was a business arrangement with me and no more or less.

Tezz wanted me to give up the club, but the club had been good to me and to Markus. Phillip was back on his gay shit again! Let me be clear, I had no ill feelin' for anyone or the decisions they made, but please, make up your damn mind! Phillip didn't know if he wanted to be in a pussy or a damn booty hole, and I didn't have the time or energy to explain that to our son!

Phillip and I both agreed to give him some space and time to figure things out for his life. He had been able to keep his sexuality under wraps with his football career, but he confided in a few close people about his desires. I would have been more pissed, but I had Tezz by my side. He'd been there for Markus and that lessened the sting of my hurt tremendously. But with that being said, I'd had to cover all the bills because I told Phillip I wouldn't accept his money.

I had my tips and regular customers along with Marvin's hush money whenever I wanted it. I had a goal in mind, and after I reached that, I could retire from stripping altogether. I would try to make my man happy in every way, but right now, I planned on stacking my cheese!

21

Montezz:

Actions Speak Louder Than Words

Nova's bullshit really had my mind gone for the rest of the morning. I made it to my business at a quarter of ten, and we were already packed for the damn day. I tried not to show my emotions, but the ones closest to me knew when I had something troubling me.

"Tezz." James approached me in the workstation after a client paid his bill. "Can I holla at you for a second?"

"What is it, man." I avoided eye contact with my oldest friend. I didn't have time for that shit today or any day. "You know we got a lot of cars to finish on. What's up?"

"I was just about to ask you that." James looked me up and down before speaking once more. "Now, I understand that you have a business to run, and I'm not trying to stand in the way of your paper, or mine for that matter! But I've known you since we were both knee-high to a grasshopper, so miss me with all that hard shit, okay? What's really on your mind, and don't bullshit me!"

"Now is not the time for all of this, man," I sighed and dapped up my friend. I really did need a friend to lean on, but I had to handle my business first.

"I just want you to know that I'm here for you, you feel me?" James gave me a sympathetic nod, and I appreciated it.

"I know that you got me." I let off a nervous laugh and tried to remain professional in front of our next customer. "We can link up after hours."

"Sounds like a plan to me," James replied and looked over the client's paperwork. "I gotta tell you about my new project that I've been working on."

"Oh, shit!" I let off a laugh and knew immediately that he found a new pussy to fuck. "Damn, my dude! I thought things were going good with the doctor assistant you been fuckin' for over a month! I can't wait to hear about this one!"

"Yeah." James shrugged his shoulders and began to check on the engine. "Things are still tight with Angela, but you know me. I get tired of the same ol' thang, and sometimes I gotta switch it up!"

"I feel ya, bruh." I shrugged my shoulders and thought back to my life before Nova walked into it. "I used to be on the same thing as you. Going from skirt to skirt and bitch to bitch, but after a while, a nigga gotta get tired of that shit. You know what I'm sayin', bruh?"

"You trippin', Tezz!" James joked at my expense. "We still in our prime, and ain't nobody tryin' to hear all that locked-down bullshit! Stop talkin' crazy, and don't let Nova cloud your head with all that mess!"

"You leave her outta this!" I felt my blood boil and tried to hold my composure in my place of business.

"Look at you, man." James tried to check me. "She's changin' you, fam! Don't let yourself go through this bullshit, not again! Not again!"

James walked away and finished with our customer. I headed to my office and buried my head on my desk. What was I thinking, and was I wrong for feeling the way I did about Nova? For some reason, I felt unsure about my feelings. Did I have the right to second-guess it?

"Tezz? Are you busy right now?"

I snapped out of my confusion and heard my sister's voice over the intercom. "No, Carol." I cleared my throat and sat back in my office chair. "I'm good. What did you need?"

"I'll be in there," she replied. "Just give me a few minutes."

"All right," I replied and looked over my schedule for the rest of the day.

I refused to become one of those sappy and love-sick niggas I had seen my whole life. Nova was not going to change me. Shit, I was good to her ass! I didn't need to say a few words to define the way I felt. My actions should have been good enough, and if they weren't, the hell with it then.

I pulled out my phone and checked it for any messages from my lady. As much as I wanted to deny it, my feelings were so real for her, and I had fallen in love with her. She deserved to hear me say those three words, but I couldn't muster up the strength to say them out loud. I felt that by showing her, that would be enough. But maybe it wasn't.

"Hey, bruh." Carol tapped on my office door and cracked it open.

"Come on in." I sat back in my chair and tried to maintain a poker face for my little sister. I wasn't as close to Carol as I was to Koran, but she still managed to see right through me. I was sure she remembered the pain I felt when Kyomo broke my heart. "What's up, sis? Did you need to talk to me about something?"

"Yeah." She hesitated and closed the door behind her. "It's almost so surreal that I can't believe it, you know?"

"What?" I blurted out. "I mean, no, I don't know. Is everything all right? Is there something wrong with Ma or Pops?" I felt my heart drop to my stomach in that moment. Had my father experienced another stroke? Oh God, the last one almost killed him! "Would you stop with the suspense already?" I grew impatient with my sister. "Speak up, girl!"

"It's Kyomo." Carol said her name with a slow whisper.

"What?" I stumbled over my words. "What about her?"

"She contacted Ma and Pops." Carol let out a deep breath. "I guess she remembered their address and decided to reach out to them in a letter. Ma called me about it the other day."

"Oh, really?" I fumed with a hatred that I had tried to repress over the years. "Why would she do something like that? And why wouldn't Ma call me with that bit of information? I mean, why would she just come to you?"

"Because of the way you are comin' off right now!" Carol reached across my desk and pulled my hands into hers. "Look at how upset you are right now, bruh! Ma knows how you feel about that girl. She just didn't want to upset you."

"And how do you think I am feeling right now, Carol?" I snatched my hands away from her and spun around in my chair.

My face had become so flushed, and I felt an awkwardness that brought me right back to childhood. I thought about that day in the hospital. I had Myesha in my arms. She was only a few days old. I had met up with my parents in the waiting room, and they relayed to me that Kyomo was headed back to China that very day. I wanted to run back in the room and fight with her. I wanted to grab her up and ask her why and how she could do that to me or our baby. But Pops stopped me, and I collapsed into his arms like a weak-ass bitch.

"Are you listening to me, Tezz?" Carol raised her voice, and I turned my chair around to look at her. "Are you mad at me now?"

"I'm sorry, sis." I shrugged my shoulders and gave her a wayward smile. "I kinda zoned out for a second. I hadn't thought much about Ky in years. I try not to think back to those memories or the pain. And no, I'm not mad at you. I was trippin', and I'm sorry for making you feel that way."

"It's cool, bruh." Carol smiled and felt more at ease. "I know Ky is a very touchy subject for you, and that's understood by all of us. I was saying that she wants to get in touch with you. Ma said that she asked about you and Myesha."

"Oh, no." I felt my anger rise to the top once more. "I have nothing, do you hear me, nothing to say to her. She walked out on her own daughter. Her flesh and blood. Without so much as a goodbye or a reason. There's nothing more to say about that. Can you tell Ma that for me? I'm good, Myesha is good, and we don't need her droppin' in and fuckin' up a damn thing in our lives."

"Maybe she's changed, bruh." Carol tried to remain the devil's advocate. "Y'all were just kids back then, and maybe she's had the time to feel sorry about all that. I'm not defending her in any way, so I don't want you to feel that about me. All I'm sayin' is just be open and hear her out. Did you ever think if Myesha wants to know her mother?"

"I can appreciate your concern, baby sis." I tried to maintain my composure, but Carol had me on the ledge this time. "But I'm Myesha's father and the only parent she will ever know. I'm not gonna allow that bitch to ever hurt her the way she did me. Over my dead body, do you hear me?"

Carol stood, nodded, and closed the door behind her. I wasn't sure how long I sat at my desk in awe of this news. But when I ran my hands across my face, I felt the dampness from my tears. I was ashamed of the way Kyomo still made me feel inside. It had been over eleven years and she still pulled the strings of my heart. I hated her for it, but a part of me was curious to see her once more.

*****

"Thanks for the drinks and the great meal, bruh." James let out a small belch and leaned back in the booth of our favorite steak joint. "It's really nice to kick back and chill with you, you feel me? We haven't done this in a minute."

"True." I nodded and picked at my steak. My mind was still fixed on the bombshell that Carol had hit me with earlier that day. "It's definitely nice to kick it with you."

"Damn, bruh." James finished his double shot and gazed over at me. "Ky still got your ass in the damn matrix, huh?"

"You always got the jokes, huh, bruh?" I got on the defensive and downed my rum and Coke. I signaled the waiter over to our table and ordered another round of shots. If I had to sit through another round of bullshit from my friend, I needed to be as lit as possible.

"Calm down." James made light of the situation. "I'm sorry for playin' the way that I do. I just hate to see you like this. You know, all fucked up in the head. I really thought that the problem lay with Nova, but now I see that Ky is the main issue. You gotta get over that bitch, man. She did you dirty, and I get that you are hurt by the shit."

"You don't get shit, man." I raised my voice but checked myself when I saw a few people turn their heads in our direction. "My bad, bruh. You was definitely there for me through all my mess. But I was the one who held all that shit inside of me. I just figured she was gone and wasn't never coming back. And now, over eleven years later, the bitch wants to talk to me. She can suck on this dick. Other than that, we ain't got shit to talk about."

"Answer me this question, bruh." James greeted the waiter with a smile and sipped on the new round of drinks. "Do you love Nova? Be real with me."

"C'mon with that shit." I looked away from him and felt backed into a corner. "First you wanna school me about Ky, and now you questioning me about my girl?"

"It's just a simple question between brothers." James tried to smooth over his words, but I wasn't bitin' that shit. "You know that shit won't go any further than the two of us. So, what's up?"

"I fucks with her, and you know that." I mustered up those few words and refused to say anything further about it. "Can we just drop all this shit, please? I thought you wanted to tell me about your bitches. Why we so focused on my shit?"

"You always runnin' from the truth, my dude." James let out a chuckle and I gritted my teeth. "But okay, I can take the spotlight off of you for the time being. Like I had said earlier, I like Angela. You feel me? I mean she's all the way together. Bank account, crib, personality, and she's a freak. But you know me. Shit, I always want more."

"I can feel that." I relaxed and downed my double shot of liquor. "But at some point, you gotta figure out what you want."

"Look who's talkin', bruh." James gave me a wink, and I kept a nonchalant look on my face. I hated to admit when James was right about anything. He would never let me live it down, and I just didn't want to go over my shortcomings once again. I had love for both women, but I could never say those words. I showed my love and that had to be good enough.

22

Marvin: Weathering the Storm

"Oh, yeah, baby." I played with my dick while I sucked on Nova's sweet pussy. "Damn, you taste so good. Do you love the way I eat on that pussy, baby?"

Nova rotated her hips in a hypnotic motion while I fingered her hole with my free hand.

"Stop all of that damn talkin'." She moaned uncontrollably. "Shit, I'm about to cum."

"Oh, no." I raised my head but continued to finger her vigorously. "You gotta let me get some quality time, babe. Now, get down on your knees and put this dick in yo' mouth."

Nova wanted to talk back to me, but she knew better than that. She owed me, and she was gonna pay up one way or the other. I loved our arrangement, and whether she liked it or not, I held all of the cards in my favor. She got down on her knees, gave me an angry stare, and pulled my veiny member out of my boxers.

"Be careful with your teeth this time, love," I whined and grabbed the back of her head. "I think you chafed me a little bit the last time. But damn, my shit felt so good goin' down your fuckin' throat."

She said nothing but deep throated me like a pro. I tipped my head back and enjoyed the head game to the fullest. I sat up straight and massaged her perky titties. I looked down at my side piece. I loved to watch my dick go in and out of her juicy mouth.

"Spit on that dick, baby," I commanded her, and she did just that. "Damn it, bitch. You know what you doing, don't you?"

She massaged my balls, and I pulled on her hair tracks with some force. I didn't give a damn if I pulled one out. Shit, I paid for the shit anyway. I kept that bitch fly, and all of her damn bills were paid thanks to me. I liked the fact that she had that nigga on the side. It was a nice cover story for the shit we had together.

I made sure that trick stayed on her birth control though. I didn't have the time for another slipup. That bullshit with Cristol and Chauncey almost put me in a depression a few months ago. As my mind traced back to the fatal decisions I had made, I felt my dick soften a bit. I knew I needed to refocus my mind, and I pulled my dick from Nova's juicy lips.

"Let me hit it from the back." I smacked her on the ass, and she stood to her feet. "I wanna see that fine ass jiggle. Do that for me, love."

She straddled my torso, and I leaned back in my reclining desk chair. I found such pleasure from her booty bouncing up and down on my shaft. I tried to maintain my stamina, but a pussy like hers was hard to resist. I tried to count my way to a few more strokes but felt my body explode, and I spent my nectar inside of her.

"Damn, girl." I huffed and puffed while I pulled her naked body close to mine. "You are gonna give me a heart attack one of these days. You are just too much for this old man."

"Is that a threat or a promise?" she murmured and climbed off of me.

"Why must you be so harsh with me?" I gave a slight pout.

Nova rolled her eyes, said something under her breath, and headed into my office restroom with the door closed. I opened one of my desk drawers, sprayed some air freshener, and used baby wipes to freshen up. I decided to smoke a cig and hide the smell of our sex even more.

Knock. Knock. The sound at my office door startled me, and I hurried to put my clothes back on. Nova peeked out of the bathroom door and closed it once more.

"Who is it?" I remained cool and collected as I got dressed.

"It's me, Mr. Marvin." I heard the familiar voice. "Mia."

"Oh, hey, love." I was still reluctant to make much movement. "What did you need?"

"Just needed to talk to you about a few extra slots this week," Mia replied from the other side of the door. "Can I come in and speak to you for a moment? I won't take up much of your time. I have to run a few errands. I promise, it will only take a minute."

"Um . . ." I glanced at the bathroom door but thought I could handle the situation regardless. "Give me just a minute. I was finishing up with a group conference online. Just give me a minute, all right?"

"No problem," she replied with ease.

I headed to the bathroom, and Nova sat on the toilet with her arms folded tightly.

"Why would you let her in here?" she whispered, and I handed her the rest of her clothes. "Do you want us to get caught up?"

"She doesn't know you are in here, boo." I ran my fingers through her hair, and she jerked away from me. "That's your girl, isn't it? If she did see you, it's not like she would say anything about it, right?"

"I don't want anyone to know about this shit." She squinted her eyes and frowned with discomfort.

"Just relax and stay in here." I assured her, "She won't be in here long, and then we can get back to business."

I closed the bathroom door and heard her lock it from the inside.

"Are you still there, Mia?" I hollered at the opposite side of the door.

"Yes, Mr. Marvin."

I breathed in the air of the room, unsure about the smell. I sprayed a little more air freshener and unlocked the door.

Mia was a fine chocolate diva in her own right. She stood about five foot five, hourglass shape, with smaller titties but an ass that you could set a glass of milk on. She was rocking blond cornrows. Her eyebrows were flawless, and her nails looked freshly done. I pointed to the chair across from my desk and shut the door behind her. I wasn't sure of the perfume she wore, but I thought about gettin' lost in that smell.

"So nice to see you as always, Ms. Mia." I licked my lips and leaned back in my chair.

"Thanks for seein' me, Mr. Marvin." She smiled and showed her deep dimples. "I won't take up much of your time, I promise. I know that you are a very busy man."

"Not a problem at all." I looked her up and down as she crossed her luscious legs, and I could almost see up to her G-string. "And you said you needed some extra shifts this week. Is everything all right with you, dear?"

"Just trying to make more money, sir." She smiled and remained so professional. I felt my member harden, and I noticed her nipples were hard as well.

I opened my calendar book and tried to appear intrigued by the notations on my pages. "We have a few events lined up for the rest of this week. What days were you trying to come in?"

Mia licked her wet lips and switched her crossed legs in front of me. She noticed me watching and let out a flirtatious laugh. "I was supposed to be off Thursday and Friday. What were the times of the events?"

"Oh, I see." I felt flushed but readjusted my package in front of her. "We have a rap performance Thursday night around seven o'clock. You know the type—big-baller status. And ladies' nights on Fridays are definitely off the chain, and that starts around the same time."

"Did you need some extra girls?" She nibbled on her manicured nail. I could tell that she was tryin' to get my attention, and it worked. "I mean, I don't want to step on anyone else's ends, but I could really use the extra cash. I'm trying to move and all, you feel me?"

"Oh, really." I tapped my left leg nervously under the desk. I tried to hold my composure and remembered that Nova was held up in the office bathroom. "I'm sure I can change a few things around. A few of the girls wanted to be off."

"Could you do that?" Mia delicately placed her left hand over her right breast and never lost eye contact with me.

"I sure can, suga." I gave her a coy grin and readjusted the slight bulge in my slacks. "If you don't mind my askin', why are you moving? Is everything all right?"

"Yes, sir." She licked her lips and turned her sights on my office bathroom door. "I mean, everything is fine. I'm just upgrading my life and surroundings. You know how it is, no biggie. I'm sorry for asking, but could I use your restroom? I really need to pee."

"Sorry about that, love." I almost hesitated and took a deep breath. "That toilet is on the fritz right now. Thanks for reminding me. I will have maintenance get on that as soon as possible. But thanks for stopping by to see me. And if there's anything else, and I mean anything, that I can help you with in the future, don't hesitate to stop by and see me."

"I definitely will." She stood to her feet and gave me a curious look over. I wasn't sure if she bought that "toilet on the fritz" bullshit I fed to her, but she never showed it otherwise. I enjoyed watching her strut her stuff out of my office, and I locked the door behind her. I waited a few minutes, made sure she was gone, and tapped on the bathroom door for Nova.

"I think the coast is clear." I tapped lightly on the door and heard her unlock it.

"You play entirely too damn much, old man." Nova was fully dressed and seemingly stressed by her friend Mia. I thought they were thick as thieves, so perhaps something happened that I wasn't aware of. "You just throw your cheesy come-on lines to any bitch who will listen, don't you?"

"Aww." I wrapped my arms around her tight waist and ground my pelvis against her. "You're not getting jealous on me, are you?"

"Nigga, please." She huffed and walked over to my office window to peek out of the blinds. "Do what you want but keep me out of it."

"Why are you actin' so different?" I gave a concerned look at her while she canvased the parking lot cautiously. "Is everything all right with you and Mia?"

"Yeah," she blurted out nonchalantly, but I didn't buy it. "Why did you ask me that?"

"Just seems like there was something wrong," I replied. "And the way you keep looking out the window, it's like you expect her to pop up and smack you or something."

"Anyways"—she sucked her teeth and walked away from the window—"like I said before, I'm just being care- ful, unlike yourself. I don't like people in my business."

"And that's one of the things I love about you, girl." I focused back to the fine piece of ass in front of me. "Stay that way. But um, why did you put all your clothes back on? I wasn't done with you yet."

23

Mia: Keepin' My Enemies Closer

"What time are you coming home, baby?" Fab whined on the other end of my line. He was still on a slight punishment from that bullshit he pulled a few months back. I might have said I forgave him for fuckin' off with that Puerto Rican bitch, but I didn't forget shit.

"Don't start this shit with me today." I revved my engine and gave the club one last glance before I peeled off. "I told you I would be home in a minute."

"How long are you gonna have an attitude with me, boo?" Fab continued, and I rolled my eyes with disgust. "I have apologized over a thousand times. What else is it gonna take?"

"I told you." I came to a red light and fired up a cigarette. "We good, so why do you keep sweatin' me about it?"

"Stop playin' with me, Mia." Fab added some bass to his voice. "You say that everything is straight, but I know you. Well, I would like to think that we are good, but for some reason, I think there's something off with you. I just wish you would tell me wassup."

"Tell you wassup." I chuckled and exhaled the tobacco smoke. "I got played by the people I valued the most, and that's wassup. Yeah, I agreed to give you another chance, but don't think for one instant that I can just forget about all of that shit. Not to mention the stress of your lies and the way Nova covered shit up for you. Oh, yeah, and the miscarriage that I suffered, or did you forget about that?"

"How could I ever forget about the loss of our baby?" Fab softened his tone and took a brief pause. I hit him in his jugular with that shit. I wanted him to hurt the same as me. "I regret the way I handled my shit. But don't keep puttin' Nova and my brother in all of this. They had no idea I was bringin' that bitch to the get-together. That shit was on me."

"But Nova was supposed to be my girl." I was filled with rage and ultimately ran a red light. I felt my heart drop to my stomach and checked my mirrors for any cops who may have been close by. "I had her back from the jump, and she was supposed to have mine. I'on care how good of a dick she was gettin' from your brother. Her loyalty was supposed to be for me first. And stop takin' up for that bitch. You act like you wanna fuck her or something."

"You wilding," Fab breathed. "It's nothing like that, baby. I was only sayin' that I put her in that situation because I showed up to the dinner with a chick. If I never did that, Nova would have never had to choose."

"But she did, didn't she?" I blurted out and tried to steady my driving skills. I was three blocks from our condo, but something kept me from driving straight home. I made a left turn instead of the right and pulled into a gas station. "I'm tired of going over this shit with you. I'll see you when I get home."

I ended the call and turned off my engine. I just needed a few moments of peace and quiet, time to think and come up with a real plan of destruction. I couldn't allow my feelings for Fab to cloud my judgments and detour me from the inevitable. I didn't just want to end Nova's dancing career. I wanted to end her damn life.

I thought back to earlier days and when I first met Nova at that raggedy grocery store. She had to have been about 19 or so, nothing spectacular to look at but not that unfortunate either. She was long overdue for a relaxer, and her fingernails were chipped and worn down to the nubs. Nova would plaster on a fake smile, but her eyes always told her story of heartache and despair. She was a high school dropout, teen mom, and overworked without a real plan for life. I used to admire her work ethic and pity her all in the same breath. I didn't come from the best beginning, but I only had to live for me. Nova had her whole world dependent on her.

Ring. Ring. My phone rang and snapped me out of my flashback phase. I immediately answered the call. "Hello."

"What's tha deal, suga?" Anwar snickered on the other end. He was a familiar friend and my "candy man." "I'm sorry I'm just now getting back to ya, but I had to go out of town. You know how it goes."

"Yeah, I guess." I felt that nervous twitch that only a true cocaine lover would understand. "So, what's up? Can I come through or what?"

"What did you need, suga?" Anwar gave his seductive tone. "You know I keep that fine china."

"I know that's right." I licked my lips and grew more impatient by the second. "Just want my usual shit, and where are you gonna be?"

"I'm at the house." I knew that was code for his trap on the west side. "When was you coming to see me?"

"On the way right now," I answered and revved my engine.

Fab called me back, but I shot him a quick lie and continued my journey for a fix. Maybe it was just me, but my mind seemed so much clearer after I snorted a line or two. I had managed to keep my addiction under wraps for the past few years. I guess because I maintained my weight, didn't sniffle uncontrollably, and only spoke about it to a chosen few. But I could always tell the difference in me when I went a few days without my magic potion. Sex seemed dead, conversations with people were hazy, and I just didn't have an ounce of patience for a damn thing.

I hung a sharp left and drove against the dirt road that led to Anwar's secluded trap house. The west side of B'ham was more secluded than the rest of the city. Houses were more spread out, and privacy wasn't that big of an issue as long as you kept the music down. I saw the usual cars in the backyard and put on my Versace sunglasses before I exited my 2018 Impala.

"Hey there, MiMi," Anwar greeted me from the baby blue painted front porch. I hated the tacky color scheme, but maybe that was what attracted him to the shack. It wasn't very conspicuous, just appeared to be a run-down shack that no one would live in. "It's always such a pleasure to see you."

"Cut the crap." I playfully swatted him away, and he pulled me closer for a big hug. Truth be told, I had a lot of love for Anwar's fine mixed ass. He was six foot three, solid, with curly-straight waves and a high-yellow complexion. He always wore his tall tees, sweatpants, and Tims. Sometimes he would floss a chain but nothing that would bring a lot of attention to himself. He was smart and not arrogant like a lot of the dealers in our city.

"I see the club's been good to you." Anwar showed his pearly white teeth, and I felt my pussy pulsate. He pointed to my new ride and gave me a head nod. "Looks like my baby is doing good for herself."

"Yeah." I patted myself on the back. "You know me. I gotta stay on point by any means necessary."

"Or maybe it's that clown you've been stayin' with," Anwar joked, but I knew he was a little salty deep down. "I hear he's the big Willy DJ at that club you work at. A few of my boys been by there to check it out."

"Is that right?" I stretched out my arm to him and led him into his house. "So, when are you gonna come by the club? You know I got you for the lap dance."

"Lap dance, huh?" Anwar locked the door behind him and watched his surveillance cameras by the window. "Fuck a lap dance. I might wanna go in the champagne room."

"You are a real mess." I chuckled but grew impatient with him.

"You good over there?" he reclined on his pleather sofa and asked as if he forgot why I came by. "I'm sorry. Am I holdin' you up or something, suga?"

"You play too damn much, man." I folded my arms and pouted at him from across the room. He finally opened his safe behind a picture on the wall and pulled out a brick of Colombia's finest. I felt my pussy explode and almost felt the need to excuse myself and use his bathroom to jack off. "Damn, that's a lot of shit."

"It's a'ight." Anwar shrugged his shoulders and chopped off a few pieces with a fresh razor. "I had to go out of town and holla at my plug. Now, that guy knows how to party. I told him to make a trip to Bama and kick it with us country boys. Maybe I could get a few strippers and really show him a good time."

"I'm down for that." I walked over to the sofa and sat beside him while he chopped on the brick.

"I had you in mind, suga." Anwar caressed my face with his free hand and tongued me down passionately.

He had what I wanted, so there was no way that I could deny him. I moved closer to him and allowed him to roam his hands all over my needy body. Me and Anwar fucked a few times in the past, but he always pumped his brakes on me. He made like he couldn't be with me fully because my habit was too strong. Whatever. He just knew I would be in his stash on a regular.

"I want you to go easy on this shit, baby." Anwar fixed me two lines, and I was happy to oblige him. "I haven't cut this shit yet."

"Damn." I wiped my nose off and felt absolutely nothing. I had achieved that familiar tingle down my spine, and it sent my hormones into overdrive. I just wanted to fuck and suck him down. "I feel so . . ."

He gave me two more lines and ran his fingertips along my back and booty. I started to rotate my hips and massage my breasts in front of him.

"How's about that lap dance right now?" I removed my tank top and miniskirt slowly and seductively. Anwar sat back on the couch and made himself very comfortable. I pretended there was music playing and danced with the art of true seduction. I was turned on by the way he stared at me and bit his juicy bottom lip. I mounted my body on top of his and we close burned for a few minutes or two.

"I bet you make a grip on tips, don't you, suga?" Anwar pulled out his money clip and dropped a few hundred on me. "I'd be broke as a joke messin' with you."

I said nothing but tongued him down and placed his strong hands on my supple breasts. I wanted him to want me in that moment and hoped he would throw me an extra gram or two.

"You gettin' me all hot and bothered, fuck." Anwar tugged at his sweatpants, and I felt his python against my inner thigh. "It's been a long time for us. You gon' let me play wit' it for a minute?"

"How do you want it?" I stroked on his meat, and he stood to his feet with me wrapped around his waist.

"You know I like you face-down and ass up." He winked, and I did as I was told.

I helped myself to another line of the candy, and Anwar pounded into my guts.

"Fuck me, daddy," I hollered with such conviction, and he did as I had asked.

"Damn, bruh." I heard a familiar voice across the room. "I guess I came in here at the wrong time. My bad."

Anwar's annoying brother Stanley plopped his ass in the loveseat and watched us fuck. I had to admit, I was a little turned on and glanced over at him from the corner of my eye.

"Can't you come back a little later, nigga?" Anwar huffed and slapped me on my ass. "We a little busy in here."

"Shit." Stanley stood up and walked a little closer. "Mia got her eyes on me like she's curious about something."

"Fuck you, Stanley," I hollered and bit my lip from the pounding I received.

"You can definitely get it." Stanley stroked his hard dick and teased me with it. "I'm a little bigger than bruh, and I'd love to see you suck on my dick. Shit, I'm payin'. What you want? I see you eyein' that shit on the table. I wanna see you suck the coke off this anaconda. You down for that?"

"Bruh." Anwar came to a halt but kept his dick inside of me. "You got to the count of three to get the fuck out this room. If I reach under this sofa cushion, I promise it's gon' get ugly in here."

"A'ight, damn." Stanley backed away from us. "But if you want some King Kong dick, holla."

I watched Stanley close the door behind him and felt Anwar's dick soften in my cooch.

"He's gone now, daddy." I pushed him down onto the sofa and mounted him.

"That nigga threw me off." Anwar sucked on my titties and laid me down. "I'm good, I guess. I'ma just eat on that cat and let you get yours. I got a few stops to make."

I squirted on his face, took my four grams, and headed out the door and to my ride. I wasn't surprised to find Stanley posted by the hood of my Impala.

"Hey, Ms. Mia." Stanley blew me a kiss, but I tried to ignore him as I unlocked my car door. "Dang, you gonna do me like that?"

"Move out the way, Stanley." I started my engine. "I got shit to do."

"So, I can't get no quality time? Damn, it's like that." Stanley appeared hurt, but I didn't give a fuck.

"Don't play yourself." I gave a smart laugh.

"Well." Stanley folded his arms abruptly. "If you're not interested in gettin' this bread, why not hook me up with that fine-ass friend of yours, Nova. I seen her workin' that ass at the club. Can you hook a brother up?"

"Nova." I frowned and remembered the betrayal she showed me. "So, you're interested in her?"

"My dick is." Stanley let out a laugh, and I joined him before leaving the yard.

Stanley might be just the mark to help destroy that dumb bitch. Maybe I could arrange a meetup with him. If I could get it on tape or get Tezz around, maybe, just maybe, I can begin to destroy her happy little life.

24

Nova: Holding It Down

"I don't know about all of that, girl." I shook my head at the thought of doing a private show with Mia and her homies. I still felt some type of way about the family dinner at Tezz's. I never confessed the truth to Mia, and after she lost her baby, I just decided to drop the subject altogether. I mean, what good would it do to grind more salt into an open wound?

"C'mon, Nova," Mia pleaded on the other line. A part of me felt like I really owed her and should just shut the fuck up and dance with her. "You've been talkin' about stackin' your cheese and whatnot. This is a guaranteed two grand, so how are you losing?"

"You do have a point." I paused and thought it over while I stirred my mac and cheese on the stove. "And if things go well with the club parties this week, I should have close to five thousand."

"Exactly, friend," Mia persisted. "So, how are you losing? C'mon, it's from ten to two in tha morning. Some real easy money from some straight ballers from the hood. Plus, and I wasn't gonna tell you this, my people's plug might be there. We would be surrounded by millions. Do you hear me?"

"I definitely do," I replied with a smile and heard a key turning at the kitchen door. That could only be Tezz. I glanced at the time and thought of a way to get off the phone with Mia.

"So, are you down to get this cheese or what?" Mia kept drilling me.

"Hey, baby," Tezz replied with a smile and kiss for me.

I winked at him and took a deep breath on the phone.

"I see that you are tied up right now," Mia joked but caught the hint. I didn't want Tezz in my private parties. He was already on my ass about the club. I didn't want him showing up at a party and messin' my money up. "I will check you tomorrow. What's a good time to link up?"

"Sounds good to me." I played it cool and nibbled on Tezz's left ear. "We could do lunch at the Carrot Top tomorrow around noon."

"That's a bet, girl." Mia ended the call, and I wrapped my arms around Tezz's strong neck. "How's my hard-working man this evening?"

"He's doing much better now that he's seein' you." Tezz was always the smooth talker, and he stuck his tongue down my throat.

We embraced for a few minutes more, and I noticed my cheese sauce began to bubble a bit.

"Damn, boo." I giggled and removed the pot from the heat. "I don't want to start a fire in here. But for real, how was your day?"

"I'm good, boo." Tezz gave a slight hesitation as he made his way to the kitchen table. "Nothing I can't handle, that's for sure. Where's Markus, and how is he liking school?"

"He's in his room." I smiled and checked on the baked chicken in the oven. "He's going over his numbers in his room. He really loves school and spending time with the other kids."

"That's great," Tezz replied and glanced at the fridge.

"There's some beer in there. Help yourself." I smiled at my man and joined him at the table. "Where's Myesha?"

"Still at my parents' house." Tezz popped his neck and guzzled his first beer. "I came straight here after work. Just wanted to see you real quick."

"Quick?" I pouted at him. "But I thought you was gonna stay."

"I'm really exhausted tonight, love." Tezz lightly caressed my cheek, and I turned away from him. I had grown accustomed to lying next to him at night. But there were times that we had our space. "I was just gonna stop by, pick up My-My, and crash at the house. You know I will be here in the morning, and I'll spend the night tomorrow. I promise."

"I hear ya." I continued to frown but mustered up a wayward smile for Tezz. I didn't want him to leave me, but I knew that he had a life with or without me. "Did you want me to fix you a plate before you go?"

"And you know this." He licked his lips.

We commenced with small talk. I told him about Markus's day at school, and he recalled his heavy load of customers at the shop. I appreciated days like these, the days that were easy to hide my feelings of doubt or concern.

"So." Tezz nibbled on a piece of chicken and rewrapped his plate to go. "Was you talking to Mia on the phone earlier?"

"Yeah." I sipped my iced tea and avoided eye contact.

"And how are things between the two of you?" Tezz raised an eyebrow and let out a low burp.

"We good," I blurted out and walked over to the stove. I didn't want to have that conversation with Tezz again. He thought that I should maintain a distance with her after what went down. He assumed that Fab spilled the beans on us and that neither one of them could really be trusted.

I felt that he had a valid point, but if I kept a distance, that may cause Mia to notice it. I didn't want to give her another reason to hate me. She was a good friend, and I felt bad about holding secrets from her.

"Nova." Tezz jolted my head with his lowered tone. "Are you hearing me over there? What did you have planned for tomorrow?"

"Oh, I'm sorry." I laughed nervously. "Nothing much. I'm having lunch with Mia tomorrow and then nothing until I pick up Markus from school."

"Did you have to, uh, work tonight?"

"Don't do that," I scolded my man and finished Markus's plate. "Markus, baby. Wash your hands and c'mon in here to eat."

"Okay, Mommy," Markus yelled from his room, and I heard him head into the bathroom.

"So, was that a yes or a no?" Tezz persisted.

"Yes, I have to work tomorrow night. They are throwing some concert, but I will be home by midnight. Was you still comin' over?"

"I might be here when you get off." Tezz stood to his feet, gave me a light kiss on my neck, and walked out the kitchen door.

I hated the way he acted at times. There was no need for all of that. I was doing my damn thing. *He should be glad to have such an independent woman.*

"I miss these afternoon lunches with you, bihh." Mia sat across from me in the booth of our favorite restaurant. The Carrot Top was one of the best soul food places in Birmingham. They had it all, and the fried chicken would make you slap yo' damn momma. Mia and I used to come here two or three times a week. Just loved the laid-back scenery and the great food. I missed those days before I started harboring secrets.

"I know what you mean." I plastered on a fake smile and sipped my sugary iced tea with lemon. "We definitely need to get back to days like this. I can't remember the last time I kicked it with you."

"Yeah." Mia looked away from me momentarily. "I've just had a lot on my mind, but I'm doing my best to bounce back. I'm just grateful Fab and me were able to hold it down. I just don't think my heart could take any more hurt or disappointment."

"I feel ya." I took a harsh gulp of my tea and gagged for a few seconds.

Mia walked over and patted me on the back a few times. I felt so embarrassed and noticed other guests gasping and whispering about me. I thanked her for the concern and motioned her back to her seat.

We ordered our usual meals from the restaurant. I always ordered the three-piece chicken, heavy hot sauce, potato salad, and baked beans. I was on my third buttermilk biscuit before the food made it to our table.

"So." Mia smacked her lips and lightly wiped the grease from her lips. "Are you down for the party or what?"

"Damn, girl." I cleared my throat and lowered my voice. "Did you really have to blurt it out like that? Can we at least finish eating first?"

"C'mon, Nova," Mia whined and stuffed a forkful of baked beans into her mouth. "I really need you to do this with me. Plus, you have been requested by one of the ballers."

"Me?" I said curiously. "Who requested me?"

"My homeboy's brother." Mia gave me a sly grin and nod. "Stan has been by the club a time or two. I guess he asked around and got your name and the fact that we are hella cool. He specifically asked if you was gonna be there."

"Oh, yeah?" I tilted my head slightly in deep thought. "Describe him to me."

"Six foot three," Mia recited from memory. "Chris Brown yella, muscular build, straight but curly hair, flashy but designer hood. You know the type. Probably threw all hundreds and gave deep stares while he licked his lips at you."

"Hmm." I thought back to the past few weeks, and there were a few guys who could have fit that description. "I guess, girl. But we get a lot of those types in the club. I guess I can dance with you. Count me in."

"That's my bihh," Mia said. "I knew you was down for these dollar bills. I'll call the homies up and give them the great news after I leave here. Thanks a lot, my girl."

"You know I gotcha." I gave her a fake smile, and we clinked our tea glasses together. A part of me felt cautious with her, but I felt so much shame for the lies I had told. "So, what do you have up for the rest of the day? Any plans with Fab or whatever?"

"That nigga's at the house, I guess." She rolled her eyes and continued eating. I could never read her mind, and it always bothered me. "I wanted to get down with the rest of you girls at the club tonight. I need some of that big money."

"That's cool." I finished my chicken wing and wiped the grease off my mouth. "We haven't worked an event together in ages. We need to do more of this stuff."

"I totally agree with you." Mia gave a sincere smile and cleared her throat. "Since we are being so honest, can I rap with you for a sec?"

"Of course," I replied and felt my stomach turn in knots.

"Are we good, friend?" Mia shrugged her shoulders.

"What would ever make you ask me that?" I played it off and stuffed my face with some potato salad.

"I don't know," Mia continued and searched my suspicious gaze. "Just seems like there's something bothering you. We go way back, and it's not like I don't know you. Is everything okay?"

"I'm good, girl," I lied once again. "Just things with my man. You know how that shit goes."

"Oh, yeah?" Mia raised an eyebrow and continued to eat. "Spill it and fill me in."

"Tezz keeps harpin' on me about quitting the club." I drank my iced tea. "He thinks I should get a more suitable job, and I feel like I'm good where I'm at."

"Well," Mia breathed, "I gotta say, I kinda saw that comin'. I mean, what man would want his girl shaking her ass at a club? Unless he was Fab, the slimeball nigga who plays music at that club."

"I guess." I gave a halted laugh to her remark. "But when he met me, I worked at Uriah's, so it's not something new."

"But there are feelings involved now, sis." Mia took his side. "You can't fault the man for wanting better for you. What kind of nigga would he be if he didn't? I'm not tellin' you to quit or anything like that. But if I were you, I would consider it. I mean, don't you have other dreams or things that you wanna do?"

"Don't we all?" I wiped my mouth and sat back in my booth seat. "What about you? Where do you see yourself in a few years?"

"Shit." Mia chuckled. "I don't know, for real. Unlike you, I don't have a child or someone who's dependent on me. I'm just living my life. I love to dance, and I'm good with hair and makeup."

"That you are." I applauded her skills. "You definitely got me together."

"Maybe I could go to cosmetology school or some shit like that." Mia shrugged her shoulders and let out a small belch. She excused herself and continued with her comments. "I guess I never gave it much thought, but I will from here on out. I can't thank you enough for agreeing to do this party with me. Anwar already texted me to see if you was down or not."

"Anwar?" I raised an eyebrow because I was unsure of that name.

"My 'candy man,' girl." Mia rolled her eyes across the booth.

"Oh." I smiled. "You never gave his real name before, so that threw me off. How long have you known him?"

"Since before I worked at that grocery store." She grinned uncontrollably, and I could tell that he was much more than her dealer. "Yeah, me and Anwar go way back. I always had the biggest crush on him. He's so damn fine, girl. We fucked around a few times but never on the serious tip."

"Sounds like you are down for it." I winked at her.

"I wouldn't say no to him." She laughed. "But I guess some people will always be better as fuck buddies or friends."

"I feel ya." I finished the rest of my meal.

I was glad that the two of us were hanging out and in a good place with each other. I tried not to think back to that family dinner or the lies that I covered up. The guilt ate me up inside, and I wanted to come clean about it. But how could I do that and explain to her why I kept the truth from her?

25

Montezz: Facing My Fear

You got this, Tezz, I told myself time and time again as I stared at Kyomo's cell phone number, which my sister had sent to my phone. *You can handle that bitch once and for all. You deserve the closure, and it's been long enough.*

I sat in the parking lot of my shop for what seemed to be an eternity and still failed to hit send on my phone. I felt my palms sweat, and perspiration beaded up across my brow. My heart began to race uncontrollably, and I fired up a smoke to calm my nerves. I thought long and hard about my conversation with James. I hated to admit that he was right about anything, but Ky still had her hooks in my heart. I feared that she always would, and I didn't want to fuck up what I had with Nova. There were so many unanswered questions, and I didn't know if I would ever be ready to face them.

Man up, I told myself. *Call her ass and get the shit over with.*

I dialed the digits and sighed in relief when the call went to her voicemail. Her voice was still so meek and child-like, but I grew hesitant to leave a message.

"Uh, yeah." I cleared my throat. "This is Tezz. I got your number from Carol. Uh, hit me back."

I hung up the phone and fired up another smoke to calm my nerves. Perhaps I had made a big mistake by even attempting to reach out to my ex. It wasn't like she deserved any conversation from me. She walked out of my life and never thought twice about the shit. I was left to pick up the pieces and become a single parent at the age of 15.

Ring. Ring.

"Fuck." I panicked when I saw her number pop up on the caller ID. I let it ring a few times before I answered. "Yeah."

"Tezz?" Ky replied in an almost energetic vibe.

"Yeah." I kept my nonchalant tone, but I felt like my heart might burst at any moment.

"Been a long time." She gave a brief giggle. "But you sound just the same."

"Yeah, yeah." I tried to remain uninterested in her. "So, you wanted me to call you? Although I can't imagine what you could possibly want to talk to me about in all this damn time. So, what's up?"

"Wow." She seemed hurt, and I got vast pleasure from that. "Right to the point, I guess."

"You're damn right." I huffed. "Excuse me if I'm not all excited to hear from the girl who ran out on me and my daughter years ago. Yeah, it's safe to say that you are not one of my favorite people at all."

"I know I deserve that," she replied without hesitation. "I can only imagine how my leaving made things very hard for you and your family, Tezz. I really didn't want to do this over the phone. Can we meet up?"

"Meet up?" I blurted out and chained smoked another cig.

"Yes, like a face-to-face situation," she continued. "We are not teenagers anymore. I'm sure we can have a mature conversation with one another. And you can ask me whatever you want to ask me. I know I owe you that much."

"And what if I don't want to see you at all?" I felt my blood boil. "Did you ever consider that? Maybe my life was going just fine without you in it. Myesha has gotten used to the fact that her momma went ghost on her, and she's doing very well. Did you consider that you coming back would be a bad thing for our daughter? Because I'm sure you don't plan on staying here long."

"I know you are very upset with me, Tezz." Ky remained calm, and it made me even madder than before. "You don't owe me anything, but I was just hoping that we could meet up today. I'm available right now if that's agreeable to you."

"Wow," I said sarcastically. "Such big words, huh, Ky? I guess marrying a big-shot ambassador can do that to a person. Sorry the rest of us are not up to those standards for you."

"Don't be so ridiculous." She huffed. "Can you meet with me or not?"

"I guess I could." I paused and took a deep breath. "I will have to check my schedule for the day. I'm sure my sister told you that I run my father's business now, so I need to check the workload for the day."

"She did tell me about that," Ky replied. "Congrats on that."

"Yeah," I cut her off. "So, I will check my schedule and hit you back with a time to meet up."

"All right."

I hung up the line and felt as if I wanted to throw up. Damn, after all this time, she still had my heart in her hands. I hated her more and more for that shit. There was nothing in the world that I wouldn't have done for Kyomo, and she dismissed me like I was nothing.

I exited my vehicle and entered my business with the weight of the world on my shoulders.

"Hey there, bruh." Carol gave me a smile from the reception desk. She noticed right away that something was bothering me. "Is everything all right?"

"Um." I decided to choose my words wisely. "What's today's workload looking like?"

"Oh." She looked down at the appointment book and back at my wayward expression. "Work should be steady until four this evening. Why did you ask?"

"I gave Ky a call." I paused, and Carol raised an eyebrow. "She wants to meet up with me, but I said I needed to check my availability from the shop. I mean, if we are way too busy, I can always reschedule with her. It's not like I wanna see her ass anyways."

"Stop runnin', bruh," Carol stated with conviction. "There's nothing going on today that can't be handled without you. You know I can always call you if things change here. Go ahead and get closure. You need to do this. It's way overdue. And please go in there with an open mind and listen."

"Hold up." I grew defensive. "Please don't tell me that you are siding with her ass."

"Lower your voice, bruh," Carol whispered and looked around at some familiar customers as they gawked at us. "And you know I got your back, so don't go there with me. I'm just saying that you should hear her out before you start yelling and going off about shit."

"There's no excuse she could ever give me that would justify the way she left us." I lowered my tone but kept my cold stare. "I really don't want to be in the same space as her. I'm not sure how I will react, and I don't have time to be bailed out of jail for choking that ho."

"I hope it doesn't come to that." Carol shook her head. "I doubt she would have travelled all the way back here just to stir up some shit with you."

"I can't imagine her coming back for any other reason."
I shrugged my shoulders. "And why now?"

"I guess those are some good questions that you can
ask her for yourself." Carol sighed. "I wish I could go with
you. Do you want me to see if I can get someone to fill in
for me?"

"Naw," I blurted out. "I'm not scared of her ass. I can
manage on my own."

"Are you sure?" Carol searched my broken spirit, and I
tried to fight back my tears.

"I said I got it." I turned away from her and took another deep breath. "All right, I will make a quick stop in
my office and call her ass back."

"I'm proud of you, bruh." Carol gave me a big smile and
nodded as I walked past her.

I tried to come up with a game plan of questions and
possible responses for when I met up with Kyomo, but
the more I played things out in my mind, the more
confused I felt. I wanted to call Nova and hear her voice
for inspiration. I called her line, but it went to voicemail.
I assumed she was either at the club or running errands
for the morning. I lied and told her the shop would be
rather busy for the day and that I would be over to see her
that night.

"I'm glad you agreed to meet up with me, Tezz," Ky
replied with a sense of delight. "Did you get my text with
the directions to my suite?"

"Uh, yeah." I stumbled over my words and revved my
engine. "I'm from here, remember? I know where the
Carrington Suites are, Ky."

"Still so touchy, huh, Tezz?" She giggled, and I gave a
wayward smile.

"Don't try to get on my good side, Ky." I straightened
my composure as I drove like a bat out of hell. "It's way
too late for that."

"Never say never to me," she replied and ended the call.

I felt the large lump form in my throat and couldn't shake it for the duration of my drive. *What is the real purpose of this visit?* I thought as I came to a red light. *What is she really up to?*

I wanted to pull over and empty my stomach contents, but I managed to make it to the Carrington parking lot without a hitch. Ky must be breaded up, because this was one of the most expensive hotels in the area. A one-night stay here was every bit of $400 a night. That old man must have really blessed her in their arranged marriage. For some reason, the thought of another man touching her made me feel hurt and enraged at the same damn time. She didn't deserve my concern or any feeling at all, but still I felt that way for her.

"Hello, sir." The overly feminine male receptionist gave me a programmed smile from the other side of the fancy marble receptionist's desk. "Welcome to the Carrington Suites, and how can I assist you this morning?"

"Uh, hello." I gave him a nod and glanced at my text from Kyomo. "Yes, I need to get to suite 434."

"Oh." He plastered on the charm and typed away on his computer keyboard. "I see, Mrs. Chin's suite. All right, you will want to take this elevator to the fourth floor. Turn left and follow the numbers on that wall."

"Thanks." I nodded and nervously waited on the elevator.

Mrs. Chin. I smirked in the back of my mind. *Makes me seem like a potential booty call of hers or some shit. Clearly, I'm not Mr. Chin, so I can only imagine what that guy was thinking when I mentioned her suite number.*

I felt so out of place and uncomfortable as I eased out of the elevator and onto the fourth floor. I saw several business-type dudes with expensive suits, the billion-dollar broker types. I still had on my mechanic's jumpsuit. They gave me a look over but were probably too intimidated to say a word to me. I read the number 434, stood in front of the door for a hot second, and knocked on it.

"Tezz," Ky replied from the other side of the door. "Is that you?"

"Were you expecting someone else?" I sneered back at her and covered the peephole. "Are you gonna open the door or not?"

I heard the door jingle, and it was opened for me to enter. There was a lavish food spread and expensive amenities throughout the suite. I tried my best not to seem impressed by the breathtaking view of the city, smart-house technology, or how beautiful my ex still appeared to be.

"Tezz." She smiled and showed those sexy dimples that still made my dick harden. "Oh, my, it's so great to see you."

Ky walked over to me, and I abruptly stopped her in her tracks. I had no intentions of making this meeting as pleasant as she had planned. Fuck all of that. I definitely had my guard up with her ass.

"Really, Tezz?" Ky pouted. I always hated that shit. "I can't get a little hug?"

"It's not that kind of party." I shook my head and folded my arms. "So, you wanted me over here to talk. So, talk. What do you have to say that's so important that you needed to be face-to-face with me?"

"C'mon, Tezz." Ky seductively walked over to the kitchen area and placed a bottle of champagne on the counter before she opened it. "Can you please stop acting like you aren't a little bit happy to see me after all of this time? I know I was in the wrong for the hurt that I caused, but—"

"That's just it, Ky," I stopped her. "There is no but. You are to blame for the way I'm actin' right now. All this hostility and shit is a thousand percent your damn fault. So, don't think for a damn second that seein' you is gonna make that shit go away. Because if you really wanna know, it just brings back all the shit like it was yesterday."

I stood to my feet and headed for the door. Ky ran over and blocked my escape route.

"Move outta my way," I commanded her and grabbed her soft shoulders.

"No." She looked deep into my eyes, and I felt my heart break all over again. "No, Tezz, not this time. I deserve everything that you said to me and more than that. But no more runnin'. I'm not going to let you get away from me this time."

"Get away from you?" I shook my head and again tried to move her out of the way. "I don't have time for any games, Ky. I'm way too old for that shit. I thought I was gonna come here and get an apology or an explanation for some shit. But you are actin' like we just had a lover's spat or some shit. I don't have time for this bullshit. I never should have come here."

We tussled for a few more seconds, and she managed to wrap her arms around mine. She pressed her lilac-smelling body against mine, and I tensed up instantly. She had me mesmerized, and I was so unsure about my next move.

"Please don't go, Tezz," Ky whimpered, and I saw the tears form in her eyes. "I have so much that I want to say to you."

She searched my face, and I turned away from her and walked over to the kitchen counter. I wasn't ready to feel all of this shit for her. I had spent over a decade locking my heart away, and here she was, trying to reclaim what had always belonged to only her.

"I gotta go," I almost whispered, but deep down, I was right where I needed to be.

"I don't want you to leave." Ky placed her delicate hands on either side of my face and caressed me so sensually. Before I could utter another word, she kissed my lips so sweetly and sucked me back into her heart. Dammit, man, she got to me. Now what the fuck was I going to do?

26

Mia: Killin' Her Softly

"I told you I could get the bitch to be down with us." I climbed on top of Anwar's rock-hard dick and rode him like a stallion. "She's money hungry and always down for a few bands."

"I see that, boo," Anwar moaned and placed his hands on either side of my juicy booty. "Did you have any other hoes to add to the party?"

"Damn, nigga," I cried out as he pounded my pussy walls. "How many chicks did you have in mind?"

"At least two more." He turned me around and hit me doggie style. "I sure as hell don't want you fuckin' any other niggas. So, I need you to holla at a few other dancers for my plug to smash."

"Fuck, daddy." I felt my body ready to explode from the dick he was feeding to me. "I'm about to cum."

"Oh, yeah." Anwar went harder and stronger than before. "I wanna cum with you."

He grabbed and tugged on my braids, and I felt him deep inside of my womb. We lay there motionless for a minute or so before we headed into the bathroom.

"I see you still got it." Anwar chuckled and slapped me on the booty while he turned on the shower water. "I can't fuck with you on a regular."

"And what is that supposed to mean?" I stood in the bathroom, naked and with my arms folded.

He grabbed me by the waist and kissed me passionately all over my neck and chest area. "I mean I wouldn't get a damn thing done, and I'd miss out on a lot of money because of that great pussy. That's what I meant."

"Well." I smiled and tongued him down before I climbed into the shower. "You was always the one who ran away from this pussy. Don't act like you don't know how much I rock with you."

"Yeah, yeah." Anwar climbed into the shower with me, and we commenced with another round.

Sex with Anwar was undoubtedly the best that I had ever had. Hands down, no other man had ever made me reach my peak the way that he could. Of course, I would never tell a nigga that shit. I was prideful, and I didn't want a nigga to get a big head or anything. But I was sure he had to know that I came around for more than just the great coke.

"Can I ask you something?" Anwar got his breath and lit a smoke after he found his boxer shorts.

"Yeah," I breathed and washed up in the bathroom sink.

Anwar took a pull from his cigarette and wet his juicy lips. "Where does your nigga think you are when you be coming over here to kick it with me?"

"Why would you ask me that shit?" I frowned and rolled my eyes.

"Just a fair question." Anwar showed his deep dimples and let out a chuckle. "Was that question a problem for you?"

"Naw." I smiled back at him. "And to be honest, I don't know what he thinks, and I couldn't care less about it."

"Damn, girl." Anwar gasped. "You really are cold-blooded. You see, and that's why I keep my distance from you."

"Don't you even go there with me," I teased him and sat my naked behind on his lap. "I would never treat you the way I treat him. You have no idea what I've been through with his stupid ass, but know that he deserves the way that I treat him."

"I think I want to be the judge of that." Anwar cupped my booty and kissed me softly on the back. He rolled up a few blunts, and we kicked back, smoked, and I filled him in on the lies and deceit that I had encountered over the year.

"Damn, babe." Anwar got fully dressed and shook his head for the millionth time from my story. "That's some heavy shit y'all got goin' on. I don't see why you even deal with that clown-ass nigga. I can't believe you never told me about the miscarriage."

"I tried to deal with the shit the best I could on my own." I sighed and snorted a line or two on the table. "I try not to think about the shit because it just gets me fired up."

"But with all of the rage that you seem to have inside of you," Anwar continued, "how are you able to rest your head next to that fool? I wouldn't be able to sleep next to a person I can't trust. Why do you think I stay single? Have you ever seen a bitch laid up next to me?"

"That's only because you haven't got the right chick beside you." I winked at him and saw him blush. "If you had the right one, you know your big ass would stay boo'd up."

"Oh, yeah." He laughed. "Any suggestions on who that chick might be?"

"Stop playin' yourself." I playfully ran my fingers through his curly hair. "But anyways, I guess you can now understand why I act the way that I do with those fools."

"I guess so." Anwar shrugged his shoulders. "But if it were me, I wouldn't fuck with Fab's or Nova's fake asses. If they did me like that, I would have just cut they asses off and kept it movin'. I don't give people the opportunity to cross me more than once. Once a snake, always a snake if you ask me. And the best way to rid yourself of a snake when they cross your path is to cut that bastard's head off."

"I hear what you are sayin', boo." I kissed him gently over his neck tattoo and felt his body pulsate from my touch. "But just cuttin' them off would be way too damn easy on them. And you know that easy shit has never been my style."

"Oh, shit." Anwar gave me a devilish grin. "What's that crazy mind cookin' in there?"

"Don't you stress yourself about any of that bullshit," I reassured him. "But just know that I plan on handling those snakes in due time. But for now, I will work on finding a few more girls for this party that you are throwing."

"I hear ya." Anwar seemed unsure about my next move but didn't comment on it. "So, you know my brother is really feelin' your girl Nova."

"Yeah, I know." I cackled. "I kind of like that fact."

"I bet you do." Anwar looked me up and down. "Don't you go and get my brother caught up in any shit that you got cookin' in that brain of yours. You know I don't play about him. Don't get a nigga fucked up in these streets."

"C'mon, babe." I sighed. "I would never cross you or anyone you love. I'm just glad that Stanley likes her, that's all," I lied and kept my further comments to myself. Stanley would definitely play a part in my revenge plot, but Anwar would never hear me admit that.

I spent another hour or so with my boo thang and said my goodbyes to him. I grabbed my purse and headed to my ride. I was sure Fab had blown up my phone, but I purposely left it in the car for the past few hours. I loved to raise his blood pressure and piss him off. That nigga's days were numbered, and he had no idea about it.

27

Montezz:

She Wants That Ol' Thang Back

"C'mon, baby," Ky whispered so seductively into my left ear while nibbling on my earlobe. She seemed to have remembered my spots, and I tried to fight off the temptation.

"Back that shit up, Ky." I freed myself from her grasp and stood up from the plush white sofa. She was stuck to me like glue, and I didn't want to compromise my principles, but damn, she made it hard.

"Why are you fightin' me so damn hard?" Ky frowned and gave a slight smile. "What's her name?"

"Don't come at me like that, Mrs. Chin. You have no right to ask me any questions at all," I fired back at her and sat on the arm of the loveseat.

"You know that I'm a widow now." Ky huffed and glanced away from me.

"Widow?" I was startled by her news.

"Yes." She nodded. "You heard me correctly. My dear husband has been deceased for over a year now. It's just me and my two boys now."

"Damn, Ky." I felt my guard drop momentarily. "I didn't know any of that shit."

"Yeah, it's a lot." She shrugged her shoulders, and I saw her eyes water. "There was no way for you to know, but it has been a real adjustment. As you could guess, my husband was considerably older than me. Had me by twenty years."

"Wow," I blurted out but listened to her story.

"The arranged marriage was a real struggle that first year, because I was reminded of you and our daughter every day. But Uki was very patient with me and treated me the best he could. Marrying him restored my family's respect and secured a good life for me. But not a day went by that I didn't miss you or want to be with you. I was never in love with my husband, but I did love him." She wiped her loose tears with the back of her delicate hand.

I said nothing because I didn't know how to respond to any of that. I guessed I made it through the years with the assumption that she didn't give a fuck about us and that made her decision to leave a lot easier. Now that I heard her truth, I didn't know what to think or how to feel.

"I guess that wasn't the story you wanted to hear." She waited for me to say something, but I was still speechless. "It's just so crazy the way a person's life can turn out. I was given everything that money could buy. A great education, lavish homes, and the love and respect of an entire country. But deep down, my heart was so empty, Tezz. You and our daughter were missing."

"Why are you doing this?" I asked and felt my palms sweat from anxiety.

"Whatever do you mean, my dear?" She batted her eyes and cleared her throat. "I'm only being honest with you. I thought that was what you wanted. You definitely deserve no less than that."

"But why now?" I shook my head, still in disbelief from all that I had heard. "I mean, your husband has been dead over a year. Why didn't you contact me sooner, like way sooner? I just don't know what to say or how to feel."

"I had to go through a respectful length of mourning."
She wiped her tears with a fancy handkerchief. "It's tra-
dition. Being the wife of a powerful ambassador comes
with a lot of responsibilities. Not to mention a whole
country is watching your every move."

"That's some heavy shit, Ky." I shook my head and
relaxed a bit on the plush white sofa.

"You have no idea." She gave a nervous smile and
placed her shiny jet-black hair behind her small earlobe.
I remembered the way she would always do that as a
teenager when she was nervous about something. "My
boys are adjusting to things better than I expected. They
didn't spend much time with their father because of his
political scheduling, but they admired him very deeply."

"How old are they?" I asked out of curiosity.

"Kiro and Uko are eight years old." Ky pulled out her
phone and showed me pictures of the identical twins.
"My husband insisted they go to boarding school, but I
was against it. Now that he's gone, I'm considering bringing them back to our estate and homeschooling them. I
hate being all alone, and I'm sure they would rather be
with me during this time."

We spent the next hour catching up on the last decade
and reminiscing over our rocky childhoods. I managed
to show her a few pictures of our daughter, and I could
see the hurt and pain in her eyes from each photograph.
Maybe Carol was right about Ky. We were very young
when she left, and she appeared to be sorry for the pain
she caused us.

"Tezz." Ky placed her delicate hand on my twitchy left
kneecap.

"Wassup?" I looked deep into her eyes and felt caught
up in her trance.

"I hate to ruin this remarkable moment that we are
sharing with one another." She looked away from me and

took a deep breath before speaking once more. "But do you think you could find it in your heart to ever forgive me?"

"I . . ." The words I wanted to say seemed to escape me momentarily. My tongue felt so heavy, and my palms began to sweat.

Ky eased herself closer and closer to me on the sofa, and I could feel her sweet breath on the nape of my neck. Just her presence alone had my dick harder than Chinese arithmetic, and I tried to think of anything and everything but smashing her sexy ass. Ky nibbled on my left earlobe, and my hands found their way to her perky yet revealed breasts. She mounted her frame on top of me and kissed me so passionately. I wanted her, and there was no denying that the feelings were mutual.

Ring. Ring.

Thank God, I cried out in my mind and grabbed my phone from the arm of the sofa. I felt uneasy with the fact that My-My was calling me.

"I need to take this call." I motioned for Ky to get off of me and tried to compose myself. "Hey, baby girl."

"Where are you, Daddy?" my overly protective daughter harped at me with an attitude. "Auntie Carol said you were out of the office for the rest of the day, and it's very busy in here."

"Yes, second mother," I teased her, and Ky laughed with me.

"Are you with Nova right now?" our daughter pressed on with the questioning.

"Why are you being so nosy, little woman?" I blushed uncontrollably but also felt uneasy about mentioning her mother's name on the phone.

"Why are you avoiding my questions, Daddy?" she continued. "I thought you said there would never be any secrets between us. So, what's going on?"

"We will talk about it later on today, okay?" I looked at Ky with a wayward smile. "I promise you."

"Ughh." She was growing impatient with me. She got that from the both of us. "You know I hate surprises. Did you break up with Nova and find a new chick or something? It wouldn't surprise me if you did. I overheard the two of you arguing about her job at that strip club."

"Myesha." I laughed heartily. "What have I told you about eavesdropping on my conversations? You are something else."

"Anyways." She said straightforwardly, "You're my daddy, and I have to look out for you."

"I know that's real." I chuckled once more. "I love you, sweetie."

"I love you too."

"I will talk to you soon, okay?"

"Uh-huh," Myesha hissed. "Well, you and whoever you're with have a nice afternoon."

"Bye, little lady." I shook my head and ended the call.

"She's really something." Ky smiled and showed her pearly whites.

"You have no idea." I sighed. "But I don't know what I would ever do without her. She's the greatest gift in the whole wide world, and I guess I have you to thank for that."

Ky's eyes welled up with tears. "I swear, if I could turn back the hands of time, I never would have left the two of you. Being away from you has been the hardest thing I've ever had to do. I really want you to understand that, Tezz. It's never been easy for me, but I had to make it seem like it was to protect my feelings. It was stupid and childish, but I just didn't know what else to do. I was torn between making things right with my family and hurting the one I created. I wouldn't wish that decision on my worst enemy."

"I can't say that I would ever understand where you are coming from." I gently ran the palm of my hand across her back to comfort her. "But I guess I don't hate you as much anymore. I guess it was just easier for me to hate you. It made getting over you a lot easier."

"And did you?" She blew her nose and looked deep into my eyes.

"Did I what?" I tried to play dumb, but she knew me too well for that bullshit.

"Did you get over me?" Ky stood to her feet and slowly removed her clothing one item at a time.

I felt like time had brought us back to our teenage days and we were sneaking around in her aunt's house. I admired her womanly curves and perfectly shaved pussy. She touched herself ever so slowly and got down on her knees while spreading my legs apart. My head told me to stop her, but my heart wanted her to touch me. I allowed her to unfasten my jumpsuit, and the next thing I knew I was naked on the Persian rug with her on top of me.

"We shouldn't be doing this, Ky." I moaned with pure ecstasy as she swirled her tongue around my rock-hard dickhead. "Shit, you drivin' me crazy right now."

"You know I've missed this dick." She panted and swallowed me whole. "Every time I was with my husband, I pretended I was with you. You are the only man that I could ever love, and I think you know that."

I felt like I was about to cum, but I didn't want our moment to end. I laid her down on the soft and pillowy rug while spreading her legs apart. I looked deep into her eyes, and with every stroke I felt our love and connection as if we were never apart from one another. Our bodies did all the talking, and I found the love that I tried to hide from her.

"I'm still in love with you, Montezz," she moaned, and I saw a tear roll down her face as I kept a steady tempo.

"Fuck." I kissed her passionately and placed her legs above my shoulders while I hammered her tight pussy. "I'm still in love with you too."

28

Marvin: Tryin' Not to Drown

"I know you're not tryin'a play me," Cristol barked on the other end of the phone, and I found myself very annoyed with her ass once again. "Who's the new bitch you fuckin'?"

"Woman." I had her on speakerphone while I drove through the midday traffic in B'ham. "What did I tell you about that bullshit? You know better than to question me after all the stunts you have pulled. Don't you dare come at me like that."

"Stop tryin' to avoid the issue with me, Marvin," she hissed. "I'm not your stupid-ass wife. You can't just feed me a bunch of bullshit and expect me to be cool with it."

"You leave my wife out of this." I was about to lose my cool, and I saw a flash of red before me. I pulled over into a gas station and tried to control my erratic breathing pattern. "I done told you time and time again to watch your damn mouth."

"Yeah, yeah," she hissed and popped her lips defiantly. "Stop actin' like you run a damn thing ova' here. I asked you a fuckin' question, and I want an answer."

"Now, you look here . . ." I felt my chest tighten and began to wheeze uncontrollably.

I tried to remember the calming ritual they taught us in the military that helped with anxiety. I remembered days and nights of combat while stepping over dead bodies and smelling that stench in the air. I also thought back to that night I had my hands wrapped around Cristol's ex's neck and the sound it made when I heard it pop. His body lay limp in front of me.

"Marvin," Cristol screamed through the phone. "WTF is going on over there? Where are you? Are you okay? Answer me."

"Shut the fuck up, girl." I coughed and started to breathe easier with some time. "Stop actin' like you really give a fuck if I live or die. Especially since you played a major part in the heart attack I almost had. All this fuckin' stress you keep force-feeding me, it's killin' me. Is that what you want?"

"No, baby," she whimpered. "I promise I'm so very sorry. I would never want to lose you or what we have. I know I trip about shit sometimes, but I can't help it. We have a family together, and the family doesn't work without you in it."

"If I didn't know you for the scandalous diva you are, I almost would have believed that shit."

I shook my head and took a few more deep breaths before I spoke to her once more. Cristol spent the next ten minutes trying to redeem herself for the evening. Truth be told, I was only half-ass listening to her. I thought back to my sex session with Nova. Now that bitch knew how to deep throat a dick. Had me about to bust with the thought of her sweet ass.

"Are you even listening to me?" Cristol whined through the phone.

"Yeah, girl," I lied and exited my SUV. "Did you need anything out of the store before I head your way?"

"Naw, boo." She giggled. "You just hurry up and get here to me, big daddy."

"All right then." I shook my head and ended my call.

Then I thought about the fine Ms. Mia. She had really been bringing her A game to the club lately. Always looking so flawless and flirting with me extra harder than the norm. When she came to my office the other day, I wanted to sample some of her goodies.

I pulled up to Cristol's townhouse suite, which I paid for. I shook my head at the list of expenses that hood bitch had afforded me throughout our relationship. I walked past the black Lexus SUV I purchased for the bitch last year. That bill by itself was over $50,000.

Ring. Ring.

"Yeah, girl." I sucked my teeth as I approached the front door.

"What's taking you so long, daddy?" she cried.

"Calm the hell down." I pulled out my set of keys and fiddled with the front door. I hung up the phone and opened the door. I could smell fried chicken and a pot of greens in the kitchen. "Well, it's about damn time that you got something right around here."

"Bring your ass in here," she hollered from the kitchen, and I could hear my son's rambunctious self.

"Daddy." Kalen jumped up from his chair at the table and gave me a big bear hug.

"Hey there, son." I held him close to my heart and kissed him on the top of his head. "Daddy missed his little man."

"Um, hello." Cristol stood by the stove with her caramel arms folded tightly against her big breasts. "I'm in here too. Can I get a hug or something?"

"Aww," I teased her, and our son returned to his place at the table. "Someone's getting jealous. Give me a hug, my headache."

"That's how you feel?" She seductively walked over to me. I loved her wife-beater and neon blue tights that showed every curve of hers. She held me close, and my hands freely roamed her body parts. "Um, babe. Our son is sitting at the table right now."

"You're right." I caused a slight gap between us and let out a nervous laugh.

"But if you want to show him how he got here . . ." She playfully nudged herself against me and returned to the stove. "Did you want a plate?"

"Now that's a real crazy question." I sat at the head of the table and made silly faces to my young son.

I knew I was wrong for having a whole other family and being a married man. But that was the situation, and there was nothing I could do about it. Did I think about my daughters finding out about their brother or vice versa? Yes, on a daily basis. I had the prescription bottles with refills to prove the shit. But every day was always going to be a challenge. I just happened to know the obstacles in my life. I made sure I kept all my ladies happy no matter the cost. Happy wives and a happy life.

After a fabulous meal and a great love session as a stress reliever, I lay comfortably on the king-sized bed that I also purchased for my crazy diva. The expensive bedding and plush pillow almost had me completely comatose.

"Baby," I heard Cristol whispering in my left ear. "So, are you on an imaginary business trip with your associates or just in a late-night meeting tonight?"

"Overnight business." I gave out a yawn and wrapped my arms around my other woman. "So, shut your damn mouth and put it somewhere that it's useful."

She laughed and massaged my balls without losing eye contact with me. There was just something about a bad bitch who knew how to give good head. That was always a keeper in my book, and I guessed that was why I was stuck in the bullshit I was in. I just didn't know how to say no to temptation.

"How you feeling, daddy?" Cristol gagged a little bit, and I felt my dick harden in her lips.

"You know I love when you do that shit," I moaned and gently caressed her hair and scalp. "Why you be stressin' me the way that you do?"

"I don't know." She nibbled on my shaft and kissed it a few times. "But I'm sorry, and I will try to work on it, okay?"

"That's more like it," I replied. There was no way I was going to snap on her ass when she had my dick in her mouth. I would save that conversation for a better day. As for now, I was going to enjoy my special treatment and plan a new love interest and conquest. I was thinking hard about Ms. Mia, and I wanted to test those waters ASAP.

29

Nova: About My Bag

With all the unnecessary drama that Tezz was putting in my ear about the club, I really gave his words some thought for a change. Maybe he had a point about me doing something more with my life. Mia gave me an opportunity to make some major dollars at that party she planned, and I had to admit, I still had some mixed feelings about getting involved with her, but it was because of my own guilt.

I tried to call Tezz a few times and apologize for the way I left things with us, but for some reason I couldn't reach him. Maybe they were really swamped at the shop today. I thought about bringing him some lunch, or maybe I could cook him a big dinner later on. I decided to call the shop and surprise him with a sex snack if he was available.

Ring. Ring.

I waited patiently and frowned when I heard his work voicemail. I decided to connect to Carol's line and ask her a few questions.

"This is Carol." She always sounded joyous. "How can I help you?"

"Hey, Carol." I smiled and opened my fridge door to scan my groceries. "I been trying to reach your brother today. Is it very busy in there today?"

"Umm, yeah," she said with some hesitation, and I heard chatter in the background. I decided to think nothing of it for the time being because I was used to their peak season being this time of year.

"All right." I sighed and decided to fix steaks for dinner. "I will let you get back to it. Just tell your brother to hit me up whenever he gets a minute, all right?"

"Will do, Nova," Carol replied cheerfully. "You have a nice day."

"You do the same." I frowned and ended the call.

My baby had enough going on at work to deal with. I was just being selfish again. Sometimes I hated the way I thought about things. I had to remember that there were consequences to my decisions now, especially since Tezz and I made things official. I just didn't know how to be less independent. I'd been living this strong life for so long, and it would be an adjustment to change that now.

I felt my phone vibrate in my back pocket, and a slight grin came to my face. Mia had hit me up. I had the steaks marinating for the time being, so I decided to give her a call.

"What up, bihh?" she replied as only she could.

"Nothing, girl." I smiled and cut up some potatoes for the potato salad. "Just chilling at the house and preparing this meal. What's good with you?"

"The same on the chilling part." She laughed. "But as you know, I'm not cooking a damn thang. What's on the menu for the night? I may need to come by and get a plate."

"Nothing too fancy." I shrugged my shoulders modestly. "Marinating some ribeye steaks, potato salad, and green beans. Maybe some banana pudding for dessert. I'm not sure yet. Just depends on how I feel."

"I hear ya, bihh." Mia giggled. "I'ma need you to tell me when the food is done. Can I pre-order a plate or naw?"

"You so silly." I smiled with satisfaction. It was really nice having my friend back. Mia and I always shared a special bond, and the past months without her had been rough. As much as I appreciated this moment, it also made me sad. I needed to get this guilt off my chest, but I didn't want to spoil what we had right now.

Mia cleared her throat. "But on some real shit, I really appreciate you doing this party with me. I always knew I could count on you. And, bihh, the money we gon' make from this shit will definitely set us up nice. I'm thinking about changing my occupation and some more shit."

"Damn." I licked my lips at the thought of real figures. "Is the money gonna rain like that?"

"Let me put it to you this way." Mia paused with anticipation. "The nigga we doing the party for could basically buy a professional b-ball or football team. If that's not bread, I don't know what is. I figure, we show him a good time or two, circulate with ballers in that circle, and retire at the top. Like I always say, finish out strong."

"I've really been giving retirement a thought in the past few days. There are other things I might wanna do. I just don't know how to get that easy money up. I've been straight ever since we had that performance interview a few years back. It definitely changed my life for the better."

"I can definitely feel you on that," Mia agreed.

"So." I paused before asking a question. "How are you and Fab doing? You never really bring him up anymore."

"Same ol' shit, girl," she said rather dryly. "Fab gonna be Fab. Still thinking he's the shit because he be DJing and shit. Nothing new over here."

"I guess some things will never change," I replied.

She gave a slight yawn. "Well, boo, I think I might kick back for a minute or two. But be sure to call me when that food is ready, all right?"

"I gotcha, girl." I smiled and ended the call.

Since my man was busy working and my homegirl seemed preoccupied, I put my energy into preparing my meal. All the anxiety and unanswered questions I had about the unknown were temporarily pushed to the side. I turned on the radio and allowed the smooth songs to calm my spirit and allow me to cook in peace.

Over an hour passed, and I still hadn't heard back from Tezz. I simply shrugged my shoulders and sent him a few pics of the meal and silly emojis. I was sure he would hit me up whenever he got a minute. I was so proud of him and the accomplishments he'd made with that auto shop. He really turned it into his own, and I loved that he built his brand the honest way.

The banana pudding was nicely layered in a ceramic bowl, and I placed it in the fridge to chill. I dialed Mia's line and let her know she could head on over. She seemed a little faded, but I was used to that by now. I wished I had a joint or something to mellow me out. Perhaps Mia could hook me up when she got here. I gave my father a call and checked on my son. All was well with them, and my pops agreed to keep him for the night. I wanted to share a romantic moment tonight with Tezz. I was going to get rose petals, candles, and the whole nine.

"Hey, girl." Mia had called me.

"What's up, bihh? Where you at?" I plopped down on the couch and surfed through a few television channels.

"I was wondering what you got to drink over there." She cackled and turned her radio down.

"I have juice, soda, and bottled water," I joked with her.

"That figures," she said sarcastically. "No worries, I'm stopping by the hood store for some cigs anyways. I will grab us something to sip on."

"All right then," I rejoiced.

"See you in a few, boo." She ended the call.

I gave my house a quick cleaning and checked on my banana pudding one last time. I decided to sit on the front porch and enjoy some of the cooling spring air from my porch swing. I could hear a sound system booming from the next street over and assumed it was my super-ghetto friend. She approached my street and managed to turn down her jam a few notches before she pulled into my driveway.

I stood to my feet and folded my arms across my chest with a smile. Me and this chick had been through a lot together. More than anything, I always wanted to keep our friendship near to my heart.

"I'm starving like a mu'fucka," Mia breathed as she toted her grocery bags, and I opened the screen door for her. "You got it smelling great in here, girl. Tezz got him one hell of a cook. I might need to borrow you from time to time."

"Girl, stop it." I felt my cheeks blush. "I told you that I would teach you some recipes."

"I don't have the patience to cook." Mia placed the liquor in the freezer and eyeballed the plates and stove area. "Can I dig in?"

"Be my guest." I gave a slight bow, and we made our dinner plates.

Our conversation continued after a portion of banana pudding and half a blunt. I could feel myself floating on a cloud, and everything seemed so refreshed and stress free. I couldn't remove the smile from my face, and Mia seemed joyous too.

"You put your foot in that meal, my girl." Mia licked her lips and took our plates into the kitchen. "I might need to get one of those to go."

"I'm sure there's some leftovers." I rubbed my aching neck and shoulders in pain. "You are always welcome, boo."

I felt the chronic flow through my veins and ease my tension slightly, and with my eyes closed, I continued to massage my strained neck and shoulder.

"I washed the dishes and put away the food for you." Mia sat next to me on the sofa. "I even fixed your man a plate and placed it in the microwave for ya."

"Thanks, girl." I sighed and began to feel another set of hands easing my pain. "Aw, that feels a lot better."

"Just sit back and relax." She giggled. "Let the master do her thing."

I was more than happy to oblige her and enjoy my deep body massage. I felt relaxed enough to drift into a state of sleep, and then I felt a tingly sensation on my left and right breasts. I was shocked to see my homegirl sucking on my nipples and in between my legs.

"Mia," I whispered and was surprised more than anything else. "What tha hell are you doing?"

"I said relax." She placed her freshly manicured fingertips across my lips and continued with her pleasure. I felt a hand slightly massage my pussy print.

"This is very, very awkward." I gave a nervous laugh as I squirmed around in my seat.

"You know I like to play from time to time," she whispered but never stopped her kisses or hand gestures. "It's not like anyone's gonna hear about it. So, please don't act like you've never been curious about sex with a chick."

"I just never thought . . ." I moaned and tried to be cool about it.

"This is the perfect time for it." Mia pulled at my tights, and I lay back on the sofa with my tank top and silky bikini-style panties on. "Just let me do this and you relax."

I started to object but felt her lips sucking on my clit vigorously. I moaned uncontrollably and tugged at her fresh cornrows.

"That's it." She licked her lips and inserted two fingers into my tight pussy hole. "Try not to cum for me. Only makes me work at it harder."

I screamed out passionately and squirted in her face a time or two. I thought that would satisfy my new lover, but she continued further, and I found myself kissing on her body as well.

"That's it, Nova." She moaned and licked her juices off of my fingers. "Let yourself go and enjoy this shit. It feels so good."

I did exactly as she asked me, and we fucked one another a few more times. It was truly amazing, but it was definitely something I would take to the grave with me.

30

Montezz: Right Back at One

I lay motionless, exhausted, and confused in the lavish king-sized bed in Ky's hotel suite. We had made love for what seemed like an eternity. And the reality just set in that I had a whole damn woman at home.

What the fuck was I thinkin'? The guilt from the joy I experienced just wrenched in the pit of my stomach. All the smiles and resolved issues with Ky were now replaced with shame for what I had done to the trust Nova and I had built. I promised I would never hurt her, and look at what I had done. There was no way she would ever forgive me for that shit.

"What's on your mind, love?" Ky lay naked and wrapped her yellow legs around mine. Her soft, pedicured toes tickled me, and I squirmed a tad bit.

"Cut that out." I chuckled slightly.

"Still ticklish, I see." She seemed pleased with herself and planted a kiss on my tired lips. "But seriously, where did you go? Seemed like you checked out on me, mentally."

"I just had a few things on my mind." I shrugged my shoulders shamefully. I didn't want this moment to end, but reality was bound to finish us anyway.

"What kind of things?"

"I guess there's no way to sugarcoat it." I took a deep breath and glanced away from her hypnotizing stare. "I do have a woman. Her name is Nova, and we have been together for a while now. I didn't expect all of this to happen when I first came here to see you. I really didn't know what to expect or how I was going to feel. I guess some feelings never die. Now I just feel guilty about the shit. She's really been there for me, and we had a solid thing going for the most part."

"Oh." Ky sat up in the bed and appeared rather disappointed. "Well, I guess I can't say anything about that. It was foolish of me to think that you would be single. I mean, look at you. Not to mention you are a very successful man with your life together."

"I really thought I had my life together." I looked at her teary eyes and wiped away a stray tear. "But you had a way of making me reevaluate that notion. Now, I'm feeling confused, and I just don't know."

"You still love me, Tezz?" she harped once more.

"Yes," I said honestly. "I still do, and I feel that I always will. The way we ended was so raw, and there was never any closure. Just a lot of unanswered questions and tons of hurt."

"I don't ever want to lose you again." Ky climbed on top of me, and I allowed her to kiss my face and neck gently. "I feel sorry for your girl, and I'm sure she's a nice person. But what we have doesn't come around very often, and I'm not willing to give up on that. I waited around all this time to tell you my truth. Being without you and our daughter was one of the hardest things I ever had to do. I'm not ready to go back to that kind of hell."

"Baby." I held her tightly against my chest. "Trust me. I understand completely. And now that I have you in my arms, I really don't want to let you go. But what am I going to do?"

"You're just gonna have to come clean about this." Ky kissed me passionately, and I found myself mounted on top of her once more. "Does she know about our history?"

"She knows about the portion you left me with. The way you hurt me and left our daughter, that's what she knows." I inserted my semi-hard cock inside of her pounding coochie.

"Hmm." She widened her legs and placed them on my shoulders. "So, basically, she hates me."

"With a passion." I thrust into her hard and intensely. "But that's my fault."

"I really can't blame her." Ky panted and pulled me closer to her. "But I'm not going anywhere unless it's with you. She can't have you. No one can."

Time had slipped away from me, and I glanced at the time on my phone for the first time in hours.

"Damn." I shook my head with a grin. "It's six o'clock. Where did the time go?"

"You know exactly where it went, my love." Ky winked at me and entered the bathroom. I heard her run some shower water, and I noticed the twenty missed calls and a dozen messages on my phone.

"Seems like the whole world has been trying to get ahold of me today," I hollered into the bathroom at Ky.

"It's always that way when you're busy," Ky replied and then got quiet once more.

Damn, Carol has called over eight times. I was really uneasy about the amount of times she'd tried to reach me. That was definitely not like her, and she didn't leave a voicemail. I could handle Nova a little later. My first priority was to my business and then to my personal life.

I gave my sister a call, and she answered on the second ring.

"Took you long enough, big-head boy," she rejoiced. "I was really starting to get worried. Where the hell have you been all of this time?"

"Honestly?" I hesitated.

"Of course."

"I've been here with Ky this whole time." I shrugged my shoulders and searched the nightstand for my smokes.

"Are you serious right now?" Carol laughed uncontrollably. "And you was scared to go see her. Funny how that seemed to work out, huh?"

"Shut up, ugly girl," I joked back with her.

"I know that's false," she continued. "Not to mention, your girl called up here looking for you. Apparently, she hasn't been able to reach you either. She asked if we were very busy up here, and I'm just glad I didn't have to lie for you."

"Yeah." I sighed deeply. "She's definitely been lighting my phone up, but I had it on silent all this time."

"I would ask why, but I choose not to."

"You basically did," I pointed out.

"Spare me the details," she replied. "I can piece it together, trust me. But on a good note, we had a great workday. And tomorrow should be just as hectic as today. We may need to think of some new sales pitches or discounts for all of our loyal customers. The tips were exceptional as well."

"Great things." I smiled. "Well, maybe you could come up with a game plan and we can discuss it."

"I guess I have a few suggestions," she answered. "But enough about that right now. So, what's your next move? Since you met with Ky, are you going to allow her to meet Myesha?"

"Who wants to meet me?" I heard my nosy daughter in the background. "Auntie, did you ever hear back from my daddy? I'm really getting worried because I couldn't reach him on the phone."

"As a matter of fact," Carol said, "he's on the phone right now."

"Really, Carol?" I exclaimed and watched Ky enter the bedroom with wet hair and a sexy bathrobe.

"Great," My-My rejoiced. "Let me speak to him. Daddy," she hollered. "Where have you been?"

"I, umm . . ." I stumbled over my words and placed the phone on speaker.

"Hello, sweetheart," Ky mustered up the courage to say.

"Hello?" Myesha seemed startled and pissed at the same time. "This doesn't sound like Ms. Nova. Who is this?"

"It's so amazing to hear your voice right now, my love." Ky started off very slow. "I'm Kyomo. I'm your mother."

"My what?" Myesha hollered. "I'm sorry, but could you please put my father back on the phone? There's no way that you can be who you said you are. My mom left us when I was a day old. No one has heard from her in all of this time. Furthermore, I don't appreciate you playing games on the phone like that. Definitely not cool, ma'am."

"She's not playing, My-My." I tried to calm her down.

"Are you serious right now?" My-My hollered. "You mean to say that you have been around my estranged mother all day today? The same woman you never want to talk about and whenever I asked about her, you would get mad or change the subject? You are with her right now?"

"Yes, I am." I sighed and mouthed an apology to Ky. She seemed to understand and know that she had a lot of work to do repairing her relationship with our child.

"I can't believe this." Myesha sighed. "I just don't know what to say right now. Auntie, come get the phone. I need to get out of here."

"Carol," I said, and she cleared her throat on the other end. "Where did Myesha go?"

"She just ran out the office in tears, Tezz," Carol answered honestly. "But that is to be expected. This needs to happen if the three of you want to move forward. Don't stress about it too much. I will hold down the fort on this end. Can the two of you head to your place? I have a spare key."

"Yeah." I looked around the room for my clothes, and Kyomo assisted me. "I just gotta get dressed and we will be on the way, all right?"

"Get dressed, huh?" Carol jabbed.

"Don't start, little Miss Nosy," I snapped back and headed to the bathroom to wash up.

"I'm no dummy," Carol stated. "See you two in a little bit."

We ended the call and I quickly got dressed. Ky tried to maintain small talk for the duration of the drive, but I couldn't hear most of it. I kept picturing the look of hurt and confusion on our daughter's face. I hadn't painted a pleasant picture of her mother at any time of her life. And to spring this on her now may go either way. I was unsure of how she would respond to Ky, and I just didn't want her to hate me or lose a sense of trust with me. I loved Ky to death, but my bond with our daughter gave me life.

31

Mia: Pleasure As Well As Business

"Damn, boo." Anwar seemed so turned on when I showed him the video I made of my sex session with Nova. "I had no idea you liked to lick on pussy. I fucks with you even harder now."

"Boy." I swatted his lavish kisses playfully. "Go ahead with all of that bullshit. It was that great coke that you gave me a few days ago. It really had me in a zone. What can I say? It's not something that I do on the regular. But every now and then, I like to play around."

"I can see that." Anwar unfastened his belt buckle and massaged his throbbing member. "Damn, girl, you got a great angle on that camera phone, too. Let me find out you been making flicks of us on the low."

"Chill out, boo," I reassured him and played with his balls. "You know it's always one hundred with us. And like I said before, I got a game plan for that bitch. This was just a little something to sweeten the pot, so to speak."

"I really like the way you think." Anwar allowed his jeans and boxers to hit the carpet beneath us, and I continued to jack him off while we watched the show. "You got her moaning and some more shit. My little boo is a pro with it."

"You know I'm great at everything I do." I gave a slight wink and leaned back on the opposite end of the couch.

"But enough talk about her pussy. Why don't you focus on climbing into mine right now?"

The blackmail I had over Nova's bitch-ass head had turned my boo into a sexual maniac for that day. I felt like a damn acrobat from all the different positions that nigga tried to press me into, but I wasn't complaining about it. Anwar knew how to please me, and the more I tried to fight my feelings for that nigga, the harder I seemed to fall for him. I found myself tracing my fingertips across his hard and chiseled chest as we lay across his sofa bed.

"What's on your mind, boo?" Anwar kissed me gently on the top of my head and lit a cigarette. "Why are you so quiet all of a sudden?"

"My bad." I giggled and laid my head on his chest. The sound of his heartbeat calmed me more so than any of the coke he gave me for my habit. I wanted to tell him how I really felt, but I was afraid that he might reject me, and I wasn't ready for that. "I'm good."

"Stop playing with me, girl." He rolled me over on to my back and made me look into his soft brown eyes. He searched my face for the lies I had hidden and seemed to harp on them with his. "You trust me, don't you?"

"With my life," I replied with no hesitation.

"All right then." He kissed me passionately on my neck and brought his focus back to my saddened face. "So, tell me what is up."

"It's just that . . ." I took a deep breath and felt the warm tears flow from my eyes. I hadn't cried that hard since the day I miscarried my child by myself. The hurt and despair resurfaced on that day. I just wanted to run away and hide.

"Mia." Anwar cupped my face and was so sincere with his composure. "Why are you crying, baby? Please, tell me what's wrong. Did that fool from the club hurt you again? If he did, you know I will take care of his pussy ass."

"No." I sobbed. "It's nothing like that this time. It's about us, about this. Whatever this is."

"All these tears?" he said as I wiped them from my eyes. "They are about us? What did I ever do to make you cry?"

"You are such a man." I snickered and gave a slight smile. "Always trying to be the fixer and always thinking that tears represent sadness. Did you know, sometimes a person can cry because they are happy?"

"So, those are happy tears?" Anwar handed me a few more tissues, and I gathered my composure.

"It's really deeper than that," I began. "Please, don't make me do this. I don't know if I can. I'm not the best at expressing feelings and you know that."

"Yeah, I know." He smiled and showed his platinum grill. "But I wanna see you try."

"Always with the jokes." I rolled my eyes and fired up a smoke.

"Would you stop stallin' and say what's on your mind?" Anwar snatched the cig from my lips and placed it in the ashtray. "No more distractions. Now spill it."

"I love you, all right?" I blurted it out fast, got up from the bed, and headed to the bathroom.

I immediately felt flushed and splashed some cold water on my face to calm my nerves. Anwar still had said nothing, and I regretted the words that I uttered to him. With eyes still closed, I said a quick prayer and hoped that I hadn't ruined my amazing "situationship."

"So." I heard Anwar's sultry voice behind me at the sink. His hands wrapped firmly around my waist, and I fell into his arms. "Now you running away from me? You know I'm not going for that shit, right?"

"You always think I'm about a game or something." I tried to fight my way out of his arms, but he was way too

strong for me. "I really meant what I said to you in there.
I love you."

"I believe you." Anwar remained cool and collected
while he turned me to face him. He picked me up, carried
me back to the sofa bed, and laid me down. "Can I speak
now?"

"I guess," I whined.

"I've had love for you for quite some time now," he
began. "But being in the lifestyle that I'm in, it's hard to
know who to trust and what drama they might be bringing into my life. But you have never come at me sideways
and always kept it one hundred with me. The more we
kick it, the more I want to kick it with you. I want to see
you happy, and I don't want to see you hurt by any more
of them fuck niggas. You need to always have a smile on
your face, and only the right man can do that for you."

"So," I probed further, "are you saying that you are that
man?"

"I've always been him." Anwar fired my cig back up and
took a pull from it. "But like you, I'm not the best when it
comes to expressing that shit. Not to mention, I don't like
you using that shit. If we were to be together, you gotta
stay clean from that. Weed is okay, but powder is a no. I
can't have no powder-head as my lady, ya dig? Just not
gonna happen."

"I been knowing you felt like that about the powder." I
shrugged my shoulders.

"So, are you saying that you can drop the habit to be
with me?" Anwar licked his lips and had me under his
spell. "Is that a yes or a no?"

I said nothing but climbed on top of my love and
made passionate love to him, deeper and richer than
ever before. I had found my better half and a reason to
become a better woman. No matter what happened from

that moment on, I knew that I would be cared for and loved forever.

"Baby."

I heard Anwar's voice ringing in my ears, and I yawned before I rolled over. "Huh?" I breathed.

"You've been knocked out for over an hour now." He laughed and kissed me on my cheek. "I guess I was doing too much."

"Anyways." I stretched and sat up in the bed. "I'm starving over here. Do you have anything to eat in here? I know it's the trap, but you should at least have some snacks or something in this muthafucka."

"Such a potty mouth when you wake up," he teased. "If you get up, we can go by my crib, and maybe I will cook you something to eat."

"Say what?" I felt my mouth drop to the floor. "Your house where you live at?"

"Now who's playing games with who?" Anwar slapped me on my booty, and I searched the room for the rest of my clothes. "Do you need my assistance with getting dressed?"

"I think I got it." I stood to my feet and fastened my skinny jeans and Gucci belt. "You are the main reason I'm looking for all my clothes right now. I think you have helped enough already."

Anwar locked up the trap and made a few phone calls before we made it to our vehicles.

"Do you want me to follow you in my ride?" I turned on my car from the remote on my keychain and straightened out my blouse and sunglasses.

"You can leave your car parked if you want and ride with me," Anwar suggested and opened the passenger door of his Range Rover. "No one will fuck with your shit, and you know that."

"But I'm still gonna have to come back here and get my car." I walked over to my ride. "It doesn't make sense to do all that extra back and forth for nothing."

"Maybe I wanted you to spend the night with me." Anwar opened his car door and winked at me. "Did that ever cross your mind?"

"Spend the night?" I was shocked. "Wow, you are really surprising me today. I don't know how much more of this I can take."

"Such a sarcastic mu'fucka." Anwar sat in the driver's side. "Get in here, woman. Don't make me tell you twice. We will worry about your car tomorrow. You're all mine for the rest of this night."

"Kidnapping." I chuckled. "I never figured you for that type."

"You bring out the danger in me." He laughed and revved his engine. "But for real, I want you to see where I lay my head. We been kickin' it for a minute now, and with all we said to each other, I think it's time to move forward."

"I'm down with that." I nodded.

"That brings me to my next subject." Anwar turned down his system and stayed focused on the road.

"What's that?" I raised an eyebrow.

"When are you gonna give that clown his walkin' papers?" He came to a complete stop and placed my hand in his before the light turned green again. "I'm serious about this shit, Mia. I can't have just some of you. I want all or nothing."

"I know what you mean, baby." I pouted and felt my pussy moisten. I loved the seriousness across his face. "Things have been over between me and Fab. I just haven't moved out of that condo yet. It's his shit and in his name, so all I have to do is move my shit."

"We can do that tonight if you want." Anwar had his eyes on the road. "Real talk. Just say the word and I will drive you over there right now. I wish that nigga would try me."

"In due time, baby," I reassured him. "I will gladly get my shit and put it in storage, I guess. I've been ready to move. Maybe we can look at some apartments this week."

"Now, why would you want to do all that?" Anwar turned into the ritzy suburbs, and we passed a few lavish Southern-style homes that had to be worth millions of dollars.

"I gotta live somewhere," I fired back. "That's why I've been pushin' about this party I'm throwing, to make enough money for me to retire. There's more to me than just sliding down a pole. The money is great, but I was thinking about doing something else with my life."

"I love the sound of that anyways." Anwar smiled. "I been told you to quit that ratchet-ass club. As for living somewhere, I got plenty of room in my mansion for you."

"I don't know." I was surprised with the offer he had given me. "I mean, nothing would make me happier, but are you sure about this? We could still be together. We don't have to live together to make things work between us."

"There you go again." He laughed and pulled into his four-car garage. I never knew he was living like this because he never would show it. Anwar kept his appearances and movements under the radar with everyone. I knew he must have really loved me to ever bring me this far into his world. "You are always assuming shit, little girl. My woman will stay with me and make this house our home. My woman ain't gonna be no stripper. You might own a club but never work in one, you dig me? We gotta complement each other. You are a reflection of me. That's why I never came by the raggedy muthafucka because it would hurt me too much to see you poppin' for them thirsty-ass niggas. I don't see how that bitch nigga put up with that shit."

"It was easy for him." I rolled my eyes and felt the fury form into my fists. "He was preoccupied with fuckin' most of the other bitches in there. He wasn't checkin' for me for real. The real reason he stayed around was because of the guilt of the miscarriage. He feels like he owes it to me to stay. But I've told him a thousand times that I would be fine without him."

"He gon' see very soon just how fine you are without his ass." Anwar cut off the ride. "Are you sure you don't just want to go get your shit right now? I don't want you staying another night at the nigga's place. It's gonna bother me until you are here with me full-time."

"I'm positive, baby." I smiled as I walked over and hugged my man. "Let's just get through this party next week, and I promise I'll be all yours after that."

"You belong to me right now. Fuck next week."

32

Marvin:

Something Old for Something New

"Oh, shit, baby," I moaned and tried not to drop my load too quick. Nova had the skills to pay the bills, but Mia stayed in the back of mind a lot lately. The way she moved and carried herself had me wanting her more and more each day.

"Be quiet." Nova spat my member out of her mouth and squinted her pretty eyes up at me. "Do you want us to get caught in here?"

"Stop worrying so damn much." I gently massaged her scalp and placed her mouth back on my dick. "The door is always locked, so stop trippin'."

She got back into her rhythm, and I leaned back in my office chair. The more I tried to fight my nut, the harder it tried to come forward.

"Shit." I clenched my teeth. "I'm about to—"

Knock. Knock.

"Fuuuuuck." I released my soldiers down her throat and held her head in the palm of my hands.

"Who is it?"

"It's me, Mr. Marvin," the sultry lady replied on the other side of the door. "Mia."

"Oh, shit," Nova whispered and hurriedly gathered up her clothes before entering the office restroom. "Why does she keep coming over here when we seem to be handling business?"

"Give me just a second, love." I fastened my clothing and sprayed some air freshener while cracking the office window. "I'm finishing up with a conference call."

"No problem," Mia answered from the other side of the door.

"This shit is really starting to get on my last nerve," Nova replied nervously as she sat on the toilet seat and I washed my face and hands quickly. "Just get rid of her."

"I told you to relax, baby." I tried to ease Nova's mind. "No one knows about us, and no one knows you are in here. I got this. Just be cool about it."

I took another quick scan of the room, popped a piece of gum in my mouth, and unlocked the door. "Come on in, beautiful." I smiled and smelled her sweet perfume as she sat her voluptuous ass across from my desk. I pictured her mounted on my face and tasting her sweet nectar. "It's always a pleasure to see you."

"Thank you so much." She giggled and played with a few strands of her hair. "I didn't mean to bother you. If you need me to come back a little later, I can do that."

"It's no bother, really." I licked my lips and felt my member harden in my khaki pants. "How can I help you?"

"I really wanted to thank you for all the love and appreciation you have given me over the years, Mr. Marvin," she breathed, and her perky breasts shifted slightly. "This place has really put me on my feet, and as much as I hate to say this, I believe it's about time for me to leave it."

"What?" I felt my dick go limp from her news. "Are you telling me that you plan on quitting the club?"

"Yes, sir." She sighed. "I've had a nice run, but now I think I want to focus more on other things. I never wanted to be a dancer forever."

"This really breaks my heart." I pouted and cleared my throat. I couldn't just let her walk away like that. I wanted her at least one time. "Did someone do something to you? Is there an issue that I need to handle? Was it Fab?"

"No, sir." She laughed while I tried to play it cool. "Nothing like that. It's just something I've been thinking a lot about lately, but it's not personal."

"I thought that maybe it was an in-house problem or something." I squirmed around in my seat and remembered that Nova was locked away in the bathroom. "And you are final on this decision? There's nothing I can do to change your mind? I'd really hate to lose one of my most requested girls at the club."

"That's very sweet of you to say." She smiled and stood to her feet. "But yes, I feel that it's just time for me to move forward with my life. I will try to have my locker cleared out by the end of this week."

I scribbled a few words on a sheet of paper with my personal number on it. I wasn't going to miss out on the chance to fuck her once in my life. But I didn't want Nova to hear about my plans either.

"This is such a shame, my dear." I walked around my desk and extended my hand to her. She shook it and accepted the note in my hand. "But you have to do what's best for you, and I can only respect that. Be sure to stay in touch with us, okay?"

"I will do that." She read the note and nodded. "Thanks again."

I hoped she decided to hit my line later, but for now, I had to deal with Nova's crazy ass. I locked the office door and gently tapped on the bathroom door.

Nova reemerged fully dressed and with her nasty attitude. Normally, her ways were a turn-on, but now I was just ready for her to leave me.

"We are going to have to meet elsewhere." She placed her hands firmly on her hips and tapped her stiletto on the carpet floor. "I'm sick and tired of these close calls in the office."

"Well," I fired back, "if you were paying attention, Mia said she was quitting the club. So, after next week, she will no longer be an issue."

"Yeah, I heard." She rolled her eyes. "But it will only be a matter of time before another bitch is knocking on the damn door. Fuck that. If you want to continue with me, we will do this at a hotel or something. I got too much on the line to get sloppy with it now."

"Too much on the line." I laughed heartily. "What the fuck do you have to lose that I don't?"

"Damn, you didn't have to say it like that," she huffed under her breath.

"I said what I said, Nova," I continued. "I'm the one with a wife, kids, and a side bitch. What do you really have to lose? Not to mention you are the one who came to me in the first place. I usually play this back-and-forth game with you, but to be honest, I'm about sick of it. All you do is nag and complain like the rest of these bitches in here. Nothing is ever good enough. You act like someone else can't come in here and do the same shit you be doing. Don't get it twisted, little miss."

"You know what?" Nova popped her lips and pointed her finger at me. "That's probably the smartest thing you've said to me since I met your deceitful and inadequate ass. Get another bitch to suck that dick. I'm over it and over you. Just pay me what you owe me, and we can keep it professional from here on out."

"Fine, little girl." I walked over to my wall safe and opened it. "Here you go." I threw her a stack of hundreds, and she hesitated before picking the money up from the floor. "And don't try to come back to me when things don't go your way. Remember, this was your choice."

She huffed and puffed before slamming my office door shut behind her. I heard a few female voices in the hallway as she stormed off. I was over that bitch. I didn't have to put up with her shit anymore. Pussy was easy come and easy go around here. I hoped she didn't think I was hard up for a nut.

I spent the rest of my afternoon booking a few parties, arguing with my wife about my long hours, and making sure Cristol didn't pop off about me not spending enough time with her. I was glad to be rid of Nova for the moment. She was just one less bitch to satisfy. I kept glancing down at my phone and hoping Mia would decide to take me up on my offer from earlier.

"Fab." I motioned for him to walk over to me from the DJ booth. "Do you have a minute?"

"Sure thang, boss man." He kissed one of the new girls on the cheek and headed over to the bar to talk with me. "What's up?"

"I just had a few questions to ask you." I took a sip from my cup.

"Cool, go ahead." He shrugged his shoulders.

"You and Mia are still dating, right?"

"Yeah." He seemed shocked by my question. "Why would you ask me that?"

"I just wanted to know why she decided to quit the club."

"Quit the club?" Fab seemed as surprised as I had been earlier today. "Why would you think that?"

"Because she came by my office earlier today and said that this week would be her last week here." I thought he would have been the first to know. "Seeing how you're her man, I thought you knew already."

"Well, I didn't know." Fab seemed upset and hurt. "Mia kind of goes off about the slightest things lately. Maybe she will change her mind, who knows?"

"Are the two of you having problems?" I probed further. "We friends. You know that, right? Whatever you say to me will remain between us."

"Yes and no." He rubbed his fade. "I fucked up in the past, and we've been going back and forth ever since then. But I never thought she would quit the club without telling me first."

"Women are some strange creatures, my friend." I laughed it off and poured him a shot. "You never know what emotion they will lay on you at any given time. Just talk to her about it. If she's mad about something, maybe she will cool down in a few days."

We kicked the shit for a little minute, not really talking about anything in particular. Just the regular guy shit, and we discussed hiring more strippers to cover some loose slots in the roster. After about my fifth shot, I could feel the world begin to spin, and I made sure to drink a glass of water behind it. I felt my phone vibrate in that instant.

"Hello," I replied to the unknown caller on the other end.

"Hey, Mr. Marvin." It was Mia. "You told me to give you a call."

"Oh, yes." I waved goodbye to Fab and headed back to my office. "I was wondering if you are busy this evening. I wanted to go over a few things with you and perhaps convince you to stay with us a little longer."

"I'm not too sure on the staying part," she joked. "But I don't have any plans right now. What did you have in mind?"

"Just some money opportunities for you." I stroked my member and wished I were inside of her. "It's getting crowded at the club. Is there somewhere I can meet you and discuss things further?"

"I'm at home right now."

"Would you mind if I came by to see you?" I blurted out. "I'm not crazy or anything. Just don't like everyone in my business."

"I completely understand," she answered. "It's gossip central over there."

"Exactly, love."

"All right." She sighed. "Me and Fab stay together, but as you know, he's working tonight. Do you have the address? And when did you want to come by?"

"Yeah." I licked my lips and looked for my wallet and car keys. "I know the address, and I'm on my way right now."

33

Montezz: Gotta Face the Music

The ride to my house seemed like the longest trip ever. I felt nauseated and scared for my life. I didn't know how my baby girl would react to her mother or how she would react to me being with her.

"Tezz." Ky rubbed her soft finger across my tightened arm. "Are you okay?"

"Hell no," I blurted out. "I don't know how Myesha is going to react to all of this, and Carol said she stormed out of the office when she got off the phone with us. I don't know if I can see her cry like that. I would give my life for hers, and I would never want to be the reason for her tears."

"She's not crying because of you, my love," Ky comforted me. "This heartache falls on me. However she feels or whatever happens, I've had years to prepare myself for it. I just wanted to get things straight with you first. We hashed out our differences because our love is so strong. I know our daughter has to get to know me, and I will accept whatever approach she gives me."

"I really misjudged you over the years," I continued as we neared my neighborhood. "I thought you were just cold and callous. I blame myself for salting you up the way that I did with her."

"I don't blame you for any of it, my love." She kissed me on the cheek. "You did what you had to do. If I were in your position, I would have done the same thing. I don't know if I would have forgiven you as quickly as you did me. Well, yes, I would have."

"Well." I took a deep sigh and cut off the engine. "There's no turning back now. Are you ready?"

"As ready as I will ever be, dear." Ky shrugged her shoulders, and I unlocked the garage door.

The house was mostly still and quiet, except for the television playing in the living room. "Carol," I hollered. "My-My, where are you guys?"

"I'm in here." I heard my sister's voice in the living room, and Ky walked with me. "Well, hello, you two."

"Hey there, Carol." Ky walked over and gave her a long hug. "Still beautiful as ever. You haven't changed a bit."

"I wish I could say the same." Carol gave Ky a detailed look over and smiled. "Not the same geeky teen who was puppy eyed for my big brother."

"I'm still a little puppy eyed, but yeah, I did grow up quite a bit."

"Where's Myesha?" I addressed the elephant in the room.

"She's locked up in her bedroom and said that she's not coming out of there." Carol sighed and sat back on the couch. "Believe me, I've tried to talk to her, but she doesn't want to hear it. That's a very strong-willed little girl."

"Don't I know it." I shook my head. "Well, are you ready to do this?"

Ky shook her head and walked with me to Myesha's room door. I knocked a few times, but there was no response on the other side.

"My-My, baby," I pleaded, "will you please come out and talk to Daddy? I can explain. I promise everything will be okay."

"Please, just leave me alone." She sobbed from the door. "I can't believe you, Daddy. You always said it was the two of us until the end of time. You said my mother hated us and she would never be back. You said you wouldn't let her hurt me the way she hurt you, and now you're all buddy-buddy with her. How do you think that makes me feel? I spent my whole life hatin' her, and now you want me to just forget all of that."

"I'm sorry, baby." I felt the tears form in my eyes. "You know I love you more than air, and I'm sorry for the way I talked about your mother. But I was hurt when she left, and I didn't know her side of the story. I only knew the way she left us. I was wrong to do that, but can you please come out so we can talk about it?"

"No," she hollered.

Ky attempted to talk to our daughter. "Myesha, I'm the one you have every right to be upset with. Please, don't blame your father. This pain is all on me. If you would just give me a few minutes to explain everything—"

"Why did you come back?" Myesha cried. "Why didn't you just stay gone? Everything was going fine without you."

"I'm sorry you had to live your life without me in it." Ky began to cry, and I held her tight in my arms. "I was just a kid, not too much older than you are now, and it was not my decision. I need for you to believe that. I love you and your father more than anything, and every day away from the two of you was harder than the day before."

"That's hard for us to know that on our end." Myesha blew her nose. "No phone calls, postcards, no letters, or anything. I don't even know you. Do you have any idea how that makes me feel? All of my friends know or are engaged with their mothers, and what have I had over the years? Nothing. Just me and my daddy."

"Please come out of there, baby girl," I begged her once more.

"Daddy," she sighed, "are you crying?"

"Yes, baby."

I heard the doorknob turn, and the door slowly began to open. Our daughter ran into my arms, and I held her there for what seemed to be all of eternity. The three of us stood by her bedroom door and embraced one another. That was a moment I had dreamed of so many times and couldn't believe it had finally manifested.

"Let me take a look at you, beautiful." Ky stood back and examined our baby from head to toe. "You look so much like me. You have all of my features."

"My granny and aunts used to tell me that all of the time whenever I would ask about you." Myesha glanced over at me for reassurance, and I simply nodded. "I have a darker color and my daddy's gray eyes though."

"Yes, you do." Ky smiled and Myesha relaxed a little bit. "Can I come in your room and talk with you?"

"I guess that will be okay." She shrugged her shoulders and sat down on her bed. "Daddy, can we be alone for a minute?"

"Really?" I was stunned at first. "You sure you don't want me in there with you?"

"You had your time with my mother," she replied seriously. "Can I have my time?"

"It's okay, Tezz." Ky motioned for me to leave.

"All right." I sighed and turned to walk away. "I guess I will go back to the den with Carol."

"Okay." Ky smiled. "We will join the two of you shortly."

Myesha shut the door behind her, and I slowly made my way back to the presence of my little sister.

"How did it go?" Carol questioned. "Is she still in her room?"

"She's in there." I plopped down on the love seat. "Ky is in there with her. She said she wanted some alone time with her mother. I just assumed she would want me with her, but I guess I was wrong."

"It's good that she agreed to talk with her," Carol soothed me. "They need to talk and get to know one another. Not to mention I wanna know what you plan on doing about Nova."

"Wow." I let out a gust of air. "Don't get me started on that topic. I really don't know where to begin with that."

"Did you and Ky, you know, make up?"

"I guess you could call it that." I looked away shamefully.

"You really know how to stir the pot, brotha." Carol shook her head.

"Tell me about it," I continued. "Just when I thought my life was headed in one direction, here goes another curveball. I don't even know what to say to Nova. I feel so guilty for all of this. She's a good woman and a patient woman for the most part. She accepted my lack of verbal expressions and opened her heart to me. And here I go, yet another nigga who let her down. I don't know what I'm going to do."

"I wish I had some words of wisdom for ya." Carol tried to reason with me. "But when it comes to matters of the heart, there aren't any rules for love. The heart wants what it wants. But if there's even a shred of love left between you and Ky, I think it's best for you to end it with Nova and not string her along. From what you have told me, she's been through that enough already."

"You have no idea, sis." I felt like the scum of the earth. "I promised I would never hurt her, and I did just that."

"So, what are you going to do?"

"I don't know." I placed my head in my hands.

"Have you spoken to her at all today?" Carol sat beside me and rubbed my back.

"Not really. I've been ignoring her for the most part. She cooked a great meal for us, but I told her something came up at home. That wasn't a total lie but definitely not truthful. I just don't know how I'm going to face her right now."

"Give her a call, bruh," Carol persisted. "Myesha is talking to her mother, and who knows how long that will be? While you have the time, you can at least get some things off your chest with Nova. You owe her that much."

"I guess you have a point." I pulled out my phone and noticed the missed calls and texts from Nova. I scanned through the messages and felt my eyes well up with tears when I read her most recent message.

Tezz, I hope everything is all right with you at home. I really miss and need you right now. I have so much bullshit going on, and I'm so ready to leave that ratchet club for good. I love you so much, and I'm ready to be that woman you need me to be in your life forever. Call me when you have time, okay?

34

Mia: Stickin' to tha Plan

"I don't give a fuck about none of them clowns from that damn club," Anwar screamed on the other end of the phone. "I don't want you meeting up with the owner by yourself. What if he is on some bullshit? Fuck all that. I'm on my way over there."

"Baby," I pleaded with him, "I told you I got this. I have homecourt advantage on his ass, and if he tries anything, you know I will give you a call."

"But what if something pops off and you can't call me soon enough?"

"C'mon now." I cocked my loaded Colt 45 and set it beside me. "You know I got my strap with me. I learned from the best: always stay three steps ahead of these fools."

"You muthafuckin' right," Anwar cheered. "But I still wanna be there with you, babe."

"I got this," I pleaded once more. "I promise to call you the moment he leaves, okay?"

"I'ma text you periodically, ya heard?" My man spoke to some nigga in his background. "If I feel any type of way about anything, you know I'm coming over that muthafucka."

"I love you too, baby."

"On some." He ended the call, and I smiled with delight.

I appreciated Anwar's love and concern for me, but he had to know that I got this. I dreamed and visualized these events coming to pass, and there was no way I would ever fuck it up. Everybody knew that Marvin was a pushover for a thick chick with a smile. All I had to do was give him a little extra attention, wet my lips, and let my body motions do the rest. Just like taking candy from a damn baby.

"Where you at?" I popped my gum and flipped through the channels on my TV.

"I'm about two blocks away, sweetheart," Marvin replied with anticipation.

"All right." I sighed and felt my heart race. "I'm just lounging. Call me when you pull up in the driveway."

"Will do, sexy." He laughed and ended the call.

There was no room for error today. I had everything set up on my end. Just had to remind myself to play it cool and be casual, and the drugs would do the rest.

Ring. Ring.

Shit, who is calling me? I almost panicked and gave a puzzled look when I noticed it was Nova on the other end. "Hello?" I raised an eyebrow and glanced out the door peephole to keep watch for Marvin's truck.

"Hey, girl." Nova sounded very shaky. "Were you busy?"

"Kind of," I breathed and saw the truck pulling up. "Are you good? Can I call you back?"

"Yeah, girl." She sighed. There was clearly something going on with her, but I didn't have the time to get into it. I had to stay focused.

"All right. I'll hit you back later, okay?"

"Cool." She ended the call.

I didn't give Marvin the opportunity to call. I immediately unlocked the front door and stood in the doorway. I saw his million-dollar smile from a distance and opened the door as he walked inside the condo.

"You and Fab have a very nice home here." Marvin admired the painting and color scheme.

"It's a house, but I'm not too sure if it's a home." I shrugged my shoulders and walked with him to the white plush sofa. I placed his jacket in the hallway closet and poured him a special mixed drink. We spent the first half hour talking about nothing, but I wanted to speed up the pace. I also wasn't sure when Anwar would text me again.

"So." I fired up my special blunt mixed with fine china and passed it to him. "What did you want to talk to me about?"

"I'm good, baby." He shook his head at the blunt. "I have never been a smoker. I'm okay with this drink you gave me."

"C'mon, Mr. Marvin." I pouted my juicy lips. "Sometimes you have to live a little bit. A couple pulls won't hurt you."

"Why do I have the feeling that you won't take no for an answer?" He gave me a wink before hitting the blunt a few times. "Damn, that's some strong shit you got there."

"Those were some massive hits you just took." I laughed and licked my lips seductively. "Are you sure you're not a smoker on the low?"

"I'm positive, baby girl." He moved a little closer to me and frowned when he noticed his phone vibrate. "Ughh, sorry about that. I'll get back to them later."

"You can call whoever." I appeared hurt and bothered. "I can wait."

"It's just Nova." He remained casual about it. "Just some club shit, I'm sure."

"Dang." I was intrigued. "So, she just be hittin' you up like that? I thought I was special."

He paused for a brief moment and then plastered on a smile. "It's nothing like that, love. But anyways, I appreciate you allowing me to speak with you. I'm really hurt that you plan on leaving the club. You are one of my best girls. Is there anything I can do to convince you to stay?"

"I appreciate that." I smiled. "But I really feel like my days at the club have run their course. I made a lot of good money there, but now it's time for me to do better things for me. Ya feel me? Test the waters and see what else is out there. I can't just shake my ass for the rest of my life."

"Yes, you could." Mr. Marvin admired all of me and gently caressed my thigh with his left hand. "Oh, excuse me for touching you like that, but I just can't help it. I have really been wanting you for a very long time. I just didn't know how to approach you or go about it. Plus, I wasn't trying to step on Fab's toes, seeing how he works for me."

"Fuck that nigga." I moved closer to him and cocked my legs onto his lap. I lay back on the sofa and placed a pillow under my head. "He's not the great guy everyone thinks he is."

"Yeah." Mr. Marvin continued to massage my thigh region. "You could definitely do better."

"Is that right?" I gave a wayward smile and placed my hand on top of his while guiding it to my juice box. "Any suggestions?"

"I may have someone in mind." He winked and gently removed my tight leggings and see-through black panties. "Damn, Mia. I been dreaming about this for months now. I want to taste you so damn bad."

"Well, stop torturing yourself." I pulled my pink pussy lips apart and arched my back in a perfect position. "What's stopping you right now?"

"With pleasure." Mr. Marvin teased my inner thighs at first before sucking on my lips and then clit.

I had to admit, he was a pro with that head. I grabbed the top of his head and began to grind my pussy deeper into his face.

"Oh, yes," he moaned. "Feed me, baby."

I obliged him and felt my body erupt from the inside out.

"Cum in my mouth, baby," he demanded and swirled his tongue frequently in my secret spot.

"Oh, shit," I hollered and felt lightheaded from the multiple orgasms.

"I'm not done yet." He pinned my arms down. "I want to taste some more of you."

"Damn," I cried out with pure delight. No one had ever eaten my pussy this good, and I never wanted it to end. I sat directly on his face, and he held on to my butt cheeks for a better penetration.

After an hour of oral pleasure, I lay back on the couch and offered Marvin a wet towel to wipe off my juices.

"Thank you, baby." He smiled and fired up a smoke.

"I should be the one thanking you." I laughed for several reasons. "You really know how to make a woman reevaluate her decisions. You really want me to stay, huh?"

"I really do, baby." He rubbed on my thighs once more, and I felt my knees grow weak. I saw my phone vibrate and noticed it was Anwar. I assured him that I was all right and focused back on my prey.

"So," I breathed, "I'm curious. Do you have relations with anyone else like this? At the club, I mean. It's between us if you do."

"I've had a few flings with a girl or two," he replied. "But them hoes ain't loyal, and there's always some bullshit involved."

"So, you know that I'm a different breed?" I tickled his bulging dick print with my toes.

"I was hoping you was different and not like your girl." He enjoyed the stimulation and chugged the rest of his drink.

"My girl?" I tried to appear naive, but I knew who he meant.

"Yeah." He sighed. "That girl was not the person I thought she was."

"Nova." I looked deep into his eyes and continued to tease him.

"The one and only."

"So, the two of you been fuckin' around?" I smiled. "How long has this been going on?"

"Honestly?" He thought back in his head, and I loved that all of this was on videotape. "Months now."

"So, you been going by her crib?"

"Naw. She would hit me up for extra cash and meet me in my office at certain times. We would meet once or twice a week."

"In your office?" I thought back to the many times that he always claimed to be in a meeting with the door locked. Or he would say that his office bathroom was out of order. It all made sense to me now.

"Yeah." He blushed. "You almost caught us a time or two. She used to get so mad about that shit. Said she didn't want us to get caught and we needed a new place to meet up. But all of that is over now. I'm done with her trifling ass. Always looking down on me, shit. I made her weak ass."

"That's some deep shit." I tried to appear unbothered. "I had no idea. I guess she's really good at keeping secrets."

"Yeah, the ones that involve her," he jabbed.

"What does that mean?" I raised an eyebrow.

"Oh, nothing." He laughed it off. "Just saying she's a sneaky little bitch. But I'm done with her, and I have no idea why she decided to hit me up today."

"She called me before you got here," I confessed for a little alliance with his mark ass. "It's funny how she decided to reach out to the both of us."

"It is." He thought for a second and then focused back on my pussy and breasts. "But back to the subject at hand, my love. I don't want you to leave just yet, but I can't stop you. I do wish to still see you from time to time, no matter what you decide to do. Do you think I could do that?"

"Mmm." I sighed as he pleasured me again. *Yes, I will definitely enjoy this mouth a little more before I destroy your bitch ass.*

35

Nova: Tryin' Not to Lose

"I'm really tired of going back and forth with you about all of this shit," I sobbed and pointed at Tezz from my bedroom door. "Why does it always have to be like this between us?"

"All this cryin' you doing is not changing anything, Nova." Tezz walked over to me and held me close to him. "Just stop making yourself upset like that. It's not good for you."

"So, now you wanna act like you care about me? Where have you been hiding for the past few days? You have been like a ghost around here, Tezz. It was never like that before."

"Now you wanna make this about me?" Tezz grew upset once again as we sat on the bed. "I told you what's going on with my daughter and her mother showing up. That is some real-life shit that I have to deal with. You have a son, so I would expect you to understand."

"I get it." I blew my nose. "I love your daughter just like I would my son in that situation."

"Well," he breathed. "Why are you getting all upset?"

"I know you and yo' baby mom have a twisted history," I answered. "Y'all have unresolved issues, and I know how that can play out. Do you still have feelings for her? Do I need to be concerned about the two of you?"

"There you go." Tezz appeared uneasy about something, and I felt sick to my stomach.

"Fuck." I stood up and sprinted to the bathroom. My stomach felt like it was doing somersaults. I positioned myself over the toilet brim and threw up a time or two.

"Damn, girl." Tezz stepped in the bathroom and ran some water in the sink. "Have you been drinkin' or something? What's really goin' on with you."

"I been feeling crappy and uneasy for a week or so now," I confessed and washed my face in the sink. "I can't seem to keep much down, and I'm so tired."

"Are you sure there's nothing you want to tell me?" Tezz seemed to be in a panic.

"Are you asking if I could be pregnant?" I looked away from him because I knew if I was, there was a possibility that it may not be his baby.

"Do we really need to play these guessing games?" He raised his hands and searched my face for the truth. "Keep it real."

"I guess." I sobbed once again. "It's a possibility but I don't know."

"Well, don't you think you need to be figuring this shit out?" Tezz fired up a smoke and tapped his leg nervously. "Damn it, Nova. This is so much shit on a nigga's plate right now. I told you what I got going on at home, and now you wanna drop this in my lap."

"That's great." I stood to my feet to walk away from him. "So, now all of this shit is my fault? I fucked myself and made your low-down baby momma return to your life right now. Yeah, you are right. I did all of this purposely to drive you crazy."

"Shit, Nova." Tezz walked to the kitchen after me and tugged at my shirttail. "C'mon, now. Look, I'm sorry. I shouldn't have said things the way that I did to you. It's just a shock to me. I wasn't expecting you to say that shit."

I blew my nose once more. "Yeah, well, I didn't plan for any of it to happen. Not right now at least."

"What do you mean by that?"

I huffed and poured myself a glass of water. "You know that I love you, and the thought of us having a baby did cross my mind. But I just didn't think about it happening right now. Not with the way things are: you and the baby momma shit, and me trying to get out of the club life."

"So, you really wanna give the club scene up for good?" he questioned.

"I was cool with it, but I know how much you are against it." I shrugged my shoulders and leaned against the countertop. "I don't like the friction between us, and you made some valid points in the past. Not to mention Mia plans on quitting the club very soon. She was the main reason I agreed to strip in the first place. I couldn't imagine being there without her. It just wouldn't be the same."

"And you and Mia are tight again?" Tezz was hazy on that subject.

"Don't start with the Mia shit, please."

"You need to stop playing with fire, Nova," Tezz warned me. "You know the secret that you kept from her. I don't see how you can plaster a fake smile on your face when you see her. You got bigger balls than me. If she ever found out about that dinner party we knew about, well, you already know."

"I get it." I sighed. "But we are cool and better than ever. I don't want to get into any of that shit. It's just more stress, and I can't afford it right now. Back to us. I want us to work out. I genuinely love you and want to make you happy."

"I hear you." Tezz seemed satisfied, but lately I was unsure about his feelings. There was just something different about him lately. "When are you going to buy a test or make a doctor's appointment?"

"I'm not sure." I cleared my throat. The truth was that I did take a test, several of them. I just didn't know the right time to spring it on him. And I would never know how to tell him about me and Marvin fucking around.

"Don't you think that needs to be a priority?" Tezz placed his head in his hands and rocked back and forth nervously. "Fuck, Nova. This is just so damn much right now."

"I'm sorry to crash your reunion with the baby mom," I snarled in his direction.

"That was so uncalled for," Tezz snapped back. "This shit between us has nothing to do with her. Don't do that."

"Why are you on the defensive about a bitch who left you as a single teenage father? How did she get in contact with you in the first place?"

"She remembered my parents' number and address." Tezz tried to calm down. "I'm surprised she remembered it after all of these years. But apparently, she reached out to them. My folks didn't know how to approach me with it, so they told my sister, and she told me."

"Oh, really?" I gasped. "Which one told you?"

"Not that it matters, but it was Carol."

"Oh, okay." I nodded and thought back to the day I called the job looking for Tezz. Carol knew the whole time that Tezz was meeting up with that bitch. I guessed there was no loyalty with mu'fuckas these days. I didn't know Carol that well, but I figured we were cool enough for her to give me a heads-up or something.

"Hello?" Tezz grabbed my shoulders and snapped me back into reality. "Where did you go?"

"Oh, my bad." I smiled at him. "I was just thinking about some stuff."

"Something else you wanna tell me?" he asked.

"Nothing like that." I paused. "I just want to know if we are good. Do I need to be worried about you and her?"

"Are you being one hundred with me about everything, Nova?" he said with a straight face.

"What do you think?" I said nervously and tried not to show it.

"Don't answer my question with one." He was displeased. "Are you tryin' to hide something from me? Please, do not be that girl. I've been there with many, and it doesn't turn out good for you in the end. Trust me on that. I have had enough bullshit with women, and I will not be made a fool of ever again. So, I am going to ask you one more time. Are you being one hundred with me?"

"Yes, Montezz," I lied without hesitation, and I hated myself for it. I grabbed him by his head and pulled him forcefully toward me. I wanted to feel his body next to mine, and I wanted things to go back to the way they were in the very beginning. All my lies and deceit were starting to seep from my soul. I hated myself more and more each day. But what was I supposed to do? If I confessed everything to everyone, that would leave me with nothing and no one. I was not ready to sacrifice it all for the truth.

"Damn, girl." Tezz pulled his lips away from mine and took a few deep breaths. "What are you trying to do, suffocate me?"

"I just want us to go back to the way we used to be." I climbed on top of him and pulled off my shirt and bra. "You remember the way we were from the start?"

"I remember." He smiled and reminisced with me. "So spontaneous, and we clicked on the first day."

"And I want us to always be that way." I unfastened his pants and massaged his semi-erect member. "Don't let her come between us, Tezz."

"Why do you keep bringing her into this, Nova?" He grew uneasy and his dick softened. "If you doing what you need to do, there's no reason for you to worry about the next chick. I have to deal with her because we have a child together. There's a difference, and you should understand that."

"I know you have to deal with her." I slid my body downward and kissed the tip of his dickhead gently. "I just don't want to lose my spot because of some hidden feelings or agenda she's on. I'm a woman, and I know the good man I got. I gotta make sure you stay mine."

I sucked him up and heard him moan with delight at my skills. There was nothing I wouldn't do to keep that man. He meant the world to me. I had done a lot of wrong and felt bad about it, but I was now focused on making things right.

"Damn it, girl." He rubbed my head and forced himself down my throat. "What you tryin'a do to me?"

"I just wanna do all the things that you like, babe. I want this for life, and I want you for life."

"What you saying?" He moaned continuously.

"Well." I massaged his dick and balls with my hands. "This wasn't really the way I wanted to discuss this, but it is what it is. I want you forever. I have thought about us getting engaged and married one day. If I am pregnant, maybe that's God's way of saying we should do it."

"You really on some deep shit right now, Nova." Tezz squirmed beneath me.

"You told me to be one hundred with ya." I put his hard cock inside of my tight pussy walls. I would make him remember the way we used to be. That bitch wasn't going to steal him from me, not now and not ever.

36

Montezz:

Two Options but One Right Choice

"I'm so happy I found you again, my heart." Ky kissed me passionately and laid her head on my chest.

I was able to put my feelings for Nova to the side when it came to Kyomo. She pulled at my heart in ways that no one else ever could. I knew she would always be my one true love, and now I had some real decisions to deal with.

"I love you too." I kissed her apple-fragranced hair.

"Tezz." She sat upward and got serious suddenly. "Can we talk about something?"

"Oh, no," I teased but was also concerned. "What did I do?"

"I'm sure you have done plenty," she laughed but returned with a straight face. "Seriously, what are we going to do? Is this just a fad, or are we going to really try again?"

"All of these questions right now, Ky . . ." I was uneasy and unsure how to respond. "Can't we just enjoy this and relax for a bit?"

"We can relax later, Tezz." She continued, "I love the time we are spending together. And Myesha, she is everything I imagined and so much more. I can't wait for her to meet her brothers. They will absolutely love her. I have told them all about her and things about us too."

"Really?" I was shocked at how honest she was being. Time really changes some people.

"Yes." She glared in my direction. "Why is that so hard for you to believe? I want all of my kids to have a relationship together. I'm tired of all the secrets and not being able to be free and love the person I'm destined to be with."

"What are you saying, Ky?" I smiled and kissed her passionately.

"I thought I said it and expressed it clearly." She pouted. "I'm in love with you, Montezz. You have always had my heart and you always will. I want us to try again and be better than we ever could have been as kids. I never thought I would have the opportunity to be here with you again. But now that I'm here, I won't waste another second of time. I'm willing to move back to the States, back to Alabama to be with you."

"Are you serious right now?" My jaw dropped to the floor, and my heart skipped a beat.

"Yes, I am." She shook her head in approval. "I have already discussed it with my council. With my husband deceased, I have every option to live my life as I please. I have no other ties to my country than my family. I can go and visit them whenever I choose to. I need to be back here with you and Myesha. That's what I want, but how do you feel?"

"I'm so floored right now." I felt lightheaded and grabbed a bottled water from the nightstand. "This has all happened so fast, and I still think some of it's a dream."

"And you have that Nova person." Ky rolled her eyes with jealousy.

"Don't do that." I frowned. "Did you really expect me to stay single for over a decade? Not to mention you got married and had two more kids. C'mon now, that's not being realistic or fair."

"I know." She apologized. "That is petty of me, but it's how I feel. You had every right to find someone. You had no idea that I would ever come back, and it is selfish of me to think any other way. But it is the way I feel. Just imagining you being with anyone else makes me angry."

"And how do you think I have felt all of these years?" I turned it back on her. "Wondering why you left? If you ever cared and how you could do that to our baby? That's the way you left me, so please don't frown your nose up at any of my decisions. Had you never left, who knows what could have happened?"

"Don't you think I've questioned that?" She faced me with tears forming in her eyes. "Every night, my heart brought me back to you. I could see your face as clear as day, but you were always too far away for me to touch you. Without you, I felt like a bigger part of me was always missing. It was like breathing without air."

"Oh, baby." I grabbed her roughly and kissed her deeply. I didn't have the answers to all of her questions. I didn't know what the future would hold for us. But I wasn't ready to dismiss it completely. We had a chemistry that some people would never understand. Ky was my better half.

"Does that mean that you feel the same way?" She sucked on my neck and left earlobe. Ky knew all my spots and they remembered her touch with perfection. "Can you give us another chance?"

"I don't think you will let me say otherwise." I chuckled nervously and let her have her way with me.

"I never plan on losing you again, Tezz." She climbed on top of me. "I lost you once and will never allow that to happen again. Nothing and no one will get in our way. I'm sorry Nova's feelings will be hurt, but she can't have you."

"Look at you." I smiled. "Turning into a little beast."

"I'm whatever I need to be when it comes to you." Ky laughed and undressed slowly. "I know Myesha will be so pleased. I look forward to seeing her later today. We have planned out a girls' day and everything. I have wanted this for so long."

"I'm happy that our baby is happy." I agreed on that part. "I have never seen her smile and laugh the way she does now. I thank you so much for that."

"She makes me just as happy as I make her." She kissed me gently before we began to make sweet love.

"Shit, Nova," I moaned from the feeling she gave me. "Slow it down, babe."

"Not gonna happen." She bit her lip while she ground on my sore dick. "This dick is all mine, and I'll ride it how I want to. Try to stop me."

I picked up her small frame and laid her on her stomach. I couldn't let her outdo me, but I had to admit that I was a little tired. The toll of handling two women was not the walk in the park it had been in my past. Too many feelings and concerns were brought up between these two. I had to be cautious about how I treated both of them. I tried to focus on waxin' that ass, but my mind was on my conversation with Ky from that morning.

"Shit, baby," Nova moaned in front of me. "I'm about to cum again."

"Cum on this dick, baby." I quickened my pace. I was exhausted but wanted her to get off once more before I lay down. "Let me feel it," I demanded and thrust harder than before. After a few good humps, I felt my dick feel sloppy and warm with her cum. Her body collapsed, and I fell on top of her sweaty as hell. We lay there for a few minutes before she went to the restroom to freshen up.

"That was amazing as always, babe." She winked at me and handed me a washcloth.

"I think you drained me dry this time." I lay against the soft pillows and closed my eyes for a moment. I saw Ky's face and immediately felt shame for what just happened.

"What do you think about what I said earlier?" she probed and grabbed one of my cigarettes.

"Are you sure you need to be smoking that?" I snatched the smoke from her hand and puffed it away from her. "If you are pregnant, cigarettes aren't good for you. I don't want my baby coming out with problems because you having a nicotine fit."

"Calm down, babe." She laughed it off and took her smoke from me. "I said I wasn't sure about that yet. I mean, it could be stress for all I know. Don't be snatching my cig. You got a whole pack with your greedy ass."

"Stop playing." I glared at her playfully. "I was just looking out for you."

"But enough of that." She cleared her throat. "You never answered my question."

"Which one?" I shrugged.

"About us being together forever." She grew impatient. "Marriage and all of that. Were you paying attention to anything I said to you?"

"Don't do all of that." I grew nervous and fired up a smoke before uttering another word. "So much and so fast."

"I don't see what the problem is." She grew angry. "I thought you would be happy that I wanted to leave the club for you. That's what you have been screaming for the last few months now. I just assumed you wanted us to be together for the rest of our lives. To be honest, you never would have doubted me before. But now that your baby momma is back, you seem to have a different look about you. I can't put my finger on it, but there appears to be something you aren't trying to say to me."

"Let's not go there." I flipped it. "You been pondering telling me you might be pregnant, and how long have you kept that from me? Ky showed up out of nowhere, but you could have told me about a baby as soon as you questioned it. That's a decision that will permanently change our lives."

"It's a person who will always bond us to each other." She rubbed her flat stomach. "Someone we created, and no one can ever change that."

"I will always be there for a child of mine," I said. "You already know that. But you have to acknowledge that Ky is Myesha's mother. I do have to deal with her because of that. There's no point in you having an attitude with her. She will always be a part of my life because of who she is to Myesha."

"I understand what you are saying." She nodded. "But I just don't want any problems out of her ass. Because I have no problem handling her ass."

"Too much." I laughed nervously because I knew that Ky felt the same way about her. "All this violence, when will it ever stop?"

"Always with the jokes and I'm being so very serious with you." She rolled her eyes and walked over to her closet.

"What are you looking for in there?" I yawned and took a sip of my water.

"Just a few outfits," she answered and stayed focused on her clothes.

"Outfits for what?" I stretched and tried to get more comfortable.

"I have something to do tonight," she responded with her back to me.

"That damn club again?" I grew furious. She had told me about a possible baby, and she was still willing to shake her damn ass. "You have got to be kidding me right now."

"Not the club." She continued with her movements and grabbed a clothing bag. "I'm doing a party with Mia and a few girls. There is a big payday opportunity for me. This will be the party that will make my goals accessible. I plan on quitting after this one party. I promise you that."

"You are really gonna do this shit." I sat up in the bed and formed my hands into fists. "With all the bullshit you been peddling my way, now you tellin' me that you plan on dancin' tonight? You could be carrying my fuckin' child, but you're focused on poppin' your damn pussy."

"It's just a small party that one of Mia's people is throwing." She tried to soothe me, but that shit was out the door. "Not a club, just a spot. A few of us will be dancing, and that's the end of it. The payday is hella large, and if I am pregnant, that money can only help us. Why can't you see that?"

"Help us?" I fumed. "I make damn good money at the shop right now. I don't need my woman takin' her fuckin' clothes off to pay for my kids or anything I could ever need. Don't ever try to play me like that, Nova. You doing this party ain't got shit to do with us or a baby. This is all you. You know I got you. This is just some shit you wanna do. You like all that attention, niggas on you, and being naked in front of their thirsty asses."

"It's just this one last party, damn." She pouted and picked up my clothing to get dressed. "Why do you always gotta be this way? The last one, I promise you."

I fastened my pants and buckled my belt. "I promise you I'm so done with this whole fuckin' scene. Do you know how many damn times I've heard you promise that shit? And every fuckin' time there's another one and one after that. The shit is never gonna end. I don't know what it's gonna take for you to stop. It's like a junkie needing a fix with you."

"That was so uncalled for, Tezz." She threw her clothes on the bed and followed me through her apartment and to the front door. "I just need you to give me this one night. Can you do that for me, please?"

"I said I'm outta here." I pulled away from her. I could hear her crying, but I wasn't trying to hear that shit. There was no way I could take her seriously when she was making a joke out of herself. I was so disgusted that I couldn't even look at her. "Find out those results for me, and then we can talk. Have a good work night."

I waved her off and revved my engine. I only saw the color red as I headed down the street and out of her neighborhood. I tried to keep things civil with Nova, but she made me want to forget about her altogether. I couldn't wife a damn stripper. I didn't respect that lifestyle. And I was tired of putting up with the shit. I knew where things stood with Ky, and she was doing the work that I required of her. As far as I was concerned, my relationship with Nova was about that baby. If there was a baby.

37

Marvin: Mesmerized by Something New

"Oh, yes, baby." I sucked her sweet pussy and loved the taste on my tongue. "Feed me that cum."

I watched Mia squirm, and I loved the way her body switched from my head game. I knew I had her where I wanted her when I saw her knees begin to buckle. Sex with my wife and Cristol was good, but Mia was just over the top to new. I loved exploring a new pussy, learning the ways of it, and making it all mine.

"Fuck," she hollered and grabbed on my fade. I loved a woman who guided me to that holy place. I applied more pressure and felt her juices explode onto my face with ease. "Damn, I can't hold my nut with you. No matter how hard I try."

"I don't ever want you to hold back from me." I wiped her glaze from my face with a washcloth and took a large sip from my drink she'd prepared for me. "You turn me on by the way you cum, baby."

"So, why you ain't tried to fuck me yet?" Mia asked a fair question. "Don't get me wrong, I'm not complaining about anything that you been doing. I just thought I would ask because we have been going strong for a little while now."

"I'm just happy with pleasin' you, baby doll." I shrugged and looked away from her. "And I just don't want any more slipups or dumb shit behind it. I'm good. I can always jack off."

"What you mean by slipups?" she probed further. "C'mon now. You just had your head in my crotch. I think we can stop with all the innuendo."

"I got a son by someone else." I breathed deeply when I exhaled that information. I hoped it didn't backfire in my face, but I never knew Mia to be about drama or stupid shit like Nova. "That was one of my slipups."

"You said one of them." She sat up on her couch and grabbed a cigarette from the table. "Someone from the club?"

"Yeah. My son is almost five years old now." I scratched my head nervously and fired a smoke with her. "I been maintaining everything, but it hasn't been easy. But the money from the club allows me to keep everyone happy, but it can be stressful juggling two families."

"That's deep." She shook her head and gently stroked my forearm for support. "The club really had some skeletons in it. So, what else is it? You said slipups, like plural."

"Yeah." I paused, looked away, and tried my best to face her. "I finally accepted Nova's phone call. She said she's pregnant too. Talkin' about it could be mine or that nigga she fucks with. Can you believe that shit? The whole time she was tellin' me that she was on the damn pill. How the hell did that happen?"

"Get the fuck outta here," she shrieked and said nothing for a few moments. I hoped I had not scared her away, but I felt better tellin' her my bullshit. "I forgot to hit her back the other day, but I will see her later on. That might have been what she wanted to share with me when you was coming over."

"If y'all are tight the way you claim to be," I began, "I'm sure that's what she had to tell you. I'm so fuckin' mad. That's all I need is another baby by another bitch. That's another reason why I only eat your pussy. Can't get a baby that way."

"I guess I can understand where you are coming from with that." She gave a wayward smile and poured us another drink. "That's some deep shit you laid on me just now."

"Sorry if that scared you away." I looked away from her shamefully. "I can understand if you don't wanna fuck with me anymore. That shit stresses me out, so I can only imagine what you must be thinkin' right now."

"Don't you worry about any of that, boo," she reassured me and planted a soft kiss on my lips. She straddled me and rotated her hips back and forth. "I would never come at you the way those hoes did. Never."

She reached underneath the sofa and pulled out a fresh box of unopened Magnums. I watched her open the pack and pull out my throbbing member.

"I appreciate you lookin' out for me and the way you have made me feel with that magical tongue of yours." She placed the rubber over my shaft, and I could feel it throb from her touch. "But I want to feel you inside of me. We can be safe about it."

"I won't even lie." I allowed her to straddle me once more and I fought back my nut. "I don't know how long I'm gonna last because you already had me about ready to pop."

"I'm doing this for your enjoyment." She smiled as she started off slowly. "You left me more than satisfied already, boo. I want you to get yours too."

"Damn, baby." I fought and bit my lip. She saw the beads of perspiration across my brow and softly kissed my forehead as she picked up the pace. "This pussy feels too damn good."

"Enjoy it and let yourself go." She rode me faster and harder than before. I grabbed her hips and vigorously bounced her up and down on my lap. "That's it, daddy."

"Fuck." I let out a holler. "Here it comes."

I felt my nut invade that rubber and relaxed knowing it wasn't implanted in her womb like the other bitches. She wiped me off and threw the condom away in the trash. I readjusted my clothing and finished my drink with ease. Mia made me feel right at home, and that liquor had me feelin' so loose.

"Are you feelin' better?" She winked and plopped down beside me.

"Yes, suga." I gave her a kiss on her cheek and breathed a lot easier than before. "I wanna thank you for that. But back to reality. I hope that baby of Nova's ain't mine. I am not tryin'a go through the bullshit again. I am thinking about getting myself fixed, for real. I'm older now, and I don't need any more kids."

"That might be the best way for you to go." She fired up a blunt. "I hear that it's effective, and you won't have to worry about chicks pinning a baby on you."

"Exactly," I agreed. "I will call around and see how much that will cost me. It's definitely worth every penny. I wish I had thought about it sooner, but there's nothing I can change now. Nova really had me fooled. I thought she was better than that. I wonder how her dude is taking all of this, and I wonder if she told him about us."

Mia raised her brow. "If Nova keeps secrets like that, I doubt she mentioned you in the equation. That girl is full of skeletons."

"Are you involved in any of them?" I felt it was a fair question to ask.

"I have one, but nothing like the shit you are involved in." She looked me up and down.

"What is it?" I was intrigued. "I told you my shit. You might as well spill it and free yourself."

"Me and Nova." She sighed and licked her lips. "We have messed around a time or two. Nothing too major, but you know what I mean."

"Damn, boo." I was more turned on that ever. "I didn't know the two of you got down like that. I would have loved to watch that shit. Damn, got my dick hard again just thinkin' about it."

"Funny you would say that." She turned on her TV and grabbed her phone. "I have a video or two if you would like to watch something. I just need to pair my phone to the TV."

"Hell yeah, I wanna see it all." I licked my lips and placed my hand on my dick when she played the video. "Damn. You eatin' that thang like you know what you doing. Are you trying to challenge me or something?"

"You are hands down better at it than me." She laughed. "I just get a little crazy when I'm fucked up."

"I'm surprised at Nova." I shook my head but never took my eyes off the two of them. "She just didn't seem like the type to fuck with a female. She carries herself such a different way. I guess you never really know a person for sure."

"But I been real with you about mine," she pointed out. "You can see that for yourself. Oh, here's the part where she skeets on my face. Look at it."

"Damn, that was so damn sexy." I stroked myself harder and was about to nut once more.

"Let me climb on your face and cum with you." She straddled me with my response, and I did not attempt to stop her.

We reached our peak at about the same time and decided to get washed up and relax with one another.

"So, what are you gettin' into tonight, sweetness?" I asked and poured one last shot of liquor into my glass. "I wanted to take you out and spoil you a little bit."

"Aww, that's sweet of you." She smiled and stood to her feet. "I would love for us to hang out, but like I said, I have some plans with Nova and other people."

"Oh, yeah." I was disappointed at best. "What other people?"

"Just a party we are going to," she replied nonchalantly. "Kinda like a retirement bash or something like that."

"Oh, okay." I pouted. "I guess I can feel that. I guess we can reschedule it for another evening, but I really wanted more time with your fine ass tonight."

"I'm sorry about that, boo." She kissed me softly on the cheek and gave a few stretches. "But I do need to pick out a few outfit options, and I'm not sure when Fab's ass might come home."

"You don't have to worry about him." I massaged her breasts and ass once more. "I got him handling a few things for me at the club right now. He shouldn't be here anytime soon. I made sure we wouldn't have any interruptions."

"I like the way you plan ahead," she joked.

"I try, suga." I relaxed and glanced at my phone. There were a few missed calls, but nothing that couldn't wait until later.

"We can do that another time, for sure." She motioned me closer to her and gave me a big hug. "Thanks for coming by to see me. It's always such a pleasure."

"That it is." I massaged her body once more before I approached her doorway. It was hard for me to leave her because she was like a new drug to me. I just wanted her more and more each time we were together. I hated the fact that I fell for these bitches as hard as I did. I had a real problem when it came to pussy. I thought about booking a session with my therapist, but shame wouldn't let me go that route.

"Call me later, sweetness." I gave her one last peck on the cheek before I walked out her door and made it to my vehicle. She stood in the doorway and waved goodbye as I drove off into the evening.

38

Mia: Where tha Party At?

I was so hyped and filled with all the blackmail and info to bury that bitch three or four times. There was no way anyone could intercept the shit that I was about to lay on her ass. I smiled and was joyful the whole ride to Nova's and once again on the trip to Anwar's trap house.

"Are you ready to get this money, bihh?" I sang and moved my body to the music. I hadn't realized how quiet and disoriented Nova had become until I reached Anwar's driveway. There were a few cars already there, but I wanted to pick her brain to see where her mind was at. "What's up with you? You've been quiet the whole ride, and that's not like you."

"I just got a lot of other shit going on right now." She sighed and fired up a smoke. "Now is really not the time to get into it. I don't want to fuck up the vibe, and I definitely need this bread."

"Are you sure?" I probed further but already knew her dirty little secrets. "We got some time. I don't think the boss man has made it here yet."

"It's cool." She gave a fake smile and took a few deep breaths. "So, how many niggas are supposed to show up tonight?"

"Not that big of a crowd," I said honestly. "Just a few close friends. The big man doesn't do crowds, and he just wants to be able to relax around those he considers family."

"That's cool with me as long as the money is long."

"That's the spirit." I nodded and deeply hated that bitch. "Money over everything else. And the money is definitely in here. What are your plans for your cut of the bread?"

"I'm out this life, for sure." She sighed and exhaled the cigarette smoke. I fired up a special laced blunt and passed it to her. "Me and Tezz got into it about me doing this damn party. I was just trying to be honest and let him know that this was my last show. But of course, he wasn't trying to hear any of that. He stormed out earlier today, and I haven't heard from him since."

"Damn, baby girl." I gave her a sad look but really didn't give two fucks. "I'm sure he will come around. Try not to think about him tonight, and let's just get this money. I got a few things for you to relax. You can worry about that nigga tomorrow, but tonight, we got a job to do."

"You're right." She sighed and gave me a smile. "I'm so glad I have you in my corner. You just don't know what our friendship means to me. I love you, girl."

"Aww." I grinned but for different reasons that would be discovered at a later time. "Stop trying to get all emotional on me. You want a bump of this?"

I had a few lines prepared on the dash, and she snorted all three of them.

"Damn, girl." I chuckled. "You could have saved me one."

"My bad." She wiped her nose and gritted her teeth. "I figured you had more of that."

"Damn skippy." I winked and got myself together. "C'mon, let's get out of this car."

We grabbed our travel bags filled with props and other costumes that we might decide to wear for the night and knocked on the front door.

"C'mon in, boo," Anwar hollered from the window. "I see your fine ass on my camera."

"Nice." Nova winked as we made our entrance into the living room. I saw only familiar faces: a few of Anwar's goons, his brother Stanley, and of course the man himself.

"Get your fine ass over here, girl." Anwar motioned for me to come closer, and I kept Nova by my side. I could tell that she was looser than before. Everything was going according to my plan.

"This must be the great Nova." Anwar extended his hand to greet her. "Nice to finally meet you. I have heard a little bit about you."

"Nice to meet you too." She smiled, and for some reason I wanted to knock her teeth down her throat. "All good things, I hope."

"Nothing but the complete best." Anwar was a great liar and decided to introduce Nova to a few people.

"Hello, beautiful." Stanley decided to pitch his intro while he had the opportunity. "The pleasure is all mine, and thanks for agreeing to do this party. I'm Stanley, Anwar's younger and much more handsome baby brother."

"Nice to meet you, Stanley." Nova knew how to make an impression. "Mia, is this the guy you said was asking about me?"

"The one and the same." I winked and nodded at Stanley.

"I've seen you at the club a few times." Stanley stood tall and proudly in front of her. "I must say that I'm impressed. Most strippers aren't that intriguing to me, but you definitely left me wanting more. I hope you save me a lap dance or two tonight."

Nova traced her index finger down Stanley's chiseled stomach to his belt buckle. "With words that sweet, I'll be sure to save you a dance or two."

"That's what I like to hear." He laughed uncontrollably and hit some extra bass in his voice. "We can get started whenever you get ready. Be careful with how you touch me. I wouldn't want you to wake up that monster down there. Unless you think you can handle eleven inches."

"What?" Nova almost choked on the air. "Quit playin' yourself."

"What you tryin' to say, Ms. Nova?" Anwar joined in on the fun. "My brother tells no lies. We are very well equipped in that area. You better ask somebody."

I snickered and felt my face flush. Anwar gave me a brief nudge, and the conversation shifted back to Stanley and Nova. I was glad to see the two of them hittin' it off. My plan wouldn't work if they couldn't get along.

"Can I steal you for a moment?" Anwar focused on me.

"Do your thang, bruh." Stanley gladly waved us off. "I will keep my eyes on Nova."

"I'm sure that's not all you wanna keep," I teased as the two of us walked away and into the back room.

Anwar closed and locked the door behind him, while I sat comfortably on the sofa bed.

"What's up, baby?" I smiled and fired up a smoke.

"Hm." He gave me a devilish grin and pounced on top of me with lust in his eyes.

"Baby," I whined but allowed him to kiss and suck all over me. "You're gonna mess up my hair and makeup. C'mon now."

"I know you better miss me with all of that." He laughed and pulled out a titty to suck on. "You belong to me now, and I want what I want, you feel me?"

"Mm," I moaned and tried to argue my point. "But what about your friend you are throwing the party for? He should be here any minute, and you got us back here getting busy."

"My peoples know what to tell him, and we won't be back here forever." Anwar unfastened his pants and pulled up my dress to my waist. "Take them panties off before I rip them off. You gon' give me some of my pussy right now. And I told them niggas to keep their hands off of you. Fuck the rest of them bitches, but you are all mines."

"I guess I won't be making any tips tonight," I teased him.

"I got all the tip you ever gonna need." Anwar proudly grabbed the monster in between his legs and bounced it on my stomach. That man was definitely packing, and he had such a beautiful yet veiny black dick. Watching him play with it had me turned on, and I massaged my hardened nipples from the excitement. "Are you ready for a payment right now?"

"Yes, daddy," I whined and watched him insert it into my tight pussy hole. "Damn."

The party was in full effect, and two other strippers were stackin' some major paper. Nova was preoccupied with Stanley and was tipsier than she was before. Raul Coba had a crime-mob look about him. He was five foot ten inches tall, had a stocky build and a nicely trimmed beard, and had a sharp Cuban accent. He placed $20,000 into my hands, and I wanted to climb right into his lap. I had never seen that much money at one time, and half of it belonged to me.

"I really appreciate this get-together you prepared for me." Coba puffed on his cigar and gave me a stern look. "You have given me such love, and I really feel at home here."

"I'm glad you are having a nice time, Mr. Coba."

"You don't have to be so formal with me." He gave a slight chuckle and nodded at one of his henchmen. The tall yet scary man walked over and bent down to hear his boss, nodded, and walked away. "You can call me Raul. Anwar is a real amigo of mine, and he said you are his lady. *Su familia es mi familia.*"

"Oh, okay." I nodded but didn't really follow what he said to me. I noticed Anwar eyeballin' Nova from across the room. He was very protective of his little brother, and after I told him about her baggage, he didn't trust her at all.

"I hear your amiga likes to party." Raul made a snortin' gesture, and his henchman brought over a small golden box. Raul opened the box, and I became wet from the smell of the fine china. "Feel free to sample some if you would like."

I glanced over at Anwar because I wanted to show him respect. He smiled and nodded for me to enjoy the gesture, and I obliged him. The powder was so potent it made me gag a little bit. My entire face felt numb, and I was ready to shake my ass on the dance floor. I called Nova over, and Stanley was close behind her. I made all the introductions, and Nova helped herself to some of the candy.

"I'm ready for my dance now." Stanley wrapped his hands around her tight waist.

"Right this way, sexy." Nova led him into the back room, and they left the door open only a crack.

"She's a beautiful girl." Raul admired my friend. "Do you think she would let me fuck her?"

"With the money you're dishin' out?" I replied. "I'm sure you could do anything you wanted to her."

"That's interesting." He stroked his beard and gave a slight smile. "I see that the young man is into her as well. The more the merrier. We could share her for the night.

Could you make sure the rest of my guys are entertained in here?"

Raul handed me another stack of cash and headed to the room with Stanley and Nova.

"Looks like your boss is satisfied." I planted a juicy kiss on Anwar's lips. He glanced back toward the room with concern in his eyes. He also noticed Raul's guards close to the door and resumed his focus on me. "Everything is going fine, baby. I wish you would just relax."

"I guess you are right." He plastered on a smile and swirled me around the dance floor. He saw everyone else having a good time and finally decided to let loose a bit. "I guess I was worried for nothing."

"That's one of the things I love the most about you." I wrapped my arms around his neck.

"And what's that?"

"The way you love the ones who are close to you," I replied and ground on his pelvis bone.

"I gotta look out for my family." He picked me up with ease, and I wrapped my legs around his waist. "I'd kill a whole country for the ones I love, and you know that."

"Baby, where are you taking me?" I teased and sucked on his neck.

"I can't let them have all of the fun." He nibbled on my earlobe while he walked. "I'm about to put a baby in your belly tonight, girl."

39

Nova: The Morning After

"Ugh." I felt my head pounding like I had been hit by a tractor trailer the night before. The room was still hazy, and I could barely open my eyes completely. I tried to remember where I was, but with a quick scan of the carpet and decor, I realized I was in my own bed.

Shit must have gotten wild last night. I snickered to myself. *Fuck, my whole body feels sore as fuck.*

I sat up in the bed and gave a slight yawn. I checked the nightstand. My keys, purse, and phone were right where I always kept them. I breathed a lot easier when I saw the fat stacks of cash that I had made from the party.

"That's a relief," I breathed and lay back on my soft pillow and sheets.

"Good morning, sexy." A strange voice but familiar face emerged from my bathroom all smiles. "You was down for the count."

"Stanley?" I scratched my scalp and really felt confused. "What are you doing here?"

"Damn, shawty." He shook his head and laughed heartily. "You must have been really out of it last night. Mia left with my brother, and you asked me to take you home. I've never been here before, so how else do you think I got here?"

"I guess you are right." I smiled nervously. "I'm just drowsy as fuck right now. I didn't mean to offend you or anything like that."

"You are good, shawty." Stanley plopped back down on the bed and moved closer to me. "How's that pussy feelin'? I hope I didn't punish her too heavy last night. You got some good shit, too."

"I am sore right now." I blushed and placed my hands over my throbbin' lips. "I guess you was right about those eleven inches."

"Are you telling me that you can't remember him?" Stanley got undressed, and my mouth dropped from the sight in front of me. It was every bit the size that he mentioned and had a thick girth to it. "Do you need for me to remind you?"

I opened my mouth to respond but nothing came out. I was just so mesmerized and allowed him to climb on top of my body. He sucked and kissed on me slow and gently. Stanley knew what he was doing, and I wanted that big thang he was packin'. I knew I needed to handle my issues, but for the moment I just wanted that big black cock.

"Are you ready?" He nibbled on my kitty cat at first and moistened it back up with his tongue. "Or do you need me to play with it a little bit for you?"

"Play with it, please." I ran my fingers through his straight-curly hair. "It feels so good right now."

"As you wish, sexy." He devoured me whole, and I tugged on my bedsheets for some kind of support.

"Oh, yes, baby." I rolled my hips back and forth and got my first nut from his lips. "I'm cummin' so hard right now."

"That's what I wanted to hear, boo." He laughed and wiped my juices from his goatee. "I want to get in on this action if you don't mind. Now, make some room for my monster in there."

I spread my legs as wide as I could, and he mounted me once more. I felt Stanley past my stomach and almost in my damn chest. I clawed at his back, and he talked dirty to me in my ear. I felt like we would suffocate underneath the covers, but I did not want the moment to end.

"Does it feel good to you, Nova?"

"Yes, it does." I held him tighter.

"Has anyone ever given it to you like this before?"

"No way, boo," I replied honestly because I wasn't used to a dick that size.

"Can I have it again and again?" he asked while he blew my back out.

"Yes," I moaned. "A thousand times yes."

"Shit, this pussy is so damn good." He continued to stroke me. "I gotta raise these covers up. It's hard for me to breathe."

We emerged from the blissful covering over us, and my heart stopped when I looked at my bedroom doorway.

"Oh, shit," I screamed in agony.

"What is it, girl?" Stanley looked down at me and then to the figure in the doorway. "Who the fuck is that nigga?"

"Tezz," I hollered and tried to push Stanley off of me.

"Oh, no." Tezz's eyes were fuming hot at this point. "Please, don't let me stop you. I enjoyed watching some random nigga fuck tha shit outta my girl, or should I say baby momma? I guess you are my baby momma."

"What tha fuck?" Stanley climbed off of me and covered himself with my bedsheet. "Look, dude, I don't know anything about what y'all got going on. I'm innocent in all of this, bruh."

"I already know." Tezz never took his glare off of me. I saw the hatred and disgust in his eyes. It was at that very moment that I knew I had lost him for good this time. "According to the messages and videos I received this morning, you was just an innocent bystander. My beef is not with you, bruh. You are free to leave. But, you, you little bitch, you better not fuckin' move."

"I appreciate that, bruh." Stanley smiled and gathered up his belongings. "It's been a pleasure, Nova. But um, looks like you got some shit to handle. I'ma just roll on up outta here."

"You have a good day." Tezz waved but kept his focus on me.

I covered myself shamefully with the sheet and put my shirt and panties back on. I was ready to say something, but Tezz threw a portrait of us against the wall. The slam and shatter of glass frightened me, and I felt my body shake in terror.

"You bitch." He frowned with fists of fury. "Don't you open your mouth to say a muthafuckin' thing to me. I've seen it all on tape. The video of you and Mia fuckin', and a conversation that stated you was fuckin' that sleazy club owner and me at the same damn time. Really, Nova? Bitch, you had me fooled. I really thought you was a good woman, but you know what you are? You are a triflin'-ass whore. As for that baby, I want a blood test as soon as you drop it. Don't call me, don't text me, and don't come by to see me. All we got to talk about is that baby. Do you hear me, bitch?"

I shook my head and let the tears flow down my face.

"I swear I wanna beat your ass so bad right now, but I'm not gonna risk doing a life sentence for murdering you. You're not even worth the damn charge. What the hell was I thinkin'?"

Knock. Knock.

"Damn, who tha fuck is it now?" Tezz swung his fist around the room and stormed to answer the front door.

I heard a lot of commotion from the living room and got dressed before I walked in there.

"Oh, my God," I shrieked and saw both Tezz and Marvin exchanging blows with one another. "Stop it. The both of you, please stop fightin'."

"Fuck you, you sneaky little bitch," Marvin yelled, and Tezz pinned him down on the ground. "You have ruined my damn life."

"What are you talking about?" I felt so lightheaded and heaved chunks into a garbage can nearby.

"Your friend Mia, she played me," Marvin began. "I had been visiting with her, and she videotaped the conversations we had at her house. My wife knows about us and Cristol. She's filing for divorce, and I might lose every fuckin' thing that I built. If I can get my hands on you, you're dead. Do you hear me? Dead."

"Can't let you do that." Tezz held him down and Marvin continued to fight back. "As much as I want in on the action, she's pregnant with a child and it could be mine. I can't let you hurt that baby even if the momma is a fuckin' slut."

"Get the fuck off me, dammit," Marvin hollered, and the two of them continued to tussle back and forth.

I was still trying to process that Mia set this plan into action. I thought she had been my friend, and all the while she had been setting me up for a trap. How could she do me like that? Yeah, I did some dirt but nothing to ever justify the shit she pulled. I walked back to my bedroom and checked my phone for calls and messages. My phone had been on silent the whole time, and I had more calls and messages than I could ever imagine. Mia sent me the videos with a lot of LOL emojis. She was a sick bitch. I gave her a call.

"Good day to ya, boo." She snickered and seemed so satisfied with herself. "It's such a beautiful day out. And how are you feeling?"

"You conniving bitch," I hollered and still listened to the fellas fight in my living room. "How could you do all of this to me and why?"

"Really, Nova?" She cackled with delight. "All of this is your damn fault. You betrayed our friendship, and now you know how that feels. You thought I didn't know that you was at the dinner with Fab and that Hispanic bitch. Oh, you thought I didn't know about all of that? Yeah, Fab confessed it to me months ago, bitch. But you went right along like everything was gravy. You are such a fake, and now everyone sees you for the gutter trash that you are. Checkmate, game over, and I'll holla."

"Nova," I heard Marvin holler, and footsteps seemed closer and closer to my bedroom door. I shut it, locked the door, and hid in the bathroom. I felt my body shake from the terror of it all, and then there was a loud boom-boom noise.

I shrieked and must have passed out from the stress of that morning. When I came to, I was on the bathroom floor. The rest of the house was silent, but I was still afraid to move from that spot. Curiosity got the better of me, and I eased my way to the horrific bloody scene that was once my kitchen floor.

"Marvin," I screamed and saw his lifeless body on my floor. I looked around cautiously for Tezz but saw no trace of him. I ran to the front door, and his truck was long gone.

What was I going to do now? I had really made a mess of my life, and nothing would ever be the same again. The player really played herself this time.

Epilogue

Mia: Tellin' It Like It Is

Now I told y'all I was gonna get that dumb bitch, and I hope you never doubted me from the beginning. Please don't shed a tear for that dumb bitch, Nova. She had everything coming to her and then some. If she couldn't stand the heat, she never should have had her ass in tha fuckin' kitchen. I'm so glad all that bullshit is over with, and please know that my life is better than ever.

As I promised Anwar, I moved out of Fab's condo and into his big-ass mansion. Of course, Fab tried to act hurt by my leaving, but Anwar made him an offer he couldn't refuse. And yeah, Fab doesn't contact or speak to me anymore. Last I heard, he moved to Huntsville or somewhere like that. He got the fuck outta B'ham, and that was good enough for me.

RIP to the Candy Licker, aka Mr. Marvin. I didn't expect him to get murked in the process, but I guess you can't win any good wars without some casualties along the way. His wife and kids are living the good life, especially since Marvin left most of his money to her. Cristol managed to get her piece of the pie, too. Marvin willed the club to her, so his son will be taken care of from all the future profits from Uriah's. I heard they got a new breed of hoes in there and Cristol runs a very tight ship. Nothing like the way sleazy Marvin ran his business.

But what about that boy Tezz? Well, he's a'ight for the most part. I guess Nova finally gave him a solid and never told the cops he was responsible for Marvin's death. He was never questioned about it and still runs his auto shop, the best in B'ham. Since he showed love to Anwar's brother that day he walked in on him and Nova, my babe threw more business his way. So much that he had to open up another shop to accommodate all his customers. That's right, your boy is now a business chain.

Nova's baby ended up being his after all. And since he no longer trusted her or fucked with her, he filed for full custody of the little boy and was granted it from the judge. It didn't help that Tezz had videotape of her doing drugs while she was pregnant and all the acts of infidelity. But oh, well, you win some and lose some. His heart mended properly, thanks to his wife Kyomo and new stepsons he adopted. Last I heard, they are expecting another baby of their own in the fall.

As for that bitch, she packed up her shit and ghosted the town. I don't know where she went and couldn't care less. My life and everyone else's are so much better without her in it. I'm still with Anwar, and we are going strong. He wants a baby and then marriage. I might be down for that one day, but for the time being, I love spending his money and sitting around on my ass. Yep, y'all thought Nova was that hitta, but she was only good at gettin' hit. We boss bitches move in silence because silence can be deadly. Just ask Marvin. Peace out.